Betrayal of the Band

Sarah Tipton

Betrayal of the Band
COPYRIGHT 2017 by Sarah Tipton

All scripture quotations, unless otherwise indicated, are taken from the Holy Bible, New International Version[R] NIV[R] Copyright 1973, 1978, 1984, 2011 by Biblica, Inc.™ Used by permission of Zondervan. All rights reserved worldwide. www.zondervan.com

Published in association with the Books & Such Literary Management, 52 Mission Circle, Suite 122, PMB 170, Santa Rosa, CA 95409-5370, www.booksandsuch.com

Cover Art by *Nicola Martinez*
Watershed Books, a division of Pelican Ventures, LLC
www.pelicanbookgroup.com PO Box 1738 *Aztec, NM * 87410

Publishing History
First Watershed Edition, 2017
Paperback Edition ISBN 978-1-61116-961-4
Electronic Edition ISBN 978-1-61116-962-1
Published in the United States of America

Dedication

To my parents, my husband, and my children for their
support and encouragement.

1

Where it All Begins

The never-gonna-be-a-chart-topper on stage stopped wailing, and a group in the back corner of the coffeehouse cheered.

Zoey swallowed back the feeling of psychotic moths swarming from her stomach into her throat and squeezed the paper cup of unsipped tea. One more karaoke performer down. Soon…soon…

She couldn't even finish the terrifying thought. The cup's sides started to cave, and she loosened her grip.

"Next…" The man at the mic checked a clipboard. "Zoey Harris."

Zoey stood on jittery legs and wove between mismatched tables fingering the beads at her neck. She should've bailed on her older sister, Livvy, the moment the off-key strains of the previous song had insulted her ears. She should've run out of the Downstairs Coffeehouse after seeing "Karaoke Night" on the black dry erase board. She should've stopped her sister from adding her name to the list of performers.

She stepped onto the black plywood stage and faced the latte- and tea-drinking audience. Her heart pounded so loud the microphone would probably pick up its beats. She wished Justin sat out there grinning and believing in her. But "no boyfriends" was rule number one on sisters' night. Of course, this was more like force-Zoey-to-face-her-fears night. Or, depending on what happened in the next five minutes, Zoey-kills-Livvy night.

Then the opening notes of a '90s classic blasted through the speakers. With the first word, the song swelled from deep inside sparking every nerve. She forgot her anger toward Livvy. Forgot her dread of the stage. Forgot everything except this moment.

By the time she hit the first chorus, conversations ceased. Every person stared. She owned the crowd. She danced with the mic, expressed the music with her entire body.

Mama's dream for her come true.

The music ended, and the last notes faded, replaced by the crowd's cheers. Zoey floated off the stage savoring the high that helped her forget she was motherless. But the euphoria evaporated.

Livvy was no longer alone. A college-age guy straddled the back of a chair. Lean and narrow-chested, his dark hair hung to his shoulders smooth and straight.

What happened to sisters' night out? Rule number two was no picking up guys. Zoey was already taken, and Livvy attracted losers.

Zoey dropped into her seat.

"What did I tell you?" Livvy held out a peach tea peace offering. She had on her falling-in-love face—cheeks flushed and eyes sparkling. "If this was one of those TV talent competitions, you'd totally be going on national television."

"Uh-huh." Zoey tipped her head at the strange

dude.

"This is Vance." Livvy gave him a head-over-heels smile. He winked in return.

That confirmed it. Only a loser would flirt with clichés.

"He wanted to meet you," Livvy said.

"Me?" Zoey sputtered tea onto the scarred wood table.

"You totally rocked that stage." Vance turned his green-eyed charm on Zoey. "You shouldn't be performing karaoke."

"Thanks." Zoey heard the caution in her voice. It wasn't as if she hadn't been complimented before, but not by some random guy who was hitting on her sister.

"How would you like to join a band?"

The on-stage adrenaline jolted through Zoey's veins. Was this for real, a total stranger inviting her to join his band? But the excitement passed. "I'm already in a band."

"What's your group's name?"

"We don't have one." Zoey caught his indulgent smile and looked away. A no-name band. She could barely take herself seriously, let alone expect him to.

"I'm in this progressive metal band called Aurora Fire." Vance's voice swelled with pride. "I write the songs, play lead guitar, and sing backup. Our singer's gone until fall, so we need a voice to fill in over the summer."

"Oh." She rolled a necklace bead between her fingers. He wasn't just using her as an excuse to flirt with Livvy. He hadn't even looked at Livvy since Zoey sat down. She felt her rapid pulse in her neck. Her heart had never beaten this wildly before. Not even while on stage.

No one had ever asked her to join a band. Well, no one besides Justin, but that was back in eighth grade, and they were already a couple then, so that hardly counted. "I'm sorry. I can't just abandon my friends."

"Yeah, I get that." Vance's voice fell like a kid reluctantly accepting a no. But he couldn't have wanted her to join that badly. He'd only heard her sing once. "You got a lot of concerts planned?"

"No. Only one—next Saturday." Flaming heat engulfed her head. She sounded like a silly middle-schooler playing a band-style video game.

"We've got concerts lined up over the summer here in Fairbanks, and in Anchorage, and at the state fair. We need a voice like yours."

Images danced through her mind, quickened her breath. Standing on stage under hot lights, backed by a live band, facing a crowd of cheering strangers. What a way to spend the summer before senior year.

"You wouldn't be abandoning your other band." Vance leaned even closer, his coffee-scented breath laced with something bitter, his gaze both begging and sincere. "And this would be good for them too. Trust me; that would benefit you a lot. You'd get exposure for yourself and your other band. You'd meet the people who book shows. You'd get experience."

There it was. The one thing she lacked. She had the talent. She had the determination. But she didn't have the experience.

She glanced across the table at Livvy, who nodded encouragement. But of course Livvy would be encouraging. She'd dragged Zoey here for experience, and she was still giving dreamy looks at Vance as if she'd become his number-one groupie.

"I don't know." His argument sounded

convincing, and he offered what she needed — connections, exposure, experience. The possibilities fluttered her heart and prickled her nerves.

"D'you want to meet the rest of the band? They're over there." Vance gestured at the tables behind Zoey and then stood. "C'mon. Let me introduce ya."

"OK."

Livvy started to stand, but Zoey shook her head. She didn't need to hold her big sister's hand. "I'm good."

She stayed on Vance's heels through the tight stream of back-to-back chairs until he stopped at his table.

Three guys and a bubble-gum-pink-haired girl clustered around a table littered with half-empty paper cups. They looked older than Zoey, probably in their early twenties like Livvy. And judging from their tats and piercings, they wanted to star in a reality spin-off: Fairbanks Ink.

"This is Zoey. She just finished singing." Vance pointed around the table. "That's Devin, Travis, Myles, Bailee."

The names buzzed inside Zoey's head like speaker feedback.

"As good as Gwen Stefani herself," black-bearded Myles said.

"Thanks." Zoey tried to sound confident, but off stage, she was as timid as a nun at a shock-rocker concert.

"Best all night." The three silver studs under Devin's lip flashed.

"Really?" Bailee's voice jumped an octave. She'd performed right before Zoey, a performance only the tone-deaf could've called not horrible.

"Yeah. You can't sing. She can."

"And she can fill-in for Halleigh until September." Vance's sharp-edged tone reminded Zoey of Dad cutting off her and Livvy's arguments.

"I don't know." Bailee leaned against Myles, her hand resting high on his inner thigh. "Karaoke is nothing. Who knows if she can sing worth anything with an actual band?"

"Shut up, Bailee." Devin leaned across the tiny table. "Only band members have a say."

"Bailee's right." Myles shoved Devin against his chair.

Zoey held her breath and inched one foot back. If a fight started, she was gone.

"But Zoey's worth a try." The guy with hoops in his lip like oddly-shaped fangs—Travis?—rubbed a hand over his bald head. "Else we gotta cancel next week."

Bailee shrugged a shoulder and studied her neon orange nails.

The guys eyed Zoey as if assessing a new instrument's specs. Not what she'd expected after Vance's pleading. He'd acted as if she'd be the band's savior.

"We gotta hear her with us first." Myles stuck with his girlfriend. Bailee might not have a say, but Myles gave her a voice.

"No problem." Zoey lifted her chin. She'd prove capable of singing anything they played. "When's your next practice?"

"Tomorrow. Six o'clock," Vance said. "You free?"

"Yes." She'd cancel on anything or anyone else. No way was she letting a bubble-gum-haired girl who couldn't carry a tune win.

"OK. We practice in the basement of our house." Vance asked for Zoey's number. "I'll text you the address."

"This place is getting dull." Bailee pulled away from her boyfriend and stood. "Let's go to Deadhorse."

"You wanna come?" Vance asked Zoey.

"I'm hanging out with my sister tonight." She waved toward the table where Livvy waited. She wasn't about to admit that at seventeen she couldn't get into the popular bar. Not that she'd go anyway.

"See you tomorrow?" He sounded hopeful.

"Yeah. Of course."

"You better. We need you." His tone shifted. Less hope, more demand.

Then he walked away, and it hit her. Tomorrow was Thursday. Thursday night, six o'clock, youth devotional followed by band practice with Justin and Sawyer. The realization wrapped around her lungs and squeezed. Squeezed so hard her vision blurred. How could she ditch her band?

But Justin and Sawyer would understand what this opportunity meant for her—and them. She'd be crazy to turn down concerts and exposure and connections.

They'd be crazy to let her.

2

Rain's a Comin'

Justin Conrad grabbed his cellphone off the amp in his garage and stared at the screen.

No missed calls.

No messages.

No Zoey.

But it was Thursday night. A sacred night. Band practice night. And Zoey hadn't shown up for the youth devo or practice.

"That Zoey? She finally tell you where she's been?" Sawyer Mahon asked from the back of Justin's garage. He sat on a stool behind his drum kit lightly playing a beat. His black-tipped blond spikes and three-quarter-inch gauges fit the drummer image. His skill with sticks earned him the title.

"What?" Justin set down his phone, faking ignorance, and picked up his guitar. No need to admit his missing girlfriend had him distracted. "Just checking the time. We have to quit soon."

"Right." Sawyer snorted. "She really didn't tell you she wasn't coming?"

"Nope. Probably forgot she had to work or her phone died." Justin strummed a few chords. He didn't have to look at Sawyer to know his friend didn't believe him. They fit in practice around Zoey's schedule at the ice cream shack and Sawyer's schedule at the grocery store, but they had an unspoken pact always to meet on Thursdays.

Why hadn't she answered his texts or called him?

Justin shook away his stupid fears. No reason for her to be mad at him. He hadn't done anything.

Enough about Zoey. This was band practice. An endless stream of notes played inside his head begging to blend. He struck an F chord, followed by a D minor, and a new melody filled the garage.

He repeated the chords, and Sawyer merged with a simple rhythm. By the fifth round, they'd grown bolder, the guitar and drums blending and soaring out the open garage door into Justin's sunlit neighborhood. And he soared with it, lightheaded, feeding off the adrenaline.

Lifting his head, he caught Sawyer's eye. Sawyer gave a tiny nod. Time to finish big.

Justin stood, slamming down on the final chord as Sawyer crashed the cymbals.

Nothing sounded better than a new song. Even a less-than-great new song.

"What do you think?" Justin sat back down cradling his guitar.

"Gold star." Sawyer raised his voice over his new beat. If he was sitting behind his drums, they weren't silent for a second.

Justin started his song again, playing alone, committing the chords to memory as he struggled to catch hold of lyrics that fit.

The sound of a car engine interrupted his thoughts, and a few seconds later, Mom's minivan pulled into the driveway. She stepped out.

Justin's fist tightened around the guitar's neck, the

strings biting into his fingers. It was late. Maybe not late-late, but she was a mom and married, even if her skinny jeans and red top didn't scream married-mother-of-three.

"It's almost ten. You're about finished tonight, right?" It sounded as if she wasn't asking.

"Yes, ma'am," Justin said.

"Thank you." She flashed a smile, but Justin couldn't tell if her smile was too happy for someone who'd been hanging out with a girl friend.

Mom went into the house, and Justin unplugged his guitar from the amp and put it on the stand. His acoustic occupied another slot, but the third was empty. The space echoed the hollow feeling in his chest. Zoey kept her bass there after practice.

He twisted his guitar pick between his fingers. Zoey wasn't his mom, and he wasn't his dad. She had no reason to lie or keep secrets or cheat on him.

He glanced at Sawyer. "Want a ride home?"

"Got my bike." Sawyer jabbed a stick towards the dull red bike in the grass.

"Stick it in the back of my car."

"Gonna check on Zoey, aren't you?" His accusing tone was as flat as an out-of-tune guitar.

"Maybe."

"She shouldn't have missed practice. Not without saying something."

"You want a ride or not?"

"Nothing's more important than practice."

"Let it go, man." Justin laughed despite the tightening of his gut. He didn't share Sawyer's better-be-in-the-hospital-on-life-support attitude toward missing practice. But Zoey almost did. "You coming with me?"

"Fine."

"I'll go tell my parents." Justin pulled his keys from his pocket and tossed them across the garage. They clanged into Sawyer's hand.

"You mean get their permission."

Justin ignored the insult and headed into the house. His friends only needed to tell their parents where they were going; Justin needed approval. But that's how it had always been, so he shrugged it off and trudged up the stairs.

Justin's family was hanging out in the family room, minus three-year-old Tristan. Savannah was reading, curled up in an armchair. Mom was on the couch next to Dad. A good sign, but Justin mentally measured the distance between them. About one ruler-length. Too close? Too far? They were parents, so kind of old, but if they were still in love...

"Time for bed, Savannah," Mom said.

"It's not fair." Justin's ten-year-old sister tumbled off a chair. "It's not dark out. Why can't I stay up like Justin?"

Be quiet, Savannah. Wouldn't be the first time he'd gotten stuck at home because his little sister had scored sympathy points. Forget about him being nine years older than Savannah.

"You don't have to sleep." Mom's voice had a tired, compromising tone that indicated she wanted to sleep. "You can read in bed."

Savannah stomped past Justin.

"Can I give Sawyer a ride home and stop by Zoey's?" Justin asked.

Dad glanced at his watch. "It's a little late."

"I'll be back by midnight."

Dad's mouth twisted to one side in a half-frown.

Why did he have to act like the question was difficult? "All right. But make sure you're home on time."

"I will." Justin hurried back down the stairs. When had he ever broken curfew? Never.

Maybe it was his choice of friends that made his parents strict. He and Sawyer had been friends since kindergarten, but Sawyer looked like a rule breaker with the silver barbell in his eyebrow and the gauges in his ears. Sawyer's mom only had three rules: Sawyer had to let her know where he was, he had to graduate from high school, and no getting a tattoo. They argued about the tattoo regularly.

If Justin ever mentioned a tattoo to his parents, he'd be grounded until he graduated from college.

He crossed the yard to his car and slid into the driver's seat. The car speakers blasted Christian heavy metal from Sawyer's phone.

"Took you long enough," Sawyer said.

Without bothering to answer, Justin squinted at Alaska's midnight sun, slipped on his sunglasses, and drove toward Sawyer's house.

He dropped off Sawyer, switched the music to his own playlist—a mixture of Christian pop and rock—and drove to Zoey's house. He parked in the driveway behind Zoey and Livvy's green car and stared at the split-level, flipping a black guitar pick back and forth through his fingers.

His insides felt like a loose guitar string vibrating wrong. But he had nothing to worry about. She'd have a good explanation for not telling him about missing practice or answering his texts. He'd only sent three, so she'd know he cared but wouldn't feel smothered. Because all his parents' books on relationships said that was important.

Be caring, not controlling.

Be interested, not indifferent.

Justin wouldn't make his dad's mistakes. He marched up the front steps and rang the doorbell.

A few seconds later, the door opened.

"Justin, hi." Livvy's voice swung up in a question. Probably because of how late it was. Everyone knew about his curfew.

"Hey. Is Zoey home?"

"Yeah. Come in. I'll tell her you're here."

"Thanks." He crossed the shoe-littered, Arctic entry and took the stairs down to the Harris's family room. Zoey and Livvy's gray-striped cat, Tiger, streaked past him, running the opposite direction—up the stairs.

He settled on the overstuffed couch. The furniture in Zoey's house reminded him of their practice space— worn and comfortable. Next to his garage, this was his favorite hangout. Of course, here it smelled better, like vanilla and cinnamon.

Zoey clattered down the stairs and around the corner, her purple-streaked black hair hanging loose down her back. One look at her brown eyes, dulled with something like worry, and he choked on a smile.

"Hey, you weren't at the devo tonight or practice." He tried not to sound accusing.

"Yeah." She wound her necklace around her finger and unwound it. "Um, I have something to tell you."

"OK." His heart thudded crushing the air from his lungs. Had she been avoiding him? Because right now, she definitely avoided meeting his gaze. Maybe he'd rather not know.

"Tonight, I was, um..." She stared at the floor.

Had she been out with someone else? Was she

breaking up with him?

Her head popped up, and she stared him square in the eye. "I was practicing with another band."

His heart stopped as if it had been unplugged. "You've joined another band?"

"Yeah. Aurora Fire. I met them last night at a karaoke thing at the Downstairs Coffeehouse." The words tumbled out of Zoey's mouth like a guitar solo played too fast.

Justin stared at her.

"Their lead singer left for the summer, so they need someone to fill in. They liked my voice and asked me to practice with them tonight." She paused to catch her breath, her eyes wide and unblinking, pleading for him to share her excitement.

What was he supposed to say? He slid his hand into his pocket and dug the edges of his pick into his calloused fingers. She was leaving him for another band.

Not him exactly, but him and Sawyer.

"I'm so sorry." The pleading was now in her voice. "I know I should've told you right away, but I didn't know how. It's only for the summer, though, and this is a really good opportunity for me. They've already got several gigs lined up."

Her words crawled inside him like poison. Death. Killing him. He couldn't lose her. And refusing her the freedom to sing with Aurora Fire would be the quickest way to lose her. So Justin forced down the argument swelling inside him. "Several gigs, huh? That does sound good."

"I know, right?" She almost smiled but held it back as if she didn't quite believe Justin's sincerity.

But he was doing everything right, wasn't he?

Maybe he needed to be more enthusiastic.

"I think it will be good for you, and Sawyer too, after the summer," Zoey continued. "If people like my singing, then they might want to hear us when I'm back with you guys."

"If people like you?" He took Zoey's hand and entwined his fingers with hers.

She didn't pull away, but she didn't tighten her fingers around his either.

"Of course, they'll like you." Was he really giving her a pep talk to encourage her to leave their band? "And just because you're playing with them doesn't mean you can't play with us too."

"I'll be practicing with them a lot to learn their music, and I'll need to rest my voice in between. But I can still play bass with you guys."

*Learn their music... rest my voice...*She'd be singing someone else's songs.

"And there's one more thing. Their first gig is two weeks from Saturday, and I know we were supposed to play for the youth group that night..." The hesitance returned to her voice.

"Hey, no problem." Justin forced the words past his dry throat. "Sawyer and I will figure something out."

"So you're really OK with this?"

No, don't do it. He stared at their clasped hands and then looked up fighting the urge to squash her hopefulness. "Yeah. It sounds really good for you."

"I should've realized you'd be happy for me." Zoey smiled and took two steps closer.

"Of course I am." He'd act happy about anything if it made her smile as if he was her hero. "Besides, maybe it's part of God's plan for your music career."

"Yeah, maybe." Her happiness dimmed as if she didn't believe him. Or in God's plan.

"Tell me about Aurora Fire." Justin dropped onto the couch, pulling Zoey down too.

She settled next to him and told him about this other band's music, the house they shared, the guys.

Justin forced a grin and willed himself to hide his fears.

Please, Lord, make me happy for her.

3

Watching the Bottom Fall

Sawyer stood at the kitchen sink and scrubbed a dirty plate. A drum solo blasted through his earbuds begging him to join in. He lifted his hands out of the sink and played the air drums, soap suds spraying the tiny kitchen. Skills with the sticks was the only thing Sawyer's dad had left behind seventeen years ago.

He only knew three things about his dad: his name was Toby Sawyer, he was a drummer, and he couldn't handle having a kid. But someday, Toby Sawyer would see the name 'Sawyer Mahon' listed as a band's drummer. Then he'd call or email, and Sawyer would tell him off. Sawyer and his mom hadn't needed — would never need — Toby Sawyer in their lives.

The drum solo ended, and Sawyer plunged his hands into the soapy water.

Someone tapped his shoulder.

Sawyer spun around, swearing and ripping the earbuds out of his ears.

"Don't say that." Justin gave his usual response.

"Don't go sneaking up on people."

"I knocked. You didn't answer."

Not much argument for that. Except to remember to lock the door.

Sawyer faced the sink and swiped the dishcloth

over a dinner plate.

"Doing chores?" Justin asked.

"Just washing dishes." At Sawyer's, no one made a chore list. He and Mom just did what needed to be done. They took care of each other. Sawyer yanked the drain plug and led Justin the five feet into the living room. "You talk to Zoey?"

"Yeah." Justin flopped onto the couch. "She's filling in on lead vocals for this band—Aurora Fire—and she had practice with them tonight."

"She's ditching us?" Sawyer's disbelief rose from his gut. He leaned against the edge of his living room window and stared at Justin.

"Not exactly." Justin stretched his arms across the back of the floral couch, calm and chill. As if he hadn't just found out their band was screwed.

This news stank as bad as the still-present stench of his microwaved burrito dinner. When Zoey hadn't shown up earlier, Sawyer figured she had some stupid girl reason. Like dying her hair or painting her nails or cramps. Not that Zoey ever skipped practice for a stupid girl reason—that's why she was the only girl besides his mom he could stand to be around for more than five minutes—but she was still a girl. And girls were annoying, frustrating, and unpredictable.

Sawyer hammered his fists against the wall. This was why band members shouldn't date. They worried more about each other's feelings than about the music. He swore.

"Don't say that."

Sawyer ignored Justin and stepped away from the window. Heat bubbled inside him like lava. How could Justin just sit there? It was his band too, and his girlfriend who was ditching them. Sawyer kicked a leg of the scarred coffee table. A dumpster rescue like most of the furniture, it wasn't hurt by a little abuse.

"It's just for the summer," Justin said.

Sawyer plopped down on the red chair that matched the couch only in shabbiness. "Just the summer? Summer's our best time. We can practice all day long."

"And Zoey can still practice with us, when she's free."

"What about next Saturday?" He narrowed his eyes already suspecting the answer. "Will she be playing with us?"

"No." The confidence in Justin's voice faded. "Her first concert with Aurora Fire is that night."

"Right. We finally get a chance to play in public, and we have to cancel."

"We don't have to cancel. We can play without her."

"Seriously?" Sawyer tapped his heels against the faded beige carpet. Every muscle twitched, as if he'd been binge drinking caffeine supplements.

"Why not?"

"Because she's our vocalist." An instrumental riff was one thing, but an entire set without lyrics would be lame. "We could replace her."

Justin frowned. Finally, some negative emotion from the guy.

"Just for the summer." Sawyer raised his voice in a mocking falsetto trying to push Justin over to the dark side. Way back in kindergarten, Justin had arranged search parties to hunt down the gold at the end of the rainbow, and he hadn't grown out of believing in fairytales.

"Let it go, man. This can be good for us too."

Justin flipped a guitar pick across his knuckles.

"How? We'll have more free time?"

"No. If people like Zoey, they'll follow her back to us."

"Sure they will." Just another one of Justin's fairytales. This year they'd be seniors. They needed this summer to play, to perform, to prove themselves as a band. If they failed, Justin and Zoey would be off to college. No one, including Mom, expected that of Sawyer. Drums were his only chance at a future. But what good was a drummer without a band?

"Have some faith. God will work things out for all of us."

Sawyer pounded his heels a little faster. God, Justin's never-gonna-do-anything-about-it solution.

Faith was as practical as hunting down the leprechaun's gold.

To his left, the front door opened banging against a dining table chair.

Mom walked in, the sun glowing off her pale blonde hair. She wrestled her key out of the lock. "Hi, boys." The key freed, she shut the door and sat in the corner of the couch opposite Justin.

Sawyer deepened his scowl.

"Hi, Lexi," Justin said.

"What's wrong?" She glanced back and forth between them. "You two look like your favorite band broke up."

Yeah, that sounded about right. "Our band broke up."

"We did not." Justin's voice was tight.

A tremor of pleasure ran through Sawyer at the cracking of Justin's life-is-perfect attitude.

"What happened?" Mom's concern eased the

tension in Sawyer's muscles. She cared about their band.

"Zoey quit."

"Zoey?" She looked at Justin. "Your Zoey?"

"Do you know any other Zoeys, Mom?"

"She didn't quit." Justin sounded tired of repeating himself. "She's just with another band for the summer."

"Really?" Her eyebrows shot up like her voice.

At last, someone sounded surprised.

"Apparently, her loyalty doesn't go very deep," Sawyer muttered.

"It's a good opportunity for her," Justin spoke through clenched teeth.

About time he showed some annoyance, though it was probably directed at Sawyer, not Zoey.

"You're a very good boyfriend." Mom sounded wistful.

Sawyer rolled his eyes. Everybody loved Justin. The perfect son. The perfect student. The perfect boyfriend. Only because the guy could write music and shred a guitar did Sawyer stay friends with him. That and because Justin put up with all of Sawyer's crap. The guy was the perfect friend too.

Mom glanced at the microwave clock a few feet away in the kitchen. "It's almost midnight. You going home or staying the night, Justin?"

"Going." Justin stood and looked at Sawyer. "Practice tomorrow?"

"After I get off work." Bagging groceries cut into practice time, but he had to support his music and drumming habits.

"See ya later, then." Justin let himself out.

"You don't look very happy." Mom directed her

tired attention at Sawyer.

"Gold star." Wasn't as if he was trying to hide it. Sawyer drummed his fingers on the chair arms. "Zoey didn't tell us about leaving or nothing. She just didn't show."

"I'm sorry." She sounded more disappointed than Justin had.

"Yeah. Whatever." He blew out a sigh.

"What are you working tomorrow?"

"Ten to four."

"I don't go in until one. I can walk or call Gina if you want to take the car."

"Thanks." Bagging groceries couldn't pay for music, drums, and a car. Though apparently at Justin's house, chores covered all three.

"I'm exhausted." She stood, stretching and yawning. "Watch the clock and don't stay up too late."

"I won't." At least, he wouldn't intend to. With the barely-setting summer sun, he sometimes forgot to go to bed. Not smart if he had work the next day.

"'Night." Mom headed to her room.

Sawyer moved to the couch and grabbed the remote. He jabbed a button. What would happen to their band? He didn't want to answer that question. They could play without Zoey, right? He changed channels. Like a drummer and a guitarist without a vocalist would be a big hit.

They could replace Zoey, but finding someone with the musical talent and a voice like hers would be impossible.

He switched off the TV and went to his room. After turning on the stereo low enough not to bother Mom, he tried to clear his mind with push-ups. But the only thing that became clear was that Zoey had ditched them—him.

He'd make sure she realized her mistake and came back. Because without her, he didn't have a band. And without a band, he had nothing.

4

The Hunger

Zoey hit the next-to-the-last note strong, a perfect blending with Aurora Fire's playing, but on the last word, her voice cracked. The final chord and cymbal crash faded too soon, and her coughs echoed through Aurora Fire's basement.

"She's butchering the music with that pathetic coughing." Bailee, with her sparkling diamond nose-stud, sat on the stained green couch. Aurora Fire's groupie and judge.

"Shut up, Bailee." Vance spoke through clenched teeth. "No talking during practice."

Zoey raised her water bottle to her mouth. Her hands shook and the water sloshed. Her second practice with Aurora Fire, and she was butchering the songs. The lyrics—dark, depressing, creepy—were good, but some words caught in her throat. Words that made her blush. Words she hoped Mama couldn't hear in heaven.

The Aurora Fire guys cast narrow-eyed looks her way. Vance twisted a dial on an amp; shaved-headed Travis held his hands poised over the keyboard; Bailee's boyfriend, Myles, twirled his drumsticks; Devin fingered chords on a shiny bass Zoey envied. Their fidgeting and frowns declared their doubts.

She had to prove herself. She would prove herself. With another sip of water, she swallowed her own doubts.

"You OK?" Vance asked, a hint of annoyance creeping into his voice.

Zoey nodded. "Sorry."

"Next song—'Legends of Death,'" Vance said.

Zoey licked her lips and found the right lyric sheet.

Myles led them in. When Zoey heard her cue, she joined, her words clear and certain, and she managed not to cough or stumble over a single word—because she didn't even try to sing the ones she usually choked on.

Bailee, however, watching from the couch caught every unsung lyric.

Ignore her.

But Bailee's glares and sneers and wrinkled nose broke Zoey's concentration on tone and pitch and keeping her place.

Zoey survived the first run-through of the eight song set. If feeling totally drained counted as surviving. She expected Travis and Myles to grab her by the arms and throw her out like night club bouncers evicting a drunk. And part of her, the exhausted, felt-like-a-failure part, didn't care if they did.

"Let's go through it again," Vance said without even glancing at Zoey. Apparently, she'd survived round one.

"I need to pee," Zoey lied. What she needed was a time machine so she could go back to Wednesday night and un-accept Aurora Fire's invitation.

"Hurry up."

She stepped over the cords snaking across the

concrete floor and scurried into the basement bathroom. A moment alone to breathe. She relaxed against the closed door and took a deep breath. The room smelled a little weird, but it was mostly clean.

Singing was supposed to bring her peace, but her nerves felt twitchy. The problem had to be the unfamiliar songs. If Aurora Fire didn't kick her out tonight, she'd try harder, practice harder, sing harder.

Voices drifted through the hollow door. Zoey strained to listen twisting her necklace around her finger and cutting off the circulation.

"She can't hack it." Bailee's harsh judgment was unmistakable.

"We don't have any other choice." At least Vance was on her side, sort of.

"And she keeps up with the music," Travis's gravelly voice added. "That other girl who tried out finished every song three measures late."

"But she could sing all the words." Bailee refused any praise toward Zoey.

"What's your problem, Bailee?" Vance to the almost-rescue again.

"I think she's going to bail on you guys on stage."

Zoey squeezed her eyes shut against the sting of tears. Bailee was probably right. Singing wasn't usually this hard—not with Justin and Sawyer anyway. Zoey's throat burned at the thought of them, and tears dampened her eyelashes. She pushed away from the door. She couldn't think about them right now. Regret would only make her singing worse.

She splashed water on her face and glanced at her reflection in the mirror. Her necklace, designed by Mama, peeked out at the neck of her T-shirt. Butterfly-shaped beads, iridescent pearls, and sea foam green ovals alternated in a pattern that clashed with Zoey's mostly black wardrobe, but she never took it off.

If she couldn't sing good enough for Aurora Fire, maybe she couldn't sing good enough period. Maybe Mama had been wrong, and no one would ever buy tickets to hear Zoey Harris, Live in Concert. Maybe Zoey would be forever stuck singing in coffeehouses, or garages, or church.

No. She would succeed with Aurora Fire. She had to. For Mama. Music was the only way to hang on to the memories. Without it, she'd be empty.

Zoey patted her face dry with a musty-smelling towel and returned for another run-through of torture.

~*~

A week later, after yet another pathetic practice, Zoey hurried out of the Aurora Fire house and into the sunlit evening before the last notes faded from the air. One week until the concert, and she was certain Aurora Fire still regretted their decision.

She couldn't get through the lyrics. They gummed up her throat, Bailee shot her hate-filled looks, and Zoey tried not to cry. She kept telling herself they were just words, but too much church had created a voice that disagreed. A voice that sounded an awful lot like Justin correcting Sawyer.

But she needed this too much to listen.

She pushed back the strands of hair sticking to her sweaty temples and walked a little faster down the sidewalk. As long as she could bring it Saturday night, then Aurora Fire would know they'd done the right thing.

When she stepped onto Justin's street, the faint

strains of a song floated to her ears and wrapped around her like a cozy blanket. The familiar melody carried her to his house, but she stopped at the end of the driveway mouthing the lyrics she'd helped Justin compose:

My heart beats
Fueled by memories
Of you
Every breath
Keeps me living
For you
Not forever gone
If I fight to live
For you

She'd been thinking of Mama when composing that song, and it expressed all the reasons she'd joined Aurora Fire. This opportunity was one step on the way to achieving her dream. She couldn't fail.

The music ended, and Zoey entered the garage. Justin's grin and Sawyer's glare greeted her.

The sight was like warmth from a hot pad soothing away her stress. So what if Sawyer was worse than Livvy when she was mad about something? He'd always been that way, and Justin remained his usual, upbeat self. Nothing had changed between the three of them.

"Hey." Justin slipped off his guitar and set it on the stand.

"We're still practicing." Sawyer growled the words like warning off an intruder.

"We're finished." Justin stepped around cords and amps to kiss Zoey. His lips touched hers with familiar heat and flavor like mint toothpaste. He always tasted as if he'd just brushed his teeth or used mouthwash, probably because he'd stuck with the brush-your-teeth-after-every-meal rule from his braces days.

"I'm not finished," Sawyer said.

"Then keep playing." Justin wound his fingers with Zoey's and led her over to the tan couch facing the practice area.

Sawyer pounded the drums, probably to be annoying, but the noise gave her and Justin an excuse to sit close.

"How was practice?" Justin's breath was hot in her ear. He wrapped an arm around her, pulling her into his side.

"OK." She settled next to him, not minding the sticky heat where their bodies touched. She rested her head on his shoulder and closed her eyes. One of the good things about Justin was he let her be. He didn't try to talk or kiss her whenever they were together. She could relax.

"Are those your new lyrics?" Justin asked.

Zoey opened her eyes and glanced at her papers and water bottle on the opposite end of the couch. She nodded.

"Can I see them?" He reached across her.

"No!" Zoey scrambled to block him.

"Why?" Laughter sparkled in his eyes. "What's wrong with them?"

"Nothing." Her heart rate matched Sawyer's frantic drumming.

"You said they were good," Justin reminded her.

"Yeah, well, they are." Zoey swallowed. They wouldn't meet Justin's definition of good—as in moral. And he'd never understand her compromise. She cocked her head, touched his arm, and smiled. "I just want them to be a surprise for you next weekend."

Justin looked at her funny.

She'd never been good at flirting.

Sawyer quit drumming and the garage fell into an uneasy quiet.

"You are coming on Saturday, right?" She dreaded how Justin would react to Aurora Fire's lyrics, but she wouldn't survive on stage without Justin in the audience. Watching, listening, grinning. Did believing he'd be supportive no matter what make her selfish?

"We've got our own concert Saturday, remember?" Sawyer didn't know the definition of supportive.

Heat crept down her scalp. "Yeah, I remember. But we don't go on until ten. You'll be done by then, won't you?"

"Yeah. And we'll be there to hear you," Justin assured her.

Zoey gave him a grateful smile.

"I won't," Sawyer muttered.

"Yeah, he will," Justin whispered.

Zoey giggled and cuddled back into his side.

Sawyer filled the garage with the sound of his drums again. Life was perfect.

Then the door to the house swung open, and Zoey jerked away from Justin. Not that they were doing anything wrong, but his parents acted as though they were guilty of something if they were caught closer than hand-holding distance.

"Sorry to interrupt." Mrs. Conrad stepped into the garage digging through her purse. She glanced up, eyes widening. "Hi, Zoey. I didn't know you were here."

"Hi." Zoey's voice squeaked. Goody. Now she sounded guilty too.

"I need you to babysit."

Zoey stopped breathing. Her, babysit? She didn't know what to do with kids. Losing Mama had stunted her mothering gene. But Mrs. Conrad was speaking to Justin, so Zoey's pulse slowed.

"I'm meeting your dad, and we should both be home in an hour or so." Mrs. Conrad pulled her keys from her purse with a triumphant jingle. "Tristan's already in bed, though he's probably not asleep." Her gaze shifted to Sawyer as if to blame him for Justin's three-year-old brother still being awake, and then she looked at Justin. "Savannah's watching TV upstairs."

"Uh, sure." Justin glanced at Zoey and Sawyer.

"They can stay," Mrs. Conrad said, "but if Sawyer leaves, so does Zoey."

Zoey felt the blush. What did Mrs. Conrad think would happen if she stayed when Sawyer left? She'd willingly compromise the words she sang on stage, but she wouldn't put those phrases into practice. Not with Justin. Not with anybody.

"Got it." Justin managed to say it without sarcasm. Zoey couldn't have.

"Thanks." Mrs. Conrad hurried out the open garage door.

Justin watched her leave, flipping a guitar pick through his fingers. His ever-present grin had disappeared and sadness—no, worry, and a million questions—replaced it.

"Hey, you coming inside?" Zoey tugged his empty hand, trying to bring him back from whatever land of fear he'd drifted to.

"Yeah." Justin smiled as if the thought was gone,

but he grabbed Zoey's hand in a don't-leave-me kind of grip and pulled her toward the house.

"I don't know what your parents' deal is," Sawyer said as the three of them crowded through the door and into the kitchen. "It's like they think I'll chaperone you. As if you need it. Do they know you at all?"

"At least they let you stay," Justin said.

Zoey had to agree with Sawyer. Justin was the most obedient, trustworthy, godly person she knew, yet his parents acted as if he still needed a babysitter.

She hoped Mr. and Mrs. Conrad wouldn't decide to be as supportive as Justin and show up at Aurora Fire's concert. They'd never let Zoey hang out with Justin again—with or without Sawyer. And she needed Justin. He cheered her up when nothing else in the world could. He loved her when she'd forgotten what love felt like. He reminded her of God and heaven and hope.

He reminded her of Mama.

5

Saints and Sinners

Sawyer grabbed the vibrating phone off his cluttered desk and yawned. Sunday morning. Justin. Church. He wanted to ignore the buzzing and climb back into bed. Why give up a couple of hours of sleep to listen to people talk about faith and forgiveness, sin and sacrifice?

Because after all that listening came band practice.

He yanked on a T-shirt and a pair of jeans and headed for the front door.

Justin's car idled in front of the house. Sawyer collapsed into the passenger seat squinting in the sunlight.

"Morning," Justin said.

"Why am I awake?"

"Because church is good for your soul."

Sawyer groaned. "It's way too early for bad jokes."

Justin laughed, and Sawyer drowned him out by turning up the radio volume. At this hour, even worship lyrics were better than talking. Sawyer rubbed the tired from his eyes. Back in elementary school, Mom hadn't given him a choice about church. The Conrads had offered to take him, and if she'd been scheduled to work, that was free babysitting. But now he didn't need a babysitter.

And now Justin annoyed him with phone calls and

texts if he tried to stay in bed on a Sunday. But Justin was the only person besides Mom who cared about how and where Sawyer wasted his time. So here he was, up before ten, so Justin could believe he'd save Sawyer's soul. And if heaven existed and Sawyer had a soul, maybe that counted as his good deed.

And band practice motivated Sawyer to suffer.

In the teen room at church, Zoey had saved them spots on a couch. Justin put his arm around her shoulders.

Sawyer suppressed another groan. Wasn't that against church rules?

Propping his head on his fist, he tried to pay attention to Brandon, the youth minister. Over the summer, they were studying the Sermon on the Mount. Today, Brandon was talking about peacemakers and sons of God. Whatever that meant, Justin probably had it down. Those words sounded like him. Sawyer, however, would never be accused of either one, not that he cared. He tried not to fall asleep. The study on Revelation had held his interest this past spring; they should discuss demons and dragons again.

Finally, the bell rang, and everyone stood and stretched, including Sawyer. One forty-five minute Bible lecture down; another hour-and-a-half of praising, praying, and preaching. Then drum time.

He tapped his index fingers against his thighs, matching the beat in his head.

"One more thing." Brandon stopped the mass exodus. "Don't forget about the concert Justin, Sawyer, and Zoey are doing for us Saturday night in the fellowship hall. You guys have a name?"

"Not yet." Justin, acting as the band's spokesman,

admitted that fact without sounding even a little embarrassed. But playing together for almost two years without having a name? Pathetic.

They discussed names every other week, and the discussion always played out two-against-one. So choosing a band name ended in an argument. But the name was important. People needed to remember it, to want to wear it, to stick it on their bumpers. Not forget it by the next morning—or worse, laugh at it. Which was why they were still a no-name band.

"Maybe we'll have one by Saturday," Justin continued. "But Zoey won't be there. She was asked to fill-in on vocals with another band for the summer." He said that as if it were good news.

"Really?" Brandon looked at Zoey, and she nodded, her cheeks turning pink. "Good for you."

A moment of awkward silence passed, and then people continued out the door.

Sawyer followed Justin and Zoey into the hall. "I don't know why you're bragging on her. She's the one who ditched."

"Hey!" Justin spun around, his nostrils flaring. "Don't ever call her that."

Sawyer stepped back. "Call her what? I said she ditched us. What did you think I said?"

"Oh." Justin's face relaxed. "Nothing."

"Did you think I said..." The accusation hammered his heart into this throat. His hands tightened into fists. "I wouldn't call her that. Or anyone else."

Both Justin and Zoey frowned.

"Forget it." Sawyer shoved past them and stormed down the hall. Sure, Justin was always getting onto him about cussing, but Mom only stopped him from being disrespectful toward women. So he usually avoided girls since most of them made it difficult to remain respectful. Except for Zoey. He'd never had trouble respecting her. He might be ticked off, but she was his friend.

When he reached the foyer, he paused. He couldn't exactly leave, since the church was five miles or more from his house, and he didn't have a car. Which meant he was stuck listening to the sermon. He sighed, then entered the sanctuary and slumped on an empty row.

"Sawyer? Hi." A girl in front of him twisted around, her thick, dirty-blonde-colored braid swinging over the back of the pew.

Felicia Dunn. He groaned inwardly. If only he'd been paying attention. She topped his list of girls to avoid. She'd been flirting with him since the end of the school year but hadn't picked up on his disinterest. Weird, since he wasn't subtle.

"I can't believe Zoey quit your band," she said.

"It's only for the summer." Great, now he was justifying Zoey's decision.

"But still, that's not right."

"Guess not."

"No, it isn't." Felicia stood, pulling her friend Kallie Something-or-other up too. "You look lonely."

He did? Because he was happy alone, given the alternative.

Felicia and Kallie forced their way next to him on the pew tripping over his feet. Felicia parked herself next to Sawyer, her knee bumping his.

Sawyer wrinkled his nose. She stank like unnatural flowers.

"Are you going to find someone to replace her?" Felicia asked.

Sawyer squished himself against the armrest. "I don't know."

"Does she just sing?"

"No, she plays bass."

"Oh." Felicia nodded without a flicker of understanding in her silver eyes. "Bass...that's sort of like a guitar, isn't it?"

"It's nothing like a guitar," Sawyer lied. If she wanted to discuss music with him, she should know that kind of thing.

"What should I play, if I wanted to join your band?"

Sawyer rolled his eyes. Why did people ask that? Choosing an instrument to join a band was going about it backwards. He had played the drums before he owned a set, Justin created music before he learned to play the guitar, and Zoey started singing before Justin met her. They didn't randomly assign instruments so they could be a band. The music was a part of each of them, and they became a band because they had to play. And they needed each other.

Which was why Zoey's decision had sucker-punched him.

He crossed his arms. "We're not taking new people."

"Oh." Felicia pouted for a second—not cute—but then she perked back up twisting right and left in the pew and stirring up the flower stench. "Where are Justin and Zoey?"

Sawyer sneezed.

"Bless you. You guys didn't have a fight, did you? You'll still be playing Saturday, right?"

"Yeah, we'll play, but I don't think we'll be worth listening to."

"That's not true." Felicia planted a hand on his arm. "I bet you'll be awesome."

Sawyer sneezed again. He jerked out of her grasp to shield his nose.

"Are you OK? You're not getting sick or something, are you?"

"No." He scowled, his nose twitching. "It's that disgusting perfume you're wearing. Smells like flower puke."

Felicia pulled back, her chin trembling. Maybe she'd finally read his not-interested banner.

The singing started then leaving Sawyer trapped next to her. He tried breathing through his mouth, but then he tasted the smell which was worse. So he breathed shallowly and drummed his fingers against the pew end. One thing was for sure, if they did decide to replace Zoey as vocalist, Felicia wouldn't make the cut.

After services ended, Sawyer bolted away from Felicia's suffocating fumes and beat the crowd outside. He leaned against the building, inhaling fresh air and watching for Justin and Zoey. He was still ticked off by their accusation, but he needed a ride.

When Justin and Zoey exited, hand in hand, Sawyer fell in step next to them.

"There you are," Justin said. "You coming over to practice?"

"Got nothing better to do."

"Unless you found a girlfriend?" Zoey emphasized the last word.

"Huh?"

"You and Felicia? Sitting together?" She wiggled her eyebrows.

"What? No!" Sawyer kicked a pebble. It bounced

off a car's rim.

"You make a cute couple."

Sawyer clenched his teeth and made a sound like a growl. If he ever found a girlfriend, she'd have to understand and love music. The only person who even came close to that standard was Zoey. And she belonged to Justin.

Laughing, Justin punched the unlock button on his key ring, and Zoey opened the car's passenger door.

"About accusing you earlier..." Justin stopped Sawyer before he got in the car. "Sorry, man."

That was Justin—always willing to apologize.

Sawyer, jaw still tight, wanted to tell Justin off again. But a few hours with his sticks, and he'd beat away the accusations and memories of flowery girls. "Fine, whatever. I've gotta be at work by four."

He yanked open the door and climbed inside. At least he'd be able to pretend they were still a band for a few hours.

If only he could believe they weren't doomed.

6

Smothering Walls

Zoey strummed her bass strings, the music vibrating through Justin's garage and her soul. A lazy Sunday afternoon practice—she hadn't felt this relaxed in days. Sawyer had left for work a few minutes earlier taking his negative energy.

Justin sat on the ottoman facing her and harmonized on his electric, their chords floating into the summer air. He glanced at her. "You wanna practice your Aurora Fire songs?"

And there went her relaxing calm riding out the door on a misplayed chord.

"No." Her fingers pressed against the fingerboard, the strings biting into her skin. "Not without the music."

"C'mon." Justin nudged her foot. "I'm sure you've got the words memorized by now."

"I meant, I can't sing without hearing the band."

"Haven't you memorized that too?"

"No!"

Justin flinched.

Goody, now she was neither relaxed nor nice. She forced a smile. "Sorry, but I was having fun. I don't want to practice Aurora Fire stuff now, just our songs."

"No problem." Justin shrugged it off, and some of

her calm returned. "Think you'll be able to practice here again this week?"

"I don't know." She laid the bass across her lap. "I'm working a lot, and I've got Aurora Fire..."

"Every day?"

"Yeah, pretty much. No practice today or tomorrow, but I'm working until close tomorrow."

"How about before work?"

"Livvy and I are going to the dentist."

"Oh." He hunched over the guitar watching his silent chord changes.

"You can go one day without seeing me, can't you?" She linked her hand with his free one.

He looked up. "OK, yeah. One day. Does that mean you're free Tuesday?"

"Not exactly." She pulled away. "I've got work and a late practice after that. Same on Wednesday."

"So I won't see you until Thursday?"

Thursday was Mama's birthday. Zoey rubbed her thumb along the necklace. She wouldn't want to see anybody that day.

"What? You're not free Thursday either? C'mon, Zo."

"Sorry I have to work for my instruments." She heard the annoyance in her voice. Annoyance she never felt around Justin. "What's wrong with you anyway?"

"Nothing."

But it wasn't nothing. Justin didn't get upset like this—not with her. Should she argue or apologize?

"Are you mad at me for singing with Aurora Fire?" She tilted her head watching his expression. Was he hurt? Frustrated? Seeing Justin show negative emotion was strange. But it sparked something in her blood. "Because you agreed it was a good opportunity for me. And for our band."

"But you're so busy. You have no time to practice with us."

And she missed their practices so much her soul ached. But playing with Justin and Sawyer hadn't been going anywhere. "I've gotta get the songs down by Saturday."

"Yeah. I'm sorry." Justin turned back on his I-love-you-no-matter-what expression. "Besides, you're here now."

"And I don't have to leave anytime soon." The calm returned, but instead of peaceful, Zoey felt drained.

"What d'you want to play next?"

"Uh." Her phone rang. "Just a sec."

She pulled it out and saw a text from Vance. Uh-oh.

Practice in 1 hr. B Here.

What little energy Zoey had left pooled from her. This was so not how she wanted to spend today. Yeah, she needed the practice, but she also needed a break.

"Something wrong?"

The thought of Bailee's glares, and Vance's commands, and her failures pulled her nerves into thin, tight strings. "I've got practice in an hour."

"What?" The news wiped the support off his face. "You just said you didn't have practice today."

"And until five seconds ago, I didn't." She squatted on the floor and packed up her bass. "But I've got to go."

"So maybe, if I'm lucky, I'll see you again this

weekend?"

His harsh tone snapped her tense nerves. "What do you want me to do? I can't skip practice."

He was silent as if considering Zoey's options. As if she had any. If she wanted to perform with Aurora Fire, she had to sing when they said sing.

"You could invite me."

"Invite you?" Zoey froze then glanced up. His eager face begged her to say yes.

"I don't have anything else to do."

"It's not a good idea." For her or for him. No way could his supportive boyfriend role survive an Aurora Fire practice. She wasn't sure it could survive an Aurora Fire concert, but that was Saturday's problem.

"Why not?" He knelt next to her and her bass case. "Why don't you want me there?"

How could she tell him it would be like bringing a too-loud conscience, and she couldn't deal with that? "I don't need you there distracting me."

"I won't distract you. Promise. I'll just sit and listen and not say a word."

"I said no, OK?" The words came out angrier than she expected.

"Fine." He stood up. "Forget about it."

The hurt in his voice plucked her heart. She tugged her necklace. He'd always been her biggest fan, besides Mama. Maybe she was wrong. Maybe it wouldn't be so bad especially if he promised not to speak. And maybe having him at a practice would help, not hurt, her singing.

"If you really promise not to say anything, you can come Tuesday."

"Really?" His eyes widened like an excited puppy. "Because I promise to do anything you ask."

"Yeah, sure." Zoey tried to match his excitement, but she felt annoyed. Why hadn't he just accepted her no?

"Thanks, Zo." He crossed the distance between them in three strides.

"But don't complain if you don't like it."

"You're singing. Of course, I'll like it." He pressed his lips against hers for a one-second kiss. "I'll go tell my parents I'm giving you a ride home."

He went into the house, and Zoey collapsed onto the chair. Mama's birthday, Justin at practice...how would she survive this week?

~*~

"Zoey?"

At Dad's voice, she paused on the stair landing, her bass case in her hand. "Yes?"

"Hi, there." He twisted on the couch gazing up through the stair rails. "I haven't seen much of you lately. You have a few minutes to spend with your old dad?"

She placed one foot on a step shifting her weight. "I've got band practice in forty-five minutes. And it'll take me twenty minutes to walk there."

"Then you've got twenty-five minutes to spend with me." His eyes sparkled behind wire-framed glasses. "Forty, if I let you take my car."

He was offering a chance not to walk in the heat? She'd take it. "Let me put my bass away first."

She hurried upstairs to her room, then back down to the living room.

He switched off the news and patted the cushion next to him. "You've been so busy the past week, I feel like I've barely had a chance to say hi."

"I know." She tucked one foot underneath her as she sat down. "But you've been busy teaching too."

"True. Guess we're both to blame for missing each other." He crossed his arms over his round stomach. Everything about him was round—his balding head, his glasses, his middle. "Won't be long before you're gone. One more year of school, and then you'll be out of here."

"Yeah, right." She never daydreamed about moving out, being on her own permanently. This was home. "How many years ago did Livvy graduate? Four? You haven't managed to get rid of her, so what makes you think I'll be going anywhere?"

"You got me there. But you'll be off touring with some band. Perhaps this new one Livvy was telling me about?"

Touring? She wished. At the rate she was going, she'd be lucky to survive beyond the first concert. "It's only for the summer."

"Your other band then."

"Maybe." She wished she felt an echo of his confidence. Would Mama cheer her on if she were here? Zoey glanced over her shoulder at the pictures on the wall. In the center, surrounded by a hodge-podge of school pictures and digital snapshots, sat the last family portrait—taken in the hospital. Mama was smiling, her face pale and thin, the scarf she wore to hide her chemotherapy baldness almost swallowing her head. One hand rested on a twelve-year-old Zoey, the other on a seventeen-year-old Livvy.

Six months later, she'd died.

Dad followed Zoey's gaze. "Mama would be proud of you."

"You really think so?"

"I know so." He stretched out his arm inviting her in for a hug.

She cuddled into his squishy side, and he wrapped his arm around her. For a few moments, Zoey felt like the innocent little girl who'd believed in unicorns, and fairy princesses, and miracles. The innocent little girl who didn't know the words cancer, or death, or pain. The innocent little girl who believed God answered prayers and dreams.

"Mama's birthday is next week," Dad said.

"Yeah, I know." The magic of the moment disappeared.

"I was thinking we could do something different."

"What?" She jerked away. "Different? But we always celebrate by fixing her favorite meal—pot roast and vegetables with chocolate cake for dessert. Then we play Scrabble. Every year just like when she was still...here."

"I know. But with everyone being so busy this year—"

"We're not that busy. Not too busy to remember Mama's birthday." She pulled her necklace out from under her shirt. How could he suggest not celebrating this year? He'd been married to Mama. Didn't he miss her?

"OK, OK, we'll stick with tradition." He tugged her back into his side. "If that's what you and Livvy want."

"Yes, please." Singing with Aurora Fire instead of Justin and Sawyer was the only change she could handle right now. "You still want to celebrate Mama's birthday, don't you?"

"Of course." He answered quickly, maybe too

quickly, but as long as they remembered Mama, it was good enough.

She relaxed against him. Mama's birthday and Zoey's singing—those were the things that kept Mama alive. Zoey could never let them go.

They kept her alive too.

7

Come Back Home

Justin pulled up to the curb in front of the house Zoey pointed out. The dull brown and white exterior wasn't impressive. The paint flaked, the gutters dangled, and the shutters hung crooked. But home maintenance skills had nothing to do with music.

"You promised not to say anything." Zoey gave him a pointed look, as if she didn't trust him.

"I remember." He tried not to sound offended but wasn't sure he succeeded. "Want me to put duct tape over my mouth?"

She didn't look amused. "The lyrics aren't like ours, OK? Just remember your promise."

When had Zoey stopped trusting him? He'd asked to see her lyrics again, still curious about her new songs, but she made excuses like, "I've scribbled too much on them." Scribbled what? He'd seen the notes she made to herself about pitch and pacing on her old lyric sheets—his lyric sheets. But with Aurora Fire's music, she was so secretive.

Pushing aside his worries, he climbed out of the car, and they walked through the overgrown grass. She led the way through the unlocked front door, as if she belonged. But she'd known Aurora Fire less than two weeks.

He squinted in the dark interior and took a deep breath, his nose wrinkling against the strange mixture of ramen noodles and body odor with the hint of something like pizza.

Zoey dropped his hand, and he followed her down a flight of stairs.

Stepping into the basement, he forgot his annoyance. This was the practice space he'd fantasized about. Florescent lighting shone on a rack of shining guitars—three electric, two acoustic—amps and speakers. Against one wall a computer, headphones, and recording equipment sat on a desk. He practically drooled. Maybe they could find room for him.

"Hey, Zoey."

The voice behind him tugged at a memory. He tore his gaze away from the practice setup.

"Hi," Zoey said.

Justin stared, recognition pouring over him like ice water. The hair was longer, and he was taller, but Justin knew Vance Barton. He'd been like a big brother to Justin—until everyone found out about their parents' affair.

"You moved back." Justin said the first thing that popped into his head.

Vance's face clouded for a moment. "Justin Conrad? No way." His lip curled. "I hear your parents are still pretending to be happily married."

"They are happy." Justin's hands tightened into fists.

"That's so cute. But time to grow up, kid." The big brother tone Justin remembered was now lost to bitterness. "Women lie, cheat, manipulate, destroy. You can never trust 'em."

Justin glanced at Zoey. He trusted her. But the

look on her face wasn't trusting. Too late, he remembered his promise. He hadn't even kept quiet for five minutes.

"Isn't it time to practice?" Zoey glanced back and forth between them and twisted her necklace.

"Yeah, whatever." Vance shot Justin a glare and moved to yell up the stairs. "Get down here and practice!"

Justin's shoulders ached. He didn't know what he'd expected exactly, but it wasn't this. Zoey's frown said she regretted letting him come, and he regretted it too. But what had happened between his and Vance's parents was in the past. Right now he needed to make sure he stayed in Zoey's future.

"You can sit over here." Zoey tugged him to the beat-up couch facing the amps and speakers.

Stains overlapped on the pale green cushions, and foam peaked out where the fabric had worn a hole. Justin sat down, his nostrils flaring at the stench of dog. He glanced around. The equipment looked less shiny now.

Feet thundered down the stairs. Then three guys and a girl walked into the room and took their positions.

"Who're you?" The girl flopped onto the couch beside him. Her shoulder-length hair was cotton-candy pink, and she had as many rings in her ears as she had on her hands.

"Justin." He smiled, but his friendliness wasn't reflected on her face. "Zoey's boyfriend."

"Really? Huh." Her gaze rolled over him. "I totally didn't expect her to go for the boy-next-door cliché."

Justin glanced at his striped tee and unripped jeans. At least Mom had quit ironing a crease down his pant legs.

A few feet away, Vance gave directions to Zoey and the guys, but Zoey was eyeing him and the girl. Zoey fit in with her black skinny jeans and local band tee.

"So what's your name?" He attempted conversation with the girl.

"Bailee." She smacked her gum, a fresh, fruity stick based on the smell of it and nodded toward the drummer. "I'm with Myles."

Aurora Fire started tuning. Justin watched Zoey. Her lips moved silently running over the lyrics between sips of water.

"Your girlfriend better step it up." Bailee sounded like the band's manager issuing ultimatums and threats.

Zoey glanced up.

"What d'you mean?" Justin asked.

"I mean, she better figure out whatever her problem is before Saturday. She's not going to mess things up."

Zoey lowered her gaze back to the paper in her hand, but her cheeks reddened.

"That won't happen." His hands curled into fists again. What was with this crowd and their insults? "Zoey's good."

Bailee snorted and flipped open a magazine. "You obviously haven't heard her lately."

He looked at Zoey. The edges of the paper crumpled within her fists.

"OK, let's get started," Vance said.

Justin kept his attention on Zoey while Vance led them in on his guitar. But she avoided looking at him.

Zoey comparing Aurora Fire to a heavy metal

band had been right, and her vocals made an interesting twist. Vance did the screams. Sawyer would probably like the concert Saturday night.

After a few measures, his gaze wandered to Vance's flashing fingers. Vance had spent hours with Justin on an acoustic guitar, entertaining him and teaching him when Justin's hands were barely big enough to form the chords. The awe from those days returned, and his fingers twitched to join. But watching Vance's complicated chord changes, Justin felt as if he hadn't advanced beyond D7 and C.

Then he heard the problem. Zoey's voice broke in the middle of a line, and she stuttered. Straining to catch every word, he heard her voice crack again. The lyrics sank in and formed a rock in his chest. Now he knew what Zoey meant by Aurora Fire not being anything close to Christian.

"See?" Bailee leaned over, triumph in her voice. As if she wanted to see Zoey—and Aurora Fire—fail. "Crash and burn every practice. It's pathetic, like she can't even sing."

"It's not her singing," Justin said. "It's the lyrics."

"Excuse me?" Bailee tossed aside her magazine, her eyebrows rising in twin arches. "The lyrics are excellent. Your girlfriend's the problem."

Vance slammed down the final chord and glared. "You know the rule: If you're not listening, get out."

"Whatever." Bailee flopped back into her corner of the couch and opened her magazine again.

Justin glanced at Zoey and tried to smile, but his attempt didn't erase her look of irritation. Why was she determined to choose these guys—and their cursing—over him?

He settled against the lumpy cushion. The next

song began, and he pulled a guitar pick from his pocket. After practice, he'd talk to her, get her to see she didn't belong here. If the band agreed with Bailee even a little, they probably wouldn't be upset when she bowed out.

The tension in Justin's shoulders finally eased. All Zoey needed was permission to quit, and he'd give it to her.

~*~

To Justin's relief, Zoey showed no interest in hanging around after practice. She told the guys she'd see them Thursday and then shot him a let's-get-out-of-here look.

They retraced their path through the house. He stayed on her heels. When they got outside, he launched his plan. "Why are you trying to sing with them?"

"So how weird is it to see your old friend Vance again?" She sidestepped both him and his question on the porch steps.

"Yeah, weird."

"Think you two will start hanging out again? Maybe play together?"

"Probably not." During a song about a cheater and thief, Vance had screamed the lyrics right at Justin, as if to cuss him out. Like what had happened was his fault. Wasn't as if he'd introduced Mom to Vance's dad. Anyway, it didn't matter much now. Their friendship was long over, like Vance's parents' marriage, and Justin wasn't interested in talking about it.

"You know," he began again, "you can quit."

"Why would I do that?" Zoey stopped on the edge

of the grass, crossed her arms, and shot him a heated look.

"Because you don't want to sing with them."

"And how would you know that?"

He knew because her voice cracked in every song. Why else would she have so much trouble singing unless she didn't really want to?

"This is a good opportunity for me," she added.

"But you're tripping over the words. You don't even look like you're having fun."

"Are you saying my singing isn't good?"

"No." He'd never say that to her, even if he thought it were true. Which he didn't. "Your singing was great. It always is. But some of the lyrics…you had trouble."

"I warned you that the songs weren't like yours."

"I know. But I thought you meant they didn't mention God and stuff. Not that you'd be swearing more than Sawyer. What's Livvy going to say when she hears you on Saturday? Or your dad?"

Zoey winced and glanced away, before looking back with an even fiercer fire in her eyes. "This is about Vance, isn't it?"

"What?" Why had Vance come up again?

"You don't want me in Aurora Fire because you've got some problem with Vance."

"That has nothing to do with it." A sickening feeling soured his stomach. "But since you brought him up, you really want to play with him?"

"Why wouldn't I?"

"Because of what he said about women. I don't even know why he'd want a girl in his band if he feels that way."

"Maybe he's able to put aside his feelings and do

what's best for his band."

The words smashed his core. All he ever did was put aside his feelings. Especially with Zoey. He arranged his schedule to fit hers, ate her favorite foods, listened to her favorite bands.

"I'm sorry." Zoey stepped back, head hanging. "Just take me home."

"I thought we were going to hang out at my house." He needed time with her now, to show he wasn't upset. Even if he was.

"Now I just want to go home." She climbed into the car.

He stood frozen. What had happened? She shouldn't be singing with Aurora Fire. He knew that, and she did too. So why did he feel like a jerk for offering her an out? Pulling his keys from his pocket, he got behind the wheel. "Zoey, I—"

"I have to do this, OK? I committed to Aurora Fire and I can't fail." She set her jaw and dared him to argue.

He wanted to. He wanted to assure her that admitting Aurora Fire was wrong for her wasn't failure. But he knew what she didn't want to hear, so he said nothing.

The drive was silent. When he turned into her driveway, he hoped she'd change her mind. But she got out slamming the door behind her.

He gripped the steering wheel and watched her march across the lawn. "C'mon, Zo," he muttered. "One glance." *So I know you don't hate me.*

But she didn't look back.

The storm door flashed open and swung back shutting with finality.

8

Oh, Honestly

Zoey set the pot roast platter on the round dining table. Mama's birthday dinner.

Most people would probably think it crazy that her family celebrated a dead person's birthday. Crazier, if they knew about the card she'd made Mama that afternoon. She didn't even tell Dad or Livvy about that.

But how could Dad have even thought about not celebrating this year? It would be like forgetting.

And Zoey refused to forget Mama.

"Everything smells good." Dad sniffed the air and sat down at the table.

"Thanks." Zoey slid into her seat on one side of him and played with a butterfly bead at her neck. Livvy sat across from her. The vacant fourth chair brought a twisting to Zoey's heart.

"Lord ..." Dad began.

She bowed her head.

"Today, we're remembering a special person in our lives, a person who is now with You in glory. We miss her here with us, but she remains in our hearts. Thank You for the time we had with her, and bless our time now. A—"

The doorbell cut off Dad's "amen."

Zoey glanced over the stair railing. This was not a night to just drop by. The entire world should know that.

"I'll get it." Livvy pushed away from the table. She pattered downstairs and disappeared into the Arctic entry.

"Rolls?" Dad handed Zoey a basket continuing on as if no one was interrupting.

She plucked out a warm dinner roll and strained to hear who Livvy was talking to so she'd know who to be upset with. But all she heard were indistinct murmurs.

"Zoey?" Livvy called. "It's for you."

Who would come to see her? Frowning, she rounded the dining room table kicking the edge of Tiger's cat dish. Whoever it was could just leave. Tonight was sacred. Having band practice in half an hour was bad enough. She wasn't up for socializing.

Livvy beamed at the bottom of the stairs. She looked excited about whoever hid inside the Arctic entry. Why couldn't she do the talking, and the smiling, and the getting rid of them?

Zoey stepped around her sister through the doorway and froze.

Justin stood among the discarded shoes and the winter coats that had been abandoned to their hooks since May. He shifted a bouquet of brightly colored daisies, and the cellophane crinkled.

"Hi." His grin lacked its usual confidence.

"Hi." She fingered her necklace. It felt as if it was strangling her. Did he think a bunch of flowers could earn her forgiveness? Not after he insulted her singing. Besides, he knew she wasn't a flower kind of girl.

"I forgot today was your mom's birthday. Then I

remembered." He thrust the flowers at her. "Daisies—you told me once they were her favorite."

"Uh, yeah. Yeah, they were." She held the bouquet staring at the pink, purple, and yellow petals. She didn't remember telling him about Mama's favorite flowers. Zoey had spent hours cutting daisies out of construction paper to tape on the dreary white hospital walls. She shoved back the memories. "Thanks."

"About the other night, Zoey, I'm sorry. I shouldn't have...suggested you quit." He watched her as if waiting for confirmation that he'd apologized for the right thing.

Unlike Livvy, who gazed at Justin all sappy-eyed, Zoey guarded her expression. Of course she had to forgive him. He'd remembered Mama's birthday and her favorite flower. He really was the perfect boyfriend. Why couldn't he be a little less perfect?

"It's OK." She forced a smile.

"You want to come in?" Livvy asked. "There's plenty of food."

Zoey sucked in air. Boyfriends weren't invited to Mama's birthday dinner. Family only, like every other year.

"Thanks, but I've gotta get to the youth devo."

She let out her breath. Crisis averted.

"How about after? Zoey's got band practice tonight, so we're not having cake until later." Livvy raised her eyebrows at Zoey. "You're OK with that, aren't you?"

No, no, no! She wanted to stomp her foot and scream. But she didn't. "Yeah. Cake and Scrabble later."

"OK. I'll be back around nine." He hesitated.

"Bye." She lifted her hand in a wave to save him

from deciding whether he should kiss her in front of Livvy. Livvy wouldn't care, but Zoey wasn't in the mood. He'd invaded their special night, and he'd done it in a way that Zoey couldn't say anything without sounding like a horrible girlfriend. And she'd already been horrible by joining Aurora Fire without talking to Justin first. Tonight she couldn't deal with the guilt. She couldn't deal with the sadness. She couldn't deal with Justin. And she couldn't keep him away.

Justin walked back to his car, and she pushed the door shut.

"He is so sweet." Livvy sounded more in love with Justin than Zoey felt.

"Yeah, he is." Zoey pushed around her sister and up the stairs. Was something wrong with her? Why wasn't she the one with hearts in her eyes? But all Zoey felt was...emptiness.

Livvy's footsteps echoed hers. "Want me to get a vase?"

"Sure." She carried the daisies into the kitchen.

"Justin brought you flowers?" Dad watched from the table.

"Yeah."

"He brought daisies because they were Mama's favorite," Livvy added from inside the pantry. "Isn't that sweet?"

"Thanks." Zoey accepted a vase from Livvy. She was getting tired of that word, "sweet." Yeah, Justin was sweet, romantic, perfect. And Zoey was selfish.

"Hey, you're OK with Justin coming over later, aren't you?" Livvy squinted at her. "'Cause you seem a little upset."

"No. It's fine." She filled the vase with water. Maybe if she said it enough times, she'd believe it was true.

"Good." Livvy squeezed her shoulders in a one-armed hug. "You know, I think Mama would've really liked him."

She nodded and switched off the faucet. Mama probably would've liked Justin. Everyone did. So Zoey couldn't admit she was still angry. Justin had been right the other night. She was miserable she still couldn't force out some of the lyrics. She wanted to quit. Which angered her more—that he was right or that he'd apologized? She placed the vase on the table and returned to her seat.

"Those are beautiful." Dad handed her the bowl of vegetables. "Mama would like them. And you know what else she'd be excited about?"

Zoey shook her head and passed the bowl to Livvy.

"Your concert on Saturday."

"Yes, she would." Livvy spooned potatoes and carrots onto her plate. "She'd be excited to see your dream coming true."

Ducking her head, Zoey stabbed a piece of roast. That was why she'd stick it out with Aurora Fire. She couldn't quit on Mama.

Unfortunately, her dream felt more like a nightmare.

9

Rise Above It

Justin drove from Zoey's house to Sawyer's, his car still smelling like daisies. Taking Zoey flowers had been smart. He and Zoey were solid. Nothing to worry about. He parked outside Sawyer's house and then dialed Mom's cell. He should get his parents' permission now, though it'd be easier if they let him text them.

"Justin?" Mom sounded surprised.

"Hey, is it OK if I go over to Zoey's after the devo?"

"Why? Won't you see her at the devo?"

Why did asking permission always feel like a negotiation? "No, she has practice with Aurora Fire. But she invited me over later. So can I?"

"Just a moment."

His parents' muffled voices echoed through the phone. He flipped a pick through his fingers. Mom explained his question to Dad. Dad asked the same "why?" question as Mom. Back and forth went the indecision.

"It's just a simple question!" He wanted to yell. But they acted as if he'd asked something difficult like if he could spend the night at Zoey's. That would be an easy answer: No.

"What are you doing at Zoey's?" Mom finally asked.

"Playing Scrabble and eating cake and ice cream. It's her mom's birthday."

"Her mom's birthday? But isn't she…?"

"Yeah. But they still celebrate." Justin flipped the pick faster. *C'mon, agree already!*

"You'll be home by midnight."

By curfew? He never wasn't. "Yes."

"OK. Have fun."

"Thanks." He disconnected before a new line of questioning could begin. If he'd ever given them a reason not to trust him, he might understand. But Mom was the only one who'd ever sneaked around. Maybe that was why they didn't trust him. But that seemed a little too twisted.

He texted Sawyer to let him know he was waiting, and a few seconds later, Sawyer was in the car. Now to break the news.

"We aren't practicing tonight."

"What?" Sawyer's eyes flashed. "Why not?"

"I'm going over to Zoey's."

Sawyer swore.

"Don't say that."

"We've got a concert tomorrow." Sawyer kept talking as if he hadn't noticed Justin's rebuke. "She's already ditched us, and now you're letting her mess with our practice?"

"We practiced this morning. And we'll practice again tomorrow." He glanced at Sawyer, whose glare intensified. "C'mon, man, we're ready. We can give up an hour tonight."

Sawyer looked out the window his back angled toward Justin. "What's wrong with you and Zoey?

Neither of you care about the band anymore."

"Hey!" That was a little too far, even for Sawyer. Music was important to all of them. "I care. And so does Zoey."

"You don't act like it," Sawyer muttered.

"Knock it off, man. We're still playing Saturday. And Zoey's still part of our band."

"No, she isn't. She's in Aurora Fire now."

"It's temporary." Justin clenched his teeth.

"What if it's not?"

"It is, OK?" It had to be. Things had been off between him and Zoey since she'd gotten involved with Aurora Fire. But he'd survive not practicing with Zoey until September. Barely.

"Whatever."

He glanced at Sawyer again. The guy stared out the window, slumped like Savannah when she didn't get her way. First the fight with Zoey, now this. Being caught between his best friends' mood swings was getting old. "Look, cut Zoey some slack. She's having a hard time."

"Good." Sawyer's mouth tightened. "She deserves it."

"No, she doesn't." Sometimes, he wanted to smack the angry out of his friend. "Besides, it's not just Aurora Fire. Today's her mom's birthday, and that's hard for her too."

"But her mom's dead."

"So? Zoey hasn't forgotten her mom just because she died."

Sawyer was quiet for a couple of blocks. "Fine. I'll stop beating her up over ditching us—for tonight."

"Thanks."

"But I still say it's wrong."

Justin agreed. Playing without Zoey was wrong. Listening to Zoey sing with Aurora Fire was wrong. But being with Zoey was right. And the only way he'd stay with her was to support her decisions. No matter how wrong they were.

He needed Zoey. Meeting Zoey, helping her rediscover her love of music, had healed him after that year his parents spent apart. His parents had gotten back together, but family could still be destroyed. Seeing Zoey surviving the loss of her mom—and knowing in some, small way he was helping her survive—had given him hope. "Hey, I've got the chorus to that new song figured out." He tried to shift to a neutral topic.

"If we were practicing tonight, you could show me." Apparently, Sawyer's promise to stop beating Zoey up didn't extend to Justin.

"Tomorrow."

Sawyer just grunted.

He probably shouldn't tell Sawyer this would be Zoey's song. So he hummed the new music to himself, the lyrics playing through his head.

> God wrote a dream on her heart
> I pray He lets me play a part
> Through good times and bad
> She'll go where she's led
> And I want to hold her hand
> Until she reaches the end
> Because God wrote a dream on her heart
> And I pray He lets me play a part

10

Fault Line

Sawyer biked home from work Friday night and drummed his fingers against the handlebars to the concert setlist playing through his head. Over the railroad tracks. Past the restaurant where Mom was working.

Who would want to listen to a drummer and guitarist making noise? Only people who felt obligated, like parents. Which didn't include his. Too many waitresses on vacation, so Mom couldn't get off. She was more disappointed than Sawyer, though it felt good knowing she wanted to see him on stage.

He cut through a strip mall parking lot. Up ahead in the next block was the ice cream shack. Zoey exited carrying a black garbage bag.

He scowled. If she hadn't ditched them, tomorrow night could've been a success. She'd destroyed everything.

He pedaled faster planning to zip past her.

She dropped the bag into the dumpster and leaned against the rusty metal side.

He glanced over as he passed. Was she crying? He skidded the bike to a stop. "What's wrong?" he asked over his shoulder.

She looked up. "Sawyer?"

"What's the matter?" He let the bike fall, stepping out of its way.

"Nothing." She rubbed her palms across her cheeks. "You wouldn't care."

He hesitated and shrugged. "Fine." Grabbing the handlebars, he righted the bike. Maybe it really was nothing. Mom often said when she was crying that it was for no reason other than she needed to cry.

Behind him, Zoey snuffled.

Sighing, he let the bike crash to the ground again. Even when Mom said she just needed a good cry, she also said she appreciated when he didn't leave her alone.

And Justin had asked him to cut Zoey some slack.

He walked to stand in front of her. "C'mon, what's wrong?"

"Like I said, it's nothing you'd care about." She swiped her hands over her face again, not looking at him.

"Tell me anyway. I'm not leaving until you do."

She raised her head. Her eyes were puffy, her nose pink. "I'm going to bomb tomorrow. I know it—everybody knows it." She sniffed and her mouth tightened. "Which will make you happy, won't it? You'll be glad to see me fail." She turned away. "So just leave, OK?"

"Zoey." Sawyer grabbed her shoulder pulling her around to face him. "I don't want you to fail."

"Yeah, right. That's why you've been so understanding since I joined Aurora Fire." She jerked away. "Forget it, Sawyer, and go home."

"Yeah, I've been angry because you ditched us, but that doesn't mean I want to see you fail."

Zoey rolled red-rimmed eyes.

"I don't," he insisted. "I think you should be punished, but not by failing."

"OK, thanks, I feel tons better now. You got a punishment in mind?"

"C'mon, Zoey, that's not what I mean." He sighed. He shouldn't have bothered trying to cheer her up. He didn't do nice. "You know I would've done the same thing."

"You would?" She gazed at him, tears pooling in her eyes. "You would've abandoned me and Justin?"

"Of course I would. If someone asked me to fill in for their drummer, I'd be stoked. Who'd refuse that?"

"Justin."

"Yeah, well, he's a little too good sometimes."

"Yeah, he is." She gave him a tiny smile.

"Look, you'll be awesome tomorrow." Sawyer placed both his hands on her arms and smiled back. "If anyone bombs, it'll be us without you."

"I'm sorry." Zoey's tears overflowed.

"Aw, don't do that again."

Her shoulders shook. She stepped closer and rested her forehead against his chest. "I'm so sorry." The words were muffled by her sobs and his shirt.

This wasn't working. He awkwardly patted her back. He'd just made her cry more. Women were way too complicated.

Zoey's tears mixed with the sweat dampening his T-shirt.

Now what? He racked his brain for more words. Could he cheer her up with a drum solo instead? "You're an awesome vocalist. You don't have anything to worry about."

"You don't understand." Zoey shook her head against his collar bone. "The lyrics get stuck in my throat, like I can't sing them."

"Then change 'em."

She jerked her head up. "Change them?"

"Yeah. Why not? You change lyrics all the time with Justin."

"But those are mine—I helped write them. These aren't."

"So?" He stared down at her, his hands resting on her shoulder blades. She was pressed against him, smelling like ice cream and waffle cones, and still clutching his shirt. He wanted to make her believe she could do this. Even if it meant his band failing. "Isn't changing them better than not singing them?"

"Yeah, probably." She gazed at him, her face blotchy. "Why are you being nice to me all of a sudden?"

"Because we're friends."

"Really? 'Cause I was starting to think you hated me for what I did."

His voice caught in his throat. She looked so lost with her red eyes and tear-stained cheeks.

"I can't hate you," his words came out in barely a whisper.

She licked her lips, swollen from crying. His chest vibrated with his thudding heart, or maybe it was Zoey's heart he felt, beating in time with his own. She was so close, her face angled toward him, her shallow breaths hot against his chin. Then, before he realized what he was doing, he kissed her.

And Zoey kissed him back.

She tasted sweet and salty. Her hands gripped his ribcage, and he squeezed her shoulders.

A curse exploded from him, and he shoved her away.

Zoey stumbled back, her mouth gaping.

What had he done? One moment she was crying, the next he was kissing her? He swore again.

"Sawyer?"

Ignoring Zoey, he hopped on his bike pedaling furiously. What had he been thinking? When Justin found out...

He spewed a string of curses. Long shadows chased him the three blocks home. Leaving his bike on the lawn, he entered the empty house and slammed the door shut. Justin would kill him. Then Justin, being the kind of guy he was, would give him CPR and bring him back to life.

Sawyer punched the counter and paced through the kitchen. Of all girls, the first one he ever kissed was Zoey? So what if she was the only girl he could put up with? The only girl who knew what she was talking about when it came to music? She was his best friend's girlfriend. Eternally off limits.

But the kiss wasn't his fault. If Zoey hadn't thrown herself at him crying on his shoulder, none of it would've happened. If Zoey hadn't ditched them for the summer, she wouldn't have been crying to begin with. And if Justin hadn't told him to be nice yesterday, Sawyer might have ignored her. So he wasn't to blame for any of this. But he didn't think Justin would agree.

Sawyer's entire body twitched. He needed to play, but he couldn't. His drums lived in Justin's garage, and Justin's house was the last place he wanted to be.

He went to his room and turned on his speakers drowning out his thoughts with heavy metal screams. He wanted to forget Zoey's tears and how she tasted. Lying on the floor, he did sit ups until his abs burned.

Then he forced himself to do more. The pain across his stomach blocked the pain in his heart.

The music stopped. Sawyer collapsed against the worn carpet and stared up at Mom. The black slacks of her waitressing uniform looked impossibly long from this angle. His lungs ached, but he didn't know if that was because he was breathing too hard to speak or because he hated the thought of her finding out what he'd done. She was one of three people who put up with him and still liked him at the end of the day. He'd betrayed the other two tonight. How long before he failed her too?

"What's wrong?" She crossed her arms frowning. "I could hear the music outside."

"Everything's fine." His wheezing breath covered up the lie.

"Well, keep it down, OK?" She didn't look as though she believed him, but she also looked too tired to argue. "I'm going to bed."

"OK."

With the music at background noise level and Sawyer zapped of strength, his thoughts blasted back into his head.

Zoey, Justin, the kiss.

His heart hammered against his ribs. Groaning, he pushed off the floor and scooted against his bed. Zoey couldn't want Justin to find this out any more than he did. So if they both kept quiet, Justin would never know. That was the only solution.

He picked up his cell and began texting.

Don't tell Justin about

Sawyer hesitated. Putting the word "kiss" there would guarantee Justin finding out. That's how it always worked on TV. Idiot texted girl, girl's boyfriend read text, girl's boyfriend killed idiot. And he was starring as the idiot. He deleted the message and started again.

It was a mistake. Forget about it.

That should be vague enough that if Justin read it, Zoey could make something up.

He hit send and waited.

When his phone vibrated, he glanced at the screen.

OK.

He blew out a sigh. Good. As long as they agreed to forget the kiss, everything would be fine.

His heart beat audibly, like a ticking time bomb.

He was a dead man.

11

Welcome to the Masquerade

Justin stood in the garage and ran over the pre-concert checklist in his mind.

Mini-van emptied of car seats and winter survival gear.

Seats folded down for storage.

Entire van vacuumed.

Only item left was loading their gear. But Sawyer wasn't here yet, and he didn't let anyone touch his drums. He'd taped a sign on them once: Look, live. Touch, die. But Mom tore off the sign.

Justin picked up his acoustic guitar. The one Vance had taught Justin to play back in junior high. Since then, he'd created twenty, thirty, maybe a hundred songs on that guitar. Most of them Zoey had helped him write.

His heart caved in on the empty space left by Zoey. He sat on the ottoman and filled the empty only way he knew how. With music. But the melody his fingers strummed was his new song. The unfinished song.

Zoey's song.

"We're not playing that tonight." Sawyer entered the garage on the heels of his declaration.

"Maybe we should." Justin carried the guitar to its

case.

"Don't go changing the setlist." Sawyer began disassembling the drum kit, his back toward Justin. "We're gonna suck enough."

"Do you think this is right? Playing without Zoey?"

Sawyer shrugged.

"Maybe we should've canceled."

"Too late."

Justin wound an amp cord between his palm and elbow. The garage fell silent for a few moments, except for the whistle of the cords across the concrete floor and the quiet snaps of the drum kit. His confidence about their decision to play without Zoey weakened, but nerves before a performance were normal. Though Justin was usually too busy reassuring Zoey to notice his own.

Zoey. His cell sat in his back pocket, the two texts he'd sent her earlier unanswered. She'd accepted his apology yesterday. Why was she ignoring him again? The empty space in his heart grew, expanded, filled his chest. Things had been weird since she'd joined Aurora Fire. Was it her struggle with the lyrics or Aurora Fire? Or a specific band member? One who was angry with Justin. Who hated him. Who wanted revenge.

"Zoey wouldn't cheat on me?" The question ended on a note of disbelief. He was crazy to ask.

Sawyer cursed over the cymbals crashing against the concrete.

"Would she?" His voice rose. His hands and feet went cold. He hadn't been serious.

"I don't want to talk about your girlfriend." Sawyer's tone was sharp but distant.

"What's wrong with you?" Justin clenched and

unclenched his fists forcing blood to circulate. Sawyer's attitude had nothing to do with Justin's question.

"Nothing." A growl filled every syllable. Sawyer's bad mood on steroids.

"OK."

"Why're you asking me anyway?" The growl slipped out of his voice, and his tone shifted from snarling pit bull to toothless mutt.

"I probably shouldn't. What do you know about relationships?"

"Absolutely nothing." Sawyer's edge returned. He shoved the blanket-wrapped snare into the van. It bumped against the opposite door.

Great. Justin dragged a hand through his hair. Playing without Zoey was bad enough, but Sawyer banging his drums was worse. Tonight's concert would be an epic disaster. The best they could hope for was to be loud.

~*~

The final chord blasted from the amp and into the farthest corners of the church fellowship hall. About fifty people were spread around the room. Mostly school and church friends. A few parents including Justin's. But not Sawyer's.

When the applause quieted, Justin thanked them again. "Don't forget about Zoey. With Aurora Fire, tonight, at the Polar Den." The under-eighteen crowd here wouldn't have any problem getting into the all-ages venue. He squinted at the clock in the back. "She goes on in an hour."

He switched off the mic and began packing up. No way could they get the gear loaded, back to his house, and put away in under an hour. But he wouldn't be any later than he had to. He needed to be there to cheer Zoey on—and prove he supported her.

"Good job." Dad stopped by the stage with Tristan balanced on his shoulders and Mom and Savannah trailing behind. He sounded sincere, but uncertain. He didn't know music. His digital library was stuck in the '80s.

"Thanks." The concert hadn't been a disaster, even without lyrics, but something had definitely been missing on stage, in the songs, in Justin.

"You'll be home by one?" Dad's voice rose, reminding, not asking.

"Yes, sir." Justin forced a smile so the words wouldn't come out annoyed. Negotiating that extra hour had taken two days.

"I want to go hear Zoey too." Savannah plunked down on the edge of the stage and crossed her arms.

Justin's lungs crammed into his throat. Savannah was too young to hear Aurora Fire. But he couldn't tell his parents that.

"I don't think so." The words rushed out of Mom's mouth. Because Polar Den wasn't appropriate for a ten-year-old? Or because Aurora Fire wasn't appropriate? "It's late. Time for us to go home."

"Thanks for coming." Justin's words were automatic, but sincere. He wanted his parents here, together.

And he liked watching them leave together.

"You guys rocked." Felicia climbed onto the stage aiming her band-groupie gaze at Sawyer.

"We were OK." Sawyer spoke with no feeling probably to make her go away.

"You were awesome," she said.

Sawyer's mouth tightened.

Justin bit back a smile. Poor girl. The way to get Sawyer's attention wasn't by gushing about his playing. If she liked him, she should...

Justin frowned. What would get Sawyer's interest?

Felicia tapped her fingers across a tom tom.

"Don't touch." The words burst from Sawyer's mouth so quick, there was no space between them.

Felicia jerked back and shoved her hands into her pockets.

Justin ducked his head so they wouldn't catch him laughing. That definitely wasn't the way to win him over.

"I'm thinking about going to see Zoey." Felicia rocked on her heels.

"Good." Justin stacked the cords on an amp.

"You're going, right?" she asked Sawyer.

"Nope."

"C'mon." Justin rolled another cord. "You'll like their music."

"I said no," Sawyer growled as he detached the snare from its stand.

Justin frowned. Sure, Sawyer never was a people person, but he was usually in a good mood after a performance—or even band practice. Something about beating on the drums seemed to work out his anger at the world. But not tonight apparently.

Felicia rocked back and forth a moment longer. Then she offered a tiny smile. "Well, I guess I'll see you guys at church tomorrow."

"Bye." Justin raised his free hand in a wave. "Thanks for coming."

She hopped off the stage and melted into the crowd.

Justin moved to Sawyer's side. "She's gone now."

"Good." Sawyer crouched to loosen a bracket.

"Is she really that bad?"

"Yes." Sawyer glanced up. "She knows next to nothing about music, and she touched the drums."

"Seriously?" Justin chuckled and reached toward a cymbal.

"Do it, and I'll break your finger."

"What's up with you?"

"Nothing." Sawyer stood, rolling his shoulders back. "Look, let's get this stuff back to your house. I'll stay and unload it so you're not late."

"Thanks." Justin grinned. "Good thing I don't mind you touching my guitars."

"Yeah, whatever." Sawyer crouched back down muttering something that sounded like, "I owe you."

Justin frowned. That made no sense. But before he could say something, his cell vibrated in his back pocket. He pulled it out and glanced at the screen. Zoey.

C U Soon?

Smiling, Justin typed back.

30 min. Luv U.

He slid his phone back into his pocket and finished packing up his gear puzzling over Sawyer's muttered words. He couldn't have heard right.

Why would Sawyer owe Justin?

12

Ignite

"I didn't change the meanings." Zoey watched Vance scan her lyrics sheets. She held her breath, but not because the practice space in Aurora Fire's basement smelled mustier and weirder than usual. "In some places I had to change words, but in others, I just deleted ones I'm having trouble with."

Vance studied the lyrics and Zoey studied him. Her stomach clenched so tight the psychotic moths inside couldn't flutter. He would hate her changes.

Finally, he glanced up, shrugged, and handed the papers back. "Looks fine. If you can sing them..."

"I can. Thanks." Did that mean he was OK with it?

He swept his gaze around at the rest of the band.

Travis and Devin were talking about some girls they'd hooked up with. Or maybe the same girl. Zoey couldn't follow.

Bailee's spot on the couch sat empty releasing some of Zoey's nerves. The absence was like a gift from God. Maybe He did care about her performance tonight.

"We've got two hours before we've gotta pack up our gear," Vance said. "Let's play."

They played through their set, and Zoey sang her version of the lyrics. Every word left her mouth, strong, powerful, without a single cough or stutter.

"You actually might pull it off," Myles said when they took a break. He sounded surprised but still cautious.

"Thanks." She bit back her smile. That was the closest thing to a compliment any of the guys had given her.

After practicing, they packed up the amps, instruments, and cords, and loaded a van with the words "Tundra Heating and Thawing" painted over in white.

"You riding with us?" Vance shut the rear van doors.

"I'll drive myself." She waved at Livvy's car by the curb.

"See you there." He climbed into the driver's seat. Myles rode with him while Devin and Travis got in a beat-up old car.

Zoey walked to her car. Practice went great, but didn't actors have some saying about a bad rehearsal meant a good performance and a good rehearsal meant a bad performance? Did that apply to bands too?

Please, God, don't let me fail Mama.

She turned the key in the ignition, and a blast of lukewarm air hit her face fluttering her black and pink hair. She'd re-dyed it for the concert.

The clock read 8:02. Justin and Sawyer would be playing now.

Sawyer.

A fluttering kicked off in her stomach, but it wasn't the psychotic moths. This fluttering was new, different. She'd first felt it two seconds before her lips touched Sawyer's. Two seconds before her toes curled. Two seconds before she'd destroyed her relationship with Justin.

She collapsed against the driver's seat and squeezed her eyes shut. Why had she kissed Sawyer? Because he was sympathetic? So was Justin. Justin had supported her singing with Aurora Fire. Sawyer hadn't.

But Sawyer understood. He would've bailed on their band too. And he believed she could blow everyone away.

Tears rolled down her cheeks. Justin loved her. He believed in her. He told her how great her voice was. She needed that. She needed him. So she had to do what Sawyer said.

Forget the kiss. Forget the flutters. Forget the curling toes.

Forget Sawyer.

Or lose Justin.

~*~

Zoey paced in a corner of the tiny room at the back of The Polar Den twirling her necklace and sipping from a water bottle. Across the room, Bailee sprawled across Myles in a threadbare chair that might've been blue a couple decades ago. Vance sat on the edge of a scarred table, his fingers forming chords on an invisible guitar. Devin and Travis were out in the club hitting on girls.

She kept moving in a tight circle because if she stopped, her knees would give out.

Livvy had texted, and she and Dad were in the crowd. What about Justin? Zoey hadn't seen him out there, and he hadn't texted he'd arrived. Of course, she hadn't responded to any of his messages earlier. But she wanted—no, needed him there with his reassuring grin cheering her on. She was so incredibly selfish. After Sawyer, she had no right to see Justin.

"Hey." A hand landed on her shoulder.

She yelped and spun around her heart threatening to explode out of her chest.

"Get a grip." Vance stepped back. "You want more water?"

She raised the bottle. It was empty. When had that happened? "Uh, sure. Thanks."

"I'll get you another one." He headed for the door. "Do something to calm yourself down."

"OK."

Only one thing, or person, could relax her. Even if it made her the lousiest human being on earth, she didn't have a choice. She pulled out her cell with a shaky hand and texted Justin. He responded promising to be there in 30 minutes, and a few of the psychotic moths died.

"Forgive me," she whispered.

"What?"

She jumped again at Vance's voice. "Um, nothing."

"You look like you're going to puke." He handed her a bottle of water. "Don't do that in here."

That sounded like Sawyer's comforting pre-concert pep-talk. The reminder was not helping. The only way she'd succeed at forgetting was to never see or think about him again. Was that even possible?

Travis and Devin walked into the room.

"Ten minutes," Travis announced.

She slipped out the door to use the restroom. Too bad she couldn't flush her nervousness down the toilet. But she'd never thrown up before getting on stage, and she wouldn't tonight.

Her phone beeped as she washed her hands. Hurrying back to the room, she read the message.

Here. Waiting to C U.

Her thumbs tapped out a reply.

Thanks.

She hesitated.

Luv U.

She meant it too. Kissing Sawyer hadn't changed how she felt about Justin.

A few minutes later, she walked on the stage with Aurora Fire. Vance spoke to the crowd, but she only half-listened. The bright lights blinded. She searched the audience trying not to squint. Justin would be somewhere she could see him, but everyone blended together like one of those search-and-find pictures. If he'd worn a red and white striped hat, he might be easier to see. Finally, she spotted him.

He grinned, his gaze focused on her and no one else.

Behind her, Myles counted in the first song.

All her guilty thoughts vanished on the first beat, replaced by the music. The words exploded from the depths of her soul. Through all the hours of practice, she'd concentrated only on hitting the notes, never really listening to herself. Now it was as if she heard the lyrics for the first time.

"Dragged my heart through flames."

"Revenge, ice in my veins."

"An army of those you destroyed."

Her lungs ached, pain mixing with the words. The songs turned her into a hypocrite. This was what Justin would feel if he ever found out about the kiss. She poured her regret into the mic and flooded the room with her remorse.

After the set ended, Vance thanked the crowd again, and the room filled with screams and cheers.

Zoey sought Justin's face again.

His arms were raised over his head, and he mouthed, "You were awesome."

She forced a smile. Her usual performance high hadn't come. Singing had sucked out all her energy. She exited the stage, arms and legs limp.

"You came through." Vance jabbed his finger at her, relaxed and smiling for the first time since he'd recruited her at the Downstairs Coffeehouse. "I didn't think you would, but you did."

"Yeah, you were good," Travis echoed.

"Thanks." The word came long and slow, almost floating on a sigh. She'd done it. She'd earned her place. She left the backstage and hurried to the front of the club.

Justin wrapped her in a hug and warmed her ear with his breath. "You were awesome."

She melted against his familiar side. He was the guy she belonged with.

"Want me to help you guys pack up? My parents extended my curfew tonight, so I can give you a ride home too."

She shook her head. "I've got Livvy's car, and I'm exhausted." Through the crowd she spotted Dad and Livvy. Dad flashed a cheesy thumbs up sign.

"Please?" His begging sounded playful instead of carrying the desperate note Zoey had heard too often lately. "If I don't take advantage of the extra hour, my parents might not let me have it again."

"OK. Stay, help." She tilted her chin hugging his waist. On second thought, she didn't want him to leave anytime soon.

"Thanks."

She stretched up and kissed him, tasting his minty mouth.

But her toes didn't curl and nothing fluttered.

13

Hello, Don't Go

Justin pulled into the church parking lot at five after ten on Sunday morning. If his parents found out he'd arrived late, they'd blame Zoey's concert. But he wasn't late because he'd slept in. He wasn't late because of the rain pelting his windshield. He was late because of Sawyer.

Sawyer had been too lazy to get out of bed. Justin had parked outside Sawyer's house, texted him, and called him, but Sawyer hadn't answered. First Zoey had avoided him. Now Sawyer. Maybe Justin needed to rethink his communication, or his friends, or his deodorant. Justin jogged through the rain, into the church, down the hall, and to the teen room. Cardio workout complete.

"Justin's here. We can start." Brandon, the youth minister, spoke teasingly, but Justin hoped Brandon wouldn't report the tardiness. "Thought after last night you'd gotten a record deal and left us."

"Not me." Justin crossed the room and sat on the couch next to Zoey. "But maybe that's why Sawyer couldn't come."

"Sawyer's not with you?" Zoey rolled the beads at her neck.

"Nope. Wouldn't respond to my texts."

"Good." Zoey dropped her hands into her lap.

"Good?" What kind of response was that? Sawyer was skipping church and band practice. Not good.

"I just meant..." Her eyes clouded for a moment, then widened. "Hey, have you met Chey Michaels? She just moved here." Zoey squished back against the couch.

The girl next to Zoey leaned forward.

"Chey, this is Justin. My boyfriend." Zoey slid her hand into Justin's, and the muscles across his shoulders unwound.

"Hey." Chey lifted a lace, fingerless-gloved hand in a wave and gave him a half smile. A tiny diamond stud glittered just below the left corner of her mouth.

"Hi." He returned the wave and looked at Zoey. "You wanna come over later? Hang out?"

"Sure." She smiled. Not that trying-to-pretend-everything's-OK smile she'd worn since joining Aurora Fire. But a real smile. A nothing-would-make-me-happier smile. "I'll go home for my bass and meet you."

"Sweet." Justin rubbed his thumb across the tiny bones in Zoey's hand, warmth flooding him. Maybe with her first Aurora Fire performance over, they'd return to normal.

~*~

Justin watched for Zoey through the half-open garage door. Rain darkened the concrete driveway and the edge of the garage floor, but it kept the room cool. He strummed a few chords, still searching for the lyrics of the new song. What would Zoey add with the bass?

Movement under the garage door caught his eye—

Zoey's purple shoes and bass case. A few seconds later, she ducked under the door, her hair wet from the rain. She straightened glancing around the garage, her gaze finally resting on Justin. "Just you?"

"Yeah." He set his guitar aside and stood. "I asked Sawyer, but he said he was busy. Want me to ask again?"

"No!" She spoke too loud, and the word echoed through the garage.

"OK." Yesterday, Sawyer snapped at every mention of Zoey, now she was acting the same way. "Did something happen between you two?"

"No." The word sprang fast and sharp from Zoey's lips. She dropped to her knees in front of her bass case and clicked open the latches. Her hair hung down hiding her face like a black-and-pink curtain.

"I know he's been giving you a hard time about joining Aurora Fire—"

"Yes, he has." Zoey flung her hair back. She sounded surprised, maybe relieved, as if she hadn't realized until that moment how Sawyer had treated her. "And I don't want to deal with that today."

"OK." Playing would be better without their sniping. And he'd be alone with Zoey. He'd missed that. He needed that—her.

She plugged into an amp and sat on the forest green chair facing Justin's ottoman.

"I've been working on something new." Justin picked up his electric guitar.

"Really? I wanna hear."

As he played, Zoey tapped against the shiny, black face of her bass, her body swaying with the music. His music. Their music.

He played each chord with confidence.

"I like it," Zoey said when the song ended. "Any words for me?"

Justin's heart quickened, and he glanced at the upside-down stack of papers. "Just the chorus."

"Can I see?"

"Not yet."

"All right." Her grin blasted heat through him. "Play it again, and I'll add my part."

He began the melody. Why hadn't he shown her the chorus? Zoey helped write lyrics. She also sang them. But for some reason, he wasn't ready to share. They felt too fresh, too real.

"Repeat that." Zoey interrupted his thoughts and his playing. "I can come up with something better."

They worked on new music for a while, before switching to old favorites. Zoey stood, singing the songs they'd created together.

He drank in the sound as if starved.

Yet, like every practice over the past week and a half, something was missing. Only this time, it was Sawyer and his drums. Without all three of them in harmony, the music couldn't satisfy. "I'm going to call Sawyer again." He reached for his phone.

"Don't." Zoey dropped onto the chair and grabbed his hand.

He looked at her trying to interpret her pleading. "It just doesn't sound right without him. Or you."

Her fingers tightened around his hand. She licked her lips. Her breaths came in short, rapid bursts. "We haven't hung out much lately, and I've got to be at work in an hour. So, please, just you and me."

He stared at her feeling the racing pulse in her hand. Did she really miss hanging out with just him, or was it something else? "What's going on, Zoey?"

"Nothing." She let go of his hand. "Why can't it just be us? Playing music. Together."

"Because we're a band. The three of us, we play music together."

"Not last night. Last night, you and Sawyer played. Today, it's you and me. Can't that be enough?"

"No." Two of them—any two—wasn't enough.

"Fine." Zoey walked over to her bass case. "I think I'll go to work early."

"Are you forcing me to choose between you and Sawyer?"

"What if you had to?" Zoey spun around. "If you had to choose, me or Sawyer, who would you pick?"

His throat tightened like a D-string had been wrapped around his neck. "Why?"

"Who would you choose?" Her voice echoed the fierce look in her eyes.

"To play with?"

"Yes."

"You." The answer would always be Zoey. Sawyer was his best friend. Zoey was his life.

Tears pooled in Zoey's eyes.

"Zoey, what's wrong?" He tugged her close, wrapped her in a hug.

"Nothing, I..." She relaxed against his chest. "I guess I still feel bad about abandoning you for Aurora Fire."

"It's only for the summer, right?"

"Yeah. Two more months. Then I'll be playing with you again." She stepped back and wiped her palms across her cheeks. Then she picked up her bass. "I'm sorry. Let's play. I've still got an hour."

"OK." Justin sat on the ottoman, picked up his bass, and tried to figure out what had just happened. If he really had to choose between Zoey and Sawyer, he'd die of music starvation.

Verse 1:

When she starts to sing
I hear her heart take wing
Flying to the farthest star
She wants to be where You are
And I will go along
To be part of her song

14

Anthem of the Lonely

The microwave dinged. Sawyer grabbed the hot corn dog and pushed the buttons to start the washing machine. The sound of rushing water filled the kitchen.

Sawyer leaned against the counter eating his lunch. He'd cleaned the kitchen and the tiny dining area, vacuumed the carpet, and washed two loads of laundry. Given that his cleaning rarely went further than washing his dirty dishes and dividing the clothes on his bedroom floor into two piles—probably clean and definitely dirty—he was obviously bored. But he couldn't go to Justin's house and practice. Justin's ever-present grin reminded him of Justin's loyal innocence and Sawyer's worst betrayal.

A knock sounded on the front door.

He dropped the corn dog stick into the trash on his way to answer.

Justin stood on the stoop.

"What are you doing here?" Sawyer's heart pounded his ribs like a three-year-old banging the drums—hard, loud, nonstop. Sawyer scanned Justin's face for any sign that he knew what Sawyer had done.

"You're not answering your phone." Justin stepped inside. He sounded as laid back as usual.

Sawyer shut the door and checked his cell. "Oh.

Forgot to turn it back on yesterday." He watched it power up and scrolled through the missed calls. Only Justin. Good thing. Mom got ticked if he ignored her.

"You're not working today, are you?" Justin plopped down on the couch. "Thought you'd be over to practice."

Sawyer searched for an answer that was true, but not the truth. He said the first thing that came to mind. "Had to clean first."

"Really?" Justin's voice jumped an octave. "You in trouble or something?"

"No. I just wanted to help out my mom."

"You done now?" Justin glanced around the room. "Wanna go practice for a couple hours before the youth mixer thing tonight?"

"I'm not going."

"Why not?"

"It's lame. The music, the stupid games, forcing us to become friends." All one-hundred-percent truth. Sawyer would've said the same thing before he started avoiding Justin and Zoey.

"You got something better to do? Sew some throw pillows? Put together flower arrangements?"

"No."

"Then let's go." Justin pushed off the couch. "We need to practice."

Justin was right. And playing the drums would help Sawyer forget about Zoey.

Sawyer followed Justin out the front door. If only Sawyer could stop seeing the drumstick stabbing his best friend's back.

~*~

A few hours later, after eating dinner with the Conrads, Sawyer drummed his fingers on the armrest of Justin's car. Running through their setlist earlier had pushed all thoughts of Zoey from his head—until Justin turned onto her street.

His fingers froze mid-rhythm. "Where are you going?"

"To pick up Zoey."

"Why?" Sawyer straightened in his seat, his hand reaching for the door handle. Maybe he'd open it in the middle of the street and make a run for it. That might be the safest option.

"So she can go with us tonight." Justin glanced over, brow furrowed. "Is that a problem?"

"Yes."

"Why?" He sounded on the verge of laughter. "How long are you going to stay mad about her singing with Aurora Fire? That won't make her change her mind." He pulled into Zoey's driveway. "Get in the back."

Sawyer stepped out of the car, and Justin headed for Zoey's front door.

Always the gentleman, that guy. Sawyer considered his options. He could start walking home. It was only about a mile to his house. But Justin would track him down, and how would Sawyer explain that? He jerked open the back door of the car. Staying home and trying his hand at flower arranging would've been smarter.

Justin and Zoey walked toward the car holding hands. She caught sight of Sawyer, and their eyes met. The memory of Zoey pressed against him crying into his chest flooded his mind and left him cold. Why had he stopped? He should've ignored her and biked past.

On the way to church, no one spoke. The music sounded muffled in the thick air of the car. Sawyer stared out the window, too aware of the faint scent of waffle cones and Zoey's black and pink hair peeking through the head rest.

The parking lot outside the large community church—not Justin and Zoey's church—overflowed with cars. All the church youth groups had been invited. Lots of strangers. People who didn't know Sawyer. People who didn't care what he'd done. People who could fill the space between him and Zoey.

Sawyer stalked ahead, not waiting for Justin or Zoey. All the teens were gathered in the church's gym, their voices echoing off the metal rafters. At the door, some guy with a graying military haircut held out a slip of paper. Sawyer snatched it out of his hand and shoved it into his pocket. Then he wandered through the crowd trying to get lost.

"Sawyer." A finger tapped his shoulder.

Zoey's voice and touch stung like fire. Had she followed him? Why? Didn't she want to avoid him too? He faced Zoey, then looked around the room searching for Justin.

"We need to talk."

"No, we don't." He turned to escape.

"Please, Sawyer." She grabbed his arm.

He spun around yanking his arm from her grasp. "You agreed to forget about it."

"I can't."

He glanced at the people nearby. They paid no attention, but he pulled Zoey into a corner anyway. "There's nothing to talk about."

"Yes, there is." Dozens of emotions glimmered in her eyes. "We kissed. Isn't that something we need to talk about?"

"No."

"I think it is."

"No, you don't." He stared at her. She had the same look of insecurity on her face as she had that night, and her eyes were glossy with the threat of tears. He shoved away any sympathy. Feeling sorry for her had caused all this. What had happened between them was wrong for so many reasons, and he regretted it more than the time he got caught shoplifting from the gas station. He'd sworn never to do that again, and he felt the same about Zoey. Never again. "You're Justin's girlfriend."

"But—"

"No." He darted out of the shadowed corner and bumped into a girl.

"Sorry," she said.

He glanced down. Felicia.

Out the corner of his eye, he saw Zoey watching him. He needed escape help.

"Hi." He fell into step next to Felicia.

She looked up with startled gray eyes. "Hi. How are you?"

"Fine." He forced a smile. "You?"

"Good." She sounded way too happy.

Sawyer sniffed the air. He didn't detect any fake flowers. Maybe hanging out with her could work.

"Up here, people." A voice sounded over their heads, and the noise in the room quieted. Everyone faced one end of the gym. A bald, bearded man held a microphone. "I'm your puppet master—er, director of events—tonight."

The crowd laughed.

A comedian. That made these things more fun.

"Did everyone get a piece of paper when you arrived? If not, that guy over there"—the guy pointed at the military man waving a fist full of paper—"can fix you up. Look at the picture on it, and then find at least three other people with the same picture. Got it? Go."

"This is stupid," Sawyer muttered.

"I think it's kind of fun." Felicia nibbled her lower lip. "But if you wanted to leave...I'd go too."

The suggestion was tempting. Sawyer checked the exits. One had been left unguarded. It could work. "You got a car?"

"Yeah."

"Then let's go." Sawyer forced his way through the good little children comparing slips of paper. At the door, he glanced over his shoulder. Felicia was behind him.

They slipped into the dimly-lit hall.

"What if we get caught?" Felicia whispered.

"They'll lecture us and then force us to join the party." Sawyer followed unfamiliar hallways looking for an outside door. "But no one noticed."

Felicia stayed on his heels, her staccato breaths audible.

What would happen if they were caught? Probably nothing, but Sawyer hadn't ever ditched a youth thing like this. Justin always gave him a ride so he had no way to escape if he changed his mind. But the gym wasn't big enough for him and Zoey. Not if she was determined to talk. Didn't she understand the meaning of "forget"?

They came around a corner. Light shone through double glass doors. Sawyer led Felicia into the lot on the backside of the building. "Finally."

"We did it." Felicia giggled and bounced along next to him. "Wow, I've never done anything like that before. It was exciting."

"Your life must be boring." They'd ditched a youth mixer. Not school.

"Yeah, I guess it is." She clamped her hand on his arm. "So now what? You wanna go hang out somewhere? Get some food?"

What was with girls grabbing onto him tonight? He jerked away. He hadn't thought this through. Would he be stuck with Felicia for the rest of the night listening to her babble on and on about nothing? His head hurt already.

"Or we could go see a movie." They rounded the building to the front parking lot.

"A movie?" Theaters were quiet places. Sawyer might not be stuck making conversation there. "That sounds good."

"OK. What do you wanna see?"

"Whatever. But not some stupid romance." That seemed like the type of movie she'd want to see, and he couldn't deal with more kissing in his life.

"Here's my car." She stopped next to a gray car.

Sawyer sat in the passenger seat half-listening to Felicia describe movie options, his thoughts back on Zoey. It was as if Zoey wanted to destroy their band this summer—first by leaving, now by not forgetting. But he wouldn't let her. She couldn't want to destroy her relationship with Justin. Except she wasn't the one who would destroy their relationship.

Justin would blame Sawyer.

Sawyer blamed himself.

15

Let it Roll

Zoey bounced into Aurora Fire's house Tuesday, as happy and energetic as a preschooler after a sundae at the ice cream shack. She'd proven herself Saturday. Now no one could complain.

A guitar solo drifted up from the basement, and Zoey followed the sound. Practice was no longer scary.

She skidded to a stop at the bottom of the stairs. A strange girl sat next to Bailee. Were there two of them now? How could Zoey survive two Bailees?

"You'd look great with green, Cherie." Bailee tugged a piece of the younger girl's messy red-brown ponytail. "I could do it for you."

"What d'you think, Vance?" Cherie's eager tone screamed new girlfriend. "You like green?"

He glanced up from his guitar. "Yeah. Or blue."

"Hmm." She pursed her lips, staring at some loose strands. "I don't know if I'd want to go all green. Maybe like hers."

Vance and Bailee stared at Zoey and her black hair with pink streaks.

She touched her necklace, heat creeping up her neck. People didn't look to her all-black trend for style ideas unless they were attending a funeral.

"I guess you could do that." Bailee made it sound

like the dumbest idea ever.

Goody. Today would be fun as usual.

Vance stepped around Zoey and yelled up the stairs. "Practice!"

Zoey lowered her head and moved to her spot between Vance's guitars and Devin's basses.

"Our next concert is in almost two weeks—next Saturday." Vance planted himself in front of Zoey. His lack of a smile failed to clue her in on whether he wanted her singing in another concert. "But after last night's performance, I think you'll do fine."

"Thanks." She bit the insides of her cheeks to keep her smile from spreading. Finally—finally—band practice would be fun.

"But she had to rewrite the songs to do it." Bailee delivered each word with needle-like sharpness.

"So what?" Vance shot Bailee a frown and focused back on Zoey. "I suppose if I'd known Justin Conrad was your boyfriend, I would've realized you couldn't sing 'em."

Pop. The hope of a stress-free practice vanished. "What's that got to do with it?"

"He hasn't changed at all in five years." Vance sounded disgusted, like Justin not changing was a personal offense. "He's still pretending to be a good little Christian. Guess I shouldn't be surprised. He comes from a family of great actors."

"What's your problem with him?" Zoey had heard about the Vance who'd taught Justin the guitar, but until Justin had come to practice with her, she hadn't realized Aurora Fire's Vance was also Justin's Vance. They'd sounded like two different guys. Justin had always praised his guitar-playing idol. But except for Vance's skills with a guitar, he wasn't praise or idol worthy. "I thought you two were friends before you left?"

"You mean he didn't tell you?"

"Tell me what?"

"I moved away with my mom because my dad cheated on her—with Justin's mom."

"Oh." That explained a lot. Vance's comment about Justin's parents pretending to be happily married. Justin asking if she thought his mom was dressed too nice. Justin grilling his mom about where she was going. But Justin had never explained any of this to Zoey. Not even the reason for his parents' almost-divorce.

"But apparently, his parents worked everything out in counseling. Lucky them, huh?"

"Yeah, I guess." Zoey wasn't sure if agreeing was the right answer.

What would it be like to lose a parent like that? Mama's dying was horrible, but no one had caused her death. Sometimes, she wished she could be angry at someone other than God. Then again, it wasn't as if Justin had set up his mom and Vance's dad, so why was Vance blaming Justin?

And who would Justin blame if he found out she'd kissed Sawyer? Would they work it out like his parents? Or break up like Vance's? She yanked her necklace out of her shirt. Did she even want to stay with him?

That was why she'd wanted to talk with Sawyer last night. She couldn't get the kiss out of her head. Had Sawyer felt something too? Or did he really just see her as Justin's girlfriend? But she'd cheated on Justin. Was it right to keep that a secret?

"Hey! Zoey!" Vance said.

She jumped. "What?"

"Are you ready?"

"Yeah. Sorry." She shook away the thoughts of Justin, and Sawyer, and kisses.

The music began, but singing about pain and revenge didn't keep those thoughts away for long. Her voice sounded as confused and lifeless and lost as she felt. She forced out one song after the next, aware of Bailee's glares, until the final chord ended another pathetic practice.

"So you can only sing on stage?" Bailee asked.

"You were really good on Saturday." Cherie wrinkled her forehead, as if matching today's singing with Saturday's hurt her head.

"Sorry. A lot's on my mind."

"As long as she brings it on stage, who cares?" Vance put away his guitar and pulled Cherie off the couch. "C'mon. Let's go upstairs."

Giggling, she scampered at his heels.

Zoey followed them, not wanting to be stuck with Bailee.

When she got outside, her phone beeped. She squinted against the sunlight and read the screen.

Practice w me and S?

How could she face Justin and Sawyer in the same room?

Sorry. Busy.

Her heart hadn't ached this much since right after Mama died. How long would she be able to hide what happened if she couldn't be around Sawyer? Justin wasn't stupid. He also wasn't the jealous type.

Why couldn't she forget it ever happened like Sawyer said? She walked down the street and fingered the beads on her necklace. Maybe she should tell Justin. His parents went through something much worse—an affair was way more serious than a kiss—and they'd worked things out. She and Justin couldn't work things out if he didn't know. But what if they ended up like Vance's parents? Zoey would lose her best friend, her band, her everything. So would Justin.

Mama, what advice would you give? Not that she'd have the courage to admit to Mama what she'd done, even if she could. Everyone loved Justin. She couldn't tell anyone she'd cheated on him. She was stuck making that decision alone.

16

Waiting on My Deathbed

Holding his drumsticks in one hand, Sawyer pulled his vibrating cellphone from his pocket for the third time and glared at the tiny screen. Band practice should not be interrupted. Too bad Mom made him keep the phone turned on.

"Who keeps texting?" Justin asked. He plucked his guitar strings in the garage.

"Felicia," Sawyer muttered. He shoved it into his pocket without texting back.

"You two dating?"

"No!" Sawyer tapped his sticks against the snare.

"You sure? You did go to the movies with her Monday."

"So? You and I go to the movies, and it's not a date."

"But when Zoey and I go to the movies it is a date."

"It's not a date if I go to the movies with Zoey." He cursed silently. Why did he link himself with Zoey and dating? The one time he'd gone to the movies with just Zoey, Justin was supposed to be there too, but he'd canceled at the last minute.

Sawyer drummed faster, louder.

"That's because she's dating me." Justin practically

had to yell over Sawyer's drumming.

Sawyer hit the cymbals.

"By the way, she's coming over, so be nice."

"Here?" Sawyer's muscles twitched. Being in the same room with Zoey was worse than—his cell chimed with another text—worse than Felicia thinking they were dating.

"Yeah. She's coming over here."

The sound of an engine drifted into the open garage, and a few seconds later, Zoey's green car parked by the curb.

Sawyer's phone chimed again to remind him of the ignored message.

"I've gotta go." His knee bumped a tom-tom. He cursed.

"Don't say that." Justin's rebuke carried the emotion of the sneeze-following "bless you." "Why do you have to go?"

Sawyer glanced out the door.

Zoey walked up the driveway rolling her necklace between her fingers.

He scrambled for a reason. "Felicia."

"You sure you're not dating her?" Justin asked.

"Sawyer's dating?" Zoey stepped into the garage shoving her hands into her pockets. A mixture of relief and something Sawyer couldn't identify crossed her face. "Who?"

"Felicia," Justin answered.

"No, I'm not." Sawyer clenched his teeth. "Actually, I think I'll go home."

"OK." Justin's eyebrows drew together. He looked at Sawyer as though Sawyer had announced plans to join a folk band.

Sawyer met Zoey's gaze for an instant. Emotions

Sawyer never wanted to understand swirled in her brown eyes. "Yeah, I'm going home." He grabbed his bike off the lawn and pedaled away.

~*~

Sawyer shoved open the screechy front door.

Mom glanced over the back of the couch. "What are you doing home so early?"

"Just am." He headed for the fridge and chose one of the restaurant-leftovers containers. Chicken strips and fries, good to eat cold. He carried it to the couch.

"But it's only nine o'clock." She glanced at him and then back at the TV. "Everything OK?"

"Yep." He popped a limp fry into his mouth.

On the screen was some dating reality show. Mom laughed as one woman told off another.

"I don't get it," Sawyer said. "Why be on the show if you get upset about the guy dating other women? They know that's the whole point, right?"

Mom shrugged. "Yeah, but I think it's more about being on TV than dating the man. Though there's still hope that you might be a success story."

"Would you go on a show like that?"

"Ha! No. I'm smart enough to know I don't want to compete with a dozen other women." She snagged a fry. "No man is worth that."

"Not even me?"

"I hope you're smart enough to know that love won't be found on reality television."

He had no clue where love could be found. Mom hadn't proven she did either. Sawyer gnawed on a chicken strip and watched one group of women on TV prepare for a date and another group lounge by a pool.

"Does going to the movies with a girl automatically make it a date?"

"No." Mom twisted to face him. "Why?"

He shrugged.

"Did you go to the movies Monday with a girl?" She stretched out the words, eyes twinkling.

"Yeah."

"And I'd assumed you went with Justin and Zoey. It didn't occur to me that you might have other friends." She wiggled her eyebrows. "Other girl friends."

"Stop it."

She tucked a lock of pale blonde hair behind her ear, her face turning serious again. "But it wasn't a date?"

Sawyer shook his head. "She had a car and offered to ditch the youth mixer with me."

"You're so my kid." Mom's voice was a tangle of helplessness and regret. "Why'd you go if you didn't plan to stay?"

"Justin kind of forced me into it." Going into details would risk bringing up Zoey.

"OK, so was it a date?" Her mouth twisted into a knot. "You didn't pay for this girl's ticket, buy her popcorn, hold her hand, or kiss her, did you?"

"No. Why would I pay for her? She had money."

"Someday, I hope you understand why." She stole another fry. "But if you didn't do any of those things, she probably doesn't think it's a date. Unless, of course, she likes you and wanted it to be."

He groaned.

"So she likes you?" Mom chuckled sounding more amused by Sawyer's reality than reality TV. "Sounds like you've got yourself a problem."

"Thanks."

She turned her attention back to the TV snickering under her breath.

"It's not funny," he growled.

"Yes, it is. You want my advice?"

"I don't know." Her advice was often a joke, like when she told him that jumping off the roof with a bed sheet would be as thrilling as skydiving. Luckily, he hadn't broken any bones.

"Women—girls—we tend to overanalyze things. A gesture, a look, a smile might mean nothing, but often we hope it means something. Unless it's an old guy who needs better dental hygiene. Then we hope we've misread the signals until that day when he—" Her eyes widened as if she'd just remembered who she was talking to. "Never mind about that."

"Maybe you should avoid serving creepy old guys," he said.

"Believe me, I try." She shuddered. "Anyway, back to your problem. This girl—what's her name?"

"Felicia."

"Felicia probably hopes that going to the movies with you was a date, and if you don't want her thinking that, you'll have to tell her it wasn't."

"Can't I just ignore her until she figures it out?"

"You can try, but that may take a lot longer."

The list of unanswered texts on his phone proved Mom's point.

"Next time you find yourself asking a girl to the movies or something, think about whether you want her thinking it's a date or not." Mom returned to TV viewing.

Sawyer shoved the rest of the fries into his mouth. The dating show was stupid, but it made the process simpler. The women came to the guy, and he was free to send them home, one at a time, until only the woman he wanted remained. Sawyer would probably end up sending them all home. "Women are a pain."

"Watch it." Mom elbowed him. "Men aren't any better."

"I'm going to be thirty and still living with you, aren't I?"

"And I'll be almost fifty, still living with you. Depressing, isn't it?"

"Almost as depressing as being seventeen and watching this with my mommy." He shot her a grin.

"You look so much like your dad." Her return smile seemed sad. "There's no way you'll still be living with me at thirty."

Was that a compliment? She rarely mentioned his dad. Sawyer probably wouldn't know his dad's name was Toby Sawyer if he hadn't been named for him and Mom didn't have the name tattooed across her left shoulder blade.

He shoved off the couch. "I'm going to my room."

"Keep the music down, OK? You may not find this show entertaining, but I do. And I'm two weeks behind."

Sawyer waved his hand in agreement. In his room, he pulled shoeboxes of CDs from under his bed, searching for something to match his mood.

Minor keys. Melancholy rock.

He stuck the CD in the player punching the volume down.

He grabbed a pair of sticks and drummed along against his desk, his chair, his chest of drawers trying to straighten his thoughts, but everything collided inside his head. What would he do about Felicia?

Zoey? Justin?

He couldn't concentrate on one question, forget about finding an answer. Drumming harder, he sorted through his mom's advice. Tell Felicia what? To leave him alone? And if going to the movies meant he was dating Felicia, what did Zoey think the kiss meant?

One of the sticks snapped in half and flew into the air.

Yep, that summed things up. No matter the answer, that would be the result—everything snapping to pieces.

His phone buzzed with another text from Felicia.

R U going to devo tmrrw?

He stared at the screen. Answering would encourage her, but maybe there was something worse. Like kissing his best friend's girlfriend.

Yes.

Almost immediately, she responded.

Good. R U busy now?

Sawyer flopped back onto his bed. They could talk without it meaning anything more, right? Anyway, if he talked to her, she'd probably lose interest in him. Most girls did.

His phone vibrated in his hand.

It would be a long night.

17

War is Over

"You have practice tonight?" Justin asked Zoey over the phone Thursday afternoon. He leaned against the wall outside the playroom, half-listening to Tristan's play noises.

"No. Vance and Devin have to work."

"Then you'll be at the devo? It's here. My house."

"Yeah, I'll be there."

A muted crash, plastic-on-plastic, sounded, and Justin peeked around the corner. Tristan stood in the middle of the room building a tower of clear plastic containers. No catastrophes.

"Can you come early?" Justin ducked back into the hall. "We can practice together, like on Sunday."

"Sure." He heard the smile in her voice.

Ka-dunk. Ka-dunk. Another crash, this time followed by a wail.

"I've gotta go. I love you." He headed into the playroom listening for Zoey to echo his words.

She hesitated. "Yeah, me too," she said and disconnected.

Justin didn't have time to question Zoey's delayed response. Tristan lay on the floor, a half dozen plastic bins scattered around him.

"You OK, buddy?" Justin shoved the phone into

his pocket and lifted his crying brother. "What happened? Were you climbing on the bins?"

Tristan hiccuped and nodded.

"You know you're not supposed to do that."

Tristan sniffled and squirmed to get down.

"No more building towers to climb, 'kay?"

"'Tay." Tristan nodded, and Justin set him on his feet.

Sitting on the couch, Justin kept an eye on his brother. Tristan carried toys to Justin, and a random collection grew on the cushion.

Justin shouldn't read anything into Zoey's hesitation. She wasn't as quick as he was to say "I love you" anyway. It didn't mean anything, just like Mom asking him to babysit for the fourth time in a week didn't mean anything. At least she'd taken Savannah with her today, so she couldn't be meeting anyone.

He needed to concentrate on tonight. Before the devo, he'd force Sawyer and Zoey to work out their problems. Watching one run out the garage when the other arrived was annoying. Soon, Sawyer and Zoey might try to avoid each other by never coming over. Then what would he do?

Justin flipped a pick through his fingers. The three of them were still a band. They needed to act like it.

Babysitting Tristan trapped Justin inside most of the afternoon, but after Savannah and Mom returned from the store, the guitars called from the garage, and he couldn't resist.

For two hours, Justin practiced on his own, the music changing with his thoughts.

Would Sawyer leave when he saw Zoey? Minor chords. Or would Sawyer attack Zoey's decision to sing with Aurora Fire? Allegro and crescendo. What if his plan blew up in his face? The notes blasted into every corner and slammed back into his ears. But what if it worked and everything returned to normal? Andante.

Please, Lord, let me say the right things to get us playing again as a band.

A shadow fell across the guitar, and he looked up.

"Interesting song." Zoey clutched her black bass case in two hands and bounced it off her thighs. She stood awkwardly, as if she wasn't sure of what to do or how to act. As if she hadn't been in this garage a thousand times.

"I was just messing around." He set his guitar aside.

The garage door creaked open, and Savannah bounced out. "Zoey!" She threw her arms around Zoey's waist. "You haven't been here in forever."

"I was just here Sunday." Zoey hugged her with one hand.

"But I didn't see you." Savannah pulled back, grinning up at Zoey. "Guess what?"

"What?" She set her case down.

"I got these really sweet, pink skull earrings. Wanna see them?"

Zoey glanced at Justin.

He shrugged. He liked seeing Savannah and Zoey hanging out. Made Zoey a part of the family.

"Real quick." Zoey followed Savannah to the door. "I promised Justin we'd play before the devo."

They disappeared into the house, and some of the tension eased from Justin's shoulders. Zoey belonged here. So did Sawyer. They'd eaten more meals, watched more movies, spent more hours at Justin's house than Justin had at their houses combined.

Sawyer and Zoey had to miss all that—Justin's house, Justin's family, Justin.

He stepped onto the driveway and glanced down the street. Maybe he should intercept Sawyer, or he might turn around and bike home at the sight of Zoey's car. His neck ached again. He returned to the garage and exchanged his acoustic guitar for the electric. His plan had to work. He plugged into the amp and heard the dull thump of Sawyer's bike falling against the grass. Justin put the guitar down and walked outside.

"She's here?" Sawyer jerked a thumb at Zoey's car.

"Yeah."

Sawyer swore under his breath and swung his foot at the bike wheel.

"Don't say that."

"I'm outta here." Sawyer bent over and grabbed the handlebars.

"Don't." Justin grabbed the warm metal bar. "You've got to get over your problem with Zoey. How are we going to play together again if you two won't stay in the same room?"

Sawyer stared at the ground, his knuckles turning white.

Justin dragged his hand through his hair. This wasn't going well. "C'mon, Sawyer. It's stupid to keep picking on her."

Sawyer raised his head. He swallowed, and his Adam's apple bobbed. "You don't know what you're doing." He let the bike crash to the ground and stomped into the garage.

What was with the drama? At least Sawyer was staying, but that didn't stop the knots across Justin's shoulders from tightening.

Sawyer collapsed on the plaid couch as if he didn't want to commit to practice by sitting at his drums. He tapped his feet against the concrete and avoided Justin's gaze.

The door to the house opened. Zoey stepped out, and her grin vanished. "You're here." Her voice sounded flat and almost scared.

Justin's stomach clenched echoing the emotions on Zoey's face. What was going on? Was it more than Sawyer's anger over Zoey's decision? No, couldn't be. Sawyer and Zoey wouldn't even hang out together if it wasn't for Justin and their band.

"Your boyfriend has arranged an intervention or something." Sawyer locked his gaze on Zoey, eyebrows lifting as if sending her a silent message.

"Guys. I'm tired of this." Justin looked at his friends—the two people who understood and shared his love for music. They needed this as much as he did. "We're a band, and we need to play. So get over it, Sawyer. Zoey's only with Aurora Fire for the summer. She can still practice with us, and when senior year starts, we can all focus on music. Stop beating her up about it."

Sawyer stared at Justin a moment before raising his hands in surrender. "OK, fine, I'm over it." He looked hard at Zoey. "It shouldn't have happened, but it doesn't matter now."

Zoey flinched and glanced away.

Justin looked from Zoey to Sawyer back to Zoey. What was he missing? "Can we play now?"

Shoving her hands into her back pockets, Zoey looked at him. "Yeah, OK."

"Good." His stomach unclenched, and he stepped toward her, but she turned away. He glanced at

Sawyer.

"Whatever." Sawyer stood and walked to the drums.

"And you'll stay and practice after the devo, like usual?"

"Like nothing ever happened." Sawyer clunked down on the stool, raised his sticks, and grinned like a deranged sock monkey.

That had been easy. *Thank you, Lord.*

Justin picked up his electric guitar and began tuning along with Zoey. Everything was back to normal with the three of them here playing. Almost. And as long as they kept playing together, all other problems would fade.

18

New Way to Bleed

"Judas and Peter betrayed their best friend." Brandon led the devo from his seat on a couch in Justin's living room. "But their responses to that mistake were very different."

Zoey sat on the floor hugging her knees, and tried to ignore Brandon. Betrayal. A kiss. Denials. All topics Zoey struggled to avoid every minute of every hour of every day. But she failed.

"Judas saw no hope of redemption. Peter, however, when confronted with his failure, sought forgiveness and found it. Forgiveness is always offered."

Brandon's words slipped into Zoey's ears. Was that true? She glanced at Justin sitting next to her. Would he offer forgiveness?

Sawyer sat on Justin's other side, and he caught her eye with the same hard look he'd given her earlier in the garage. She shivered as if she was underdressed in below-freezing January.

Didn't Sawyer feel the same crushing guilt? She wanted their band and relationships and lives to go back to normal too. But how could life be normal if they kept such a huge secret?

"Let's close in prayer." Brandon lowered his head.

She closed her eyes. *God, should I tell Justin? Like Sawyer says, it was just a mistake. It didn't mean anything. So Justin would forgive us, right? Oh God, what am I supposed to do?*

"Amen."

Her eyes snapped open.

Justin stood and held out a hand to help her stand. He smiled as if everything was normal. As if he loved her.

That smile wrapped around Zoey's heart like the noose around Judas's neck. She needed to be somewhere—anywhere—else. She scrambled to her feet and pushed against the crowd headed for the kitchen. Could she lock herself in the bathroom for the next hour? Probably not. But maybe she could hide for a while in Mr. Conrad's study. She darted into the room across the hall from the bathroom.

Mr. Conrad's home office was neat and organized, unlike Dad's at home. Dad kept stacks of papers and file folders looking like miniature leaning towers of Pisa on the desk, the floor, the chairs, the windowsills. Mr. Conrad had only a computer and a cup of pens on his desk. Shelves lined one wall with books grouped by subject. An entire section was dedicated to marriage.

How to Repair a Relationship After Infidelity and *Now Our Marriage Is Broken, How Do We Fix It?* stood on one row. Below were *Rekindling the Spark in Your Romance* and *Making the Light of Your Life Shine*. To tell or not to tell, what did the experts advise? She pulled *Life After The Affair* from the shelf.

A quiet click of the door opening and loud talking from the living room invaded the office.

She shoved the book back in place and spun

around.

"Sorry." The new girl, the one with the diamond below her lip, peeked around the door. "This isn't the bathroom."

"No." Zoey's heart raced as if she'd been caught hacking into Mr. Conrad's computer, not innocently browsing his bookshelves. Her interest was anything but innocent. Zoey swallowed back the thought and emotions. "It's across the hall."

"Yeah, on the right, not the left. Oops." New girl glanced over her shoulder at the hall and stepped into the room. "Zoey, right?"

"Yeah. You're...Chey?"

The girl nodded squinting at Zoey and wiggling her diamond stud. "You OK?"

"Yeah, I'm fine." A total lie. For a moment, she considered admitting the truth. She had no one to talk to. Livvy adored Justin, and Sawyer wanted to forget. Zoey was about to implode from locking up this secret.

But Chey was a stranger, so Zoey focused on the flashing stud. Maybe she should pierce something other than her ears. Dad would let her, but Justin's parents wouldn't approve. Her changing hair color disturbed them enough.

"Sweet band setup in the garage." Chey wrapped her hands behind her back and leaned against the door.

"Thanks." Zoey searched for a topic to keep Chey in the room and keep away the obsessing. "You play anything?"

"Cards?"

Zoey laughed and relaxed in a way she hadn't in days or maybe weeks.

"Actually, I play the piano."

"My sister tried to learn the piano."

"Tried?"

"Turns out she's tone-deaf. Because of that, we used to argue one of us had to be adopted."

"Nice."

Zoey rested on the edge of the desk toying with her necklace.

"Pretty cool youth group you've got, too." Chey's pink tutu-like skirt poofed around her. She didn't look like the kind of girl who worried about coolness.

"Thanks," Zoey said, as if she could take credit. Then again, if Chey thought they were cool because of their band, she could.

"And I like your youth minister. Interesting topic."

Back to thinking on that? Zoey dropped her gaze to her necklace. Betrayal was fun to talk about, not so fun to live. "Do you think he was right?"

"About what?"

"About forgiveness always being offered."

"Yeah. At least, I sure hope so." Chey's voice faded away as if she spoke the last couple of words to herself. She opened the door to the hall. "Guess I'll go find the right room now. See ya." She left pulling the door shut.

Had Chey run off because of the serious question? No, that was silly. Chey probably needed to follow through with her original errand—finding the bathroom.

Zoey's need to talk about the kiss crescendoed. But everyone would side with Justin, hating her. If she worked things out with him first...

She pushed away from the desk. After all, the kiss hadn't meant anything. Her hand trembled. She wrapped her fingers around the metal knob, but didn't twist it. What if she'd kissed Sawyer on purpose? Until that night behind the ice cream shack, she'd never thought about kissing him. Even then, she couldn't remember thinking about kissing him. Sawyer had just been there, in the right place at the right time. No, wrong place, wrong time. Very wrong time. Freak piano-falling-on-a-pedestrian wrong time. Everything that happened had been wrong. Except the fluttering in her stomach and her toes curling, right now, at the memory. That felt right.

And a million times more wrong.

19

Vacillation

Social hour was over for Sawyer. He needed to get to his drums and beat away thoughts of Judas's kiss. He headed for the garage.

"You're not leaving, are you?" Justin grabbed Sawyer's arm, as if strong enough—or bold enough—to keep Sawyer from leaving.

"No. Just out to play." Sawyer stepped back bumping into someone. He glanced over his shoulder and caught blonde-and-cinnamon-red hair and impressions of black and pink as a girl exited into the garage. "Can I play?" Sawyer focused back on Justin. "That OK with you?"

"Go ahead." Insecurity flickered in Justin's eyes. "You seen Zoey? It's like she's avoiding me. Again."

Sawyer's heart jumped to his throat. "How would I know where your girlfriend is?"

"I don't know." Justin shrugged and then grinned, the insecurity vanishing. "Go. Beat on your drums instead of me."

Sawyer marched through the garage door and slammed it behind him. Had Brandon's talk left Zoey with this nauseating guilt? He couldn't blame her for avoiding Justin after listening to fifteen minutes about kisses and betrayal. He didn't want to think about her or Justin. He needed to play.

But someone stood in front of his drums. Two-toned hair girl staring a little too hard at his instrument.

"Hey!" The word came out sharp, as if Sawyer redirected all his anger and frustration at something new. "Don't touch."

She didn't respond or even look at him for a full two seconds. Then she turned slowly, chin raised as if she hadn't decided if she wanted to obey his command. "They yours?"

"Yes." He kept his tone gruff, so she'd know he was serious. If this girl had some fantasy about being in a band or becoming a groupie, she'd better find someone else to fill the drummer role. "And no one touches them."

"Chill, drummer boy." She raised her hands, palms out and then flipped them around to show the backs. "They're clean. And I'm pretty sure I've washed them at least once today."

A funny girl. He crossed his arms wanting to find her joke stupid, but he had to press his lips against a laugh. Or at least a grin. He'd never get rid of her if she thought he found her funny.

She kept her gaze on his. Her eyes were an unusual orangey-brown, the color of flames, and a sizzle shot through Sawyer. He tightened his arms across his chest to smother the lighting fire.

"Fine." She broke the silence first. "I'm going."

"Good." Sawyer stepped around her and sat on the stool behind the drums. He picked up the sticks and waited so she wouldn't think he was providing a private concert. But she didn't move. And he needed to play. "Leave."

Her chin lifted another inch. Defiance. Like his demand that she leave made her want to stay. Exactly the opposite of most girls' reactions. Maybe a private concert for her wouldn't be terrible.

But then she reached out a finger. And touched his drums.

"Hey!" Sawyer sprang to his feet, the stool rocking.

She was already walking away, out the open garage door, pink tutu swinging, shoulders straight, as if she didn't care one bit that she'd broken Sawyer's number one rule.

If he chased her down to yell at her, he'd get to spend a few more seconds with her. That desire was as bad as thinking about Justin and Zoey. He began drumming away all his thoughts. Clearing his head. But the girl who touched his drums—now he had to find out her name—couldn't be chased away.

Neither could Felicia. She walked into the garage.

Great.

She stopped in front of him, shoved her hands in her back jeans' pockets, and bounced with the beat.

He'd wanted to avoid her tonight. Who knew someone could be annoyingly chatty while texting? Last night, he'd told her his mom said he had to go to bed. A lame excuse and a lie since Mom hadn't enforced a bedtime since sixth grade.

He definitely didn't want to give her a private concert, but he was in the middle of playing now. He couldn't stop. If he ignored her, would she eventually leave? A couple of minutes later, he had the answer. She wasn't going anywhere.

"What?" He stopped playing.

"I just wanted to listen to you play." Her voice

wavered, and she shifted away from the drums.

"OK." So the best way to get rid of her was to not play? His fists tightened around the sticks. That didn't work for him.

"Do you make stuff up, or are you playing actual songs?" Felicia's voice gained strength. "'Cause I didn't recognize anything you played last Saturday."

"Saturday, it was all our own songs. We write our music."

"So since I like your music, are there any other bands I might like?"

Sawyer listed a few bands, keeping watch on the street. Did the new girl have a car? What kind? Movement on the driveway caught his attention. Two sophomore boys.

"I've heard of them. Are they your favorites?"

"They're OK."

"Who do you like then?"

Sawyer listed heavy metal bands he knew Felicia would never listen to, even if their message was Christian.

"I don't know them." She proved him right by listing off praise-and-worship types. Figured.

Her taste in music was as far from his as Alaska from Antarctica.

"Do you have any CDs I could borrow?"

"Yeah, I guess." She'd hate anything he gave her.

"Or maybe I could—"

A blue car rolled by. The two-tone hair unmistakeable. There she was—the girl who touched his drums. A rhythm pulsed through his veins. Quick but steady. She didn't even glance toward the garage.

"What do you think?"

"Huh?" Sawyer blinked at Felicia.

"Would Sunday be a good day?"

"For what?"

"For me to come over and check out your CD collection." Felicia raised her voice like the drums had made Sawyer deaf.

He tried to process her words, but he wasn't exactly interested. He looked past Felicia. The new girl drove to the corner. Had he scared her off permanently? Was that what he wanted?

"Sunday's OK?"

"What?" Sawyer pulled his attention back to Felicia. Why was she still here? He definitely wanted to scare her off. Instead, he heard himself sort of agreeing. "I guess."

"OK. See you Sunday." Felicia flashed a fan-girl smile before turning and walking off.

What had he agreed to? He should ask, but at least Felicia was leaving.

The new girl and her blue car had disappeared.

Would he see her on Sunday? This week, he might look forward to church.

20

I Need You to Love Me

Zoey clutched the knob of Mr. Conrad's office door.

Make a decision. Justin was obviously the right guy. That should be the end of it. Nothing about Sawyer was right. He certainly didn't think anything about her was right. He argued against every suggestion she ever made—from names for their band to what to do on a Friday night instead of practicing.

But Justin let her choose every movie, every restaurant, every everything. His opinion was the same as hers. Honestly, it was kind of annoying.

Was she comparing Justin and Sawyer again? It was like trying to compare the guitar and the drums. They were too different. Justin's presence filled her like a warm melody, carrying energy right into her soul, while Sawyer pounded and crashed giving her a headache.

She needed Justin and could live without Sawyer. But she'd be haunted by the kiss until she cleared her conscience. She yanked the door open. If she wanted to rid herself of this guilt, the answer was simple. She had to confess.

The hallway and living room were empty. Had she missed the entire after-devo scene? Justin was probably looking for her. Some girlfriend she was hiding from her boyfriend all night. She checked the kitchen. Empty. But she heard Sawyer drumming in the garage. Maybe they'd started practice. She walked over to the garage door.

"There you are."

She whirled around, her hair whipping across her face. Brushing back the strands, she faced Justin's grin.

"I've been looking all over for you." He grabbed her hand, tugged her close.

She curved into his side and breathed in his scent—deodorant, toothpaste, comfort. Maybe confession was a bad idea.

"Where have you been? You OK?" He lowered his voice, eyes serious.

The back of her throat burned with the threat of tears. She couldn't break his heart. "I just wanted...to be alone."

His grip tightened with don't-do-it strength as if her wanting to be alone scared him. After a couple of seconds, he relaxed, and she could feel her fingers again. "You OK now? Ready to practice?"

She nodded.

He glanced over his shoulder and then kissed her.

And she felt less passion than when she'd made out with her own hand in fifth grade.

Absolutely none.

"I kissed Sawyer!" The words burst out of her and into Justin's mouth.

He pulled back and stared looking confused, not hurt. Not like she'd shattered his soul. "What?"

"I'm sorry. It was a mistake." Her breaths came shorter, faster, until her vision fuzzed.

"What was?"

She had to say it again? She breathed one, long, slow breath, and the world sharpened. Maybe she should just pretend she'd said something else. Anything else.

"What was a mistake, Zoey?"

"I...I..." She struggled to find other words, but her rapid pulse beat the three words she never wanted to repeat. They were the only words she had. "I kissed Sawyer."

He stepped back, glanced away. He rubbed a hand over his head as if to erase what she'd said from his mind.

She reached out wanting to touch him, to reassure him of...what? That the kiss meant nothing? That she still loved him? That the thing he'd feared most—them breaking up—hadn't happened? But none of those were true, so her hand froze in the painful space between them.

Finally, he looked at her, his face hard and his eyes clouded with something she'd rarely seen in him. Anger. Death metal anger. Hate-your-face anger. His nostrils flared, and his minty breath hit her face in audible puffs.

She wanted to suck her words back in. Or better, undo the moment and forget that a kiss could send tingles all over. Tears spilled down her cheeks. She hoped Justin would brush them away, like he always did.

But words and kisses couldn't be forgotten.

He reached around her for the door. "Get. Out."

21

The Spectacle of Fearsome Acts

Finally alone, Sawyer returned to drumming. The overflow of cars had decreased, and only the Conrads' vehicles and Zoey's car remained. He glanced at the door leading to the house. Any minute, Justin and Zoey would be out to practice. Like now.

The door banged open.

He stopped drumming.

Zoey, gray streaks down her cheeks, stumbled into the garage. Justin followed on her heels practically pushing Zoey down the step, his face red, his jaw tight, his eyes wide, wild, pained.

Justin knew.

Sawyer tensed, his insides tight and cold. Stupid, stupid, stupid Zoey.

Justin's gaze met Sawyer's, and that one look drummed straight through Sawyer. Three years of being a band. Over.

"Justin, I'm sorry." Zoey's voice cracked as if echoing her heart.

The drumsticks slipped from Sawyer's sweaty fists. She should've kept her mouth shut.

Justin stood, frozen on the single step. His glance jumped from him to Zoey and back as if he couldn't decide who to be angry with or what to do about it.

This was Justin, the guy who shrugged off the stack of CDs stolen from his car last year. He probably didn't know how to react.

But Sawyer had stolen something way more important than CDs.

Justin stomped across the garage and planted his hands on the toms. "Did you kiss her?"

Sawyer couldn't breathe. Chunks of ice jammed his lungs. How was he supposed to answer that? He couldn't. "Get your hands off my drums."

"Did. You. Kiss. Her." Justin shifted his weight and the drum stand creaked.

"I said, get your hands off my drums." Sawyer shoved his forearms.

Justin lost his balance and grabbed Sawyer's arm.

Sawyer jerked back, pulling Justin toward him.

Justin bumped against the drums.

The stand screeched against the cement floor. The cymbals clanged.

Fire sparked in Justin's eyes as though the fight ignited the years of anger he'd stuffed down. He grabbed Sawyer's shirt.

Sawyer grasped Justin's forearms. They struggled, the drums between them. The stool crashed into the bass.

It was a mistake, Sawyer wanted to yell. He'd never meant to kiss Zoey.

Justin pulled Sawyer around, slammed him into the couch, pinned him down, and stared. Justin's expression changed from anger to hurt to confusion and repeated the cycle.

Sawyer's stomach heaved under the weight of Justin's knee. But that was no match to the weight of Justin's pain. This was why Sawyer had told Zoey to forget.

Justin could never understand.

Sawyer shoved Justin to the opposite end of the couch and tensed, ready for Justin to lunge back.

But Justin didn't. His face emptied of anger, of confusion, of life. And all that was left was pain.

"Leave." Justin stood, moving slow, stiff, as if his entire body ached. "Never come back." The finality in those last words punched harder than a fist.

Justin walked past Zoey and into the house.

Sawyer hunched over and rested his forehead against his palms. This was bad. Destined-for-hell bad.

"Sawyer, I...I'm sorry." Zoey's voice sounded too loud in the silence.

"Sorry?" Sawyer raised his head. His hands twitched, ready to strangle her. "You destroyed everything."

"I just thought—"

"I don't care what you thought!" He shoved off the couch, but instead of stomping over to Zoey and beating her up—so what if she was a girl?—he walked over to his drums.

The fight had torn the snare drumhead. He swore. He'd have to replace it. Not that it mattered. What good was a drummer without a band? And he couldn't replace his band.

"I'm sorry." Zoey said those words again. As if they could repair the destruction.

Sawyer walked past her, grabbed his bike off the lawn, and pedaled home. Being sorry would never be enough. He'd known that the second his lips had touched hers. Nothing could make up for stealing Zoey.

Sawyer's gut felt as ripped as the drumhead. He'd

be lucky if Justin ever let him back into the garage. And even if Justin did, they wouldn't be friends.

Which was worse—losing his band or losing his best friend?

22

The Grey

Zoey's heart lodged in her throat choking her. She couldn't speak. She couldn't move. She could only watch Sawyer bike away from Justin's house. Sawyer was right—she'd been very, very wrong. She'd never expected Justin and Sawyer to get in a fight. The fact that the fight was about her didn't cheer her up.

"Zoey?"

She spun around. Justin's mom stood in the doorway.

"What's going on out here?" Mrs. Conrad looked around the garage. Her gaze paused on the disarranged drums, and her brows pinched together. "Are you OK?"

Tears still streamed down her cheeks, so Zoey couldn't deny not being OK. But she couldn't explain things to Justin's mom, even if she were able to talk.

Before Mrs. Conrad could ask any more questions or take a motherly interest in her, Zoey grabbed her bass in one hand, the case in the other, and rushed to her car.

She drove home blanking out of her mind Justin, Sawyer, and music. But the walled-off thoughts pressed against her temples. She parked the car in the driveway and exploded in a torrent of tears. It shouldn't hurt this much. Confession was supposed to ease her conscience, not tear out her insides. But why would she deserve to feel relief when she'd hurt Justin? She folded her arms on top of the steering wheel and rested her forehead against them. Three words, "I kissed Sawyer," and three friends had broken up. Her body jerked with sobs.

The horn blasted.

She jumped away from the steering wheel. Goody, on a day she wanted to disappear, she'd alerted the entire neighborhood to her presence. Including Livvy.

Her sister walked down the sidewalk. She squinted in the sunlight, peering through the windshield.

Zoey ducked her head to hide the tears. No luck.

The passenger door opened, and Livvy slid in. "Zo, what's wrong?"

"I...I..." Zoey swallowed. The words practically strangled her. "Justin and I broke up."

"You and Justin? Why?"

Because she'd been crazy enough to believe Justin could forgive her for cheating on him. The crying began again. She couldn't say it—not to Livvy.

"Oh, baby." Livvy reached over to wrap an arm around Zoey's shaking shoulders.

Zoey yanked away. She fumbled with the latch, stumbled from the car, and ran into the house. In her room, Zoey grabbed her mp3 player and scrolled for the song that met her mood. She jammed the earbuds in her ears and flopped back on the bed. Tiger, as if sensing Zoey needed something soft and warm cuddling her, broke out of hiding and curled up next to her. At least her cat didn't hate her.

The ceiling was painted in a swirling green, blue,

and pink aurora borealis dotted with stars. Last March, she and Justin had watched the aurora nearly every weekend. Long time natives said it was a good year. They were wrong. It was an awful year.

She closed her eyes to block out the view. She didn't want to remember those romantic nights of eating candy and God's light show—that's what Justin called it. Why did he use those words? Because it killed the romance a little. Actually, a lot. It was kind of hard to make out with a boyfriend when God was hanging out in the car too. Maybe that's why Justin said it. Justin, always good, always keeping them going to youth group, always reminding them of God.

Why couldn't she admire those traits?

She didn't need his prodding to stay on the side of good. Not like Sawyer. Sawyer lived a nudge away from the abyss. But Justin kept him from falling.

Until she'd shoved them both over the edge.

Tears leaked from under her lids. In fairytales, a kiss saved the girl's life. But a kiss destroyed hers.

Of course, she'd always known she lived in a tragedy.

23

She Mighty Mighty

Sawyer parked outside Rhythm and Notes and checked the time on his phone. Thirty minutes and he had to have the car back to Mom.

He'd needed to do something to fix what had happened two days ago. Talking to Justin wasn't an option. Justin would make the first move. He always did. Justin couldn't let a fight last.

Except this wasn't a fight. Sawyer had ripped out Justin's heart—maybe even Justin's soul—and unlike Sawyer's drums, which only needed a new drum head, their friendship wouldn't be a simple fix.

But Sawyer *could* fix his drums.

He walked up the ramp into the store. A pick screwed to the door strummed a guitar mounted over the entrance. The strings played up, and then down, as the door closed.

Two steps toward the room where the drum heads were and he froze.

"Hey, drummer boy." Two-toned-hair girl from Thursday cocked her hip against the music book bins.

His heart jumped into a rhythm normally reserved for a band announcing a tour date in Alaska. But he summoned his menacing voice. "You touched my drums."

"I did." She pursed her lips, looking sad. But the expression was faker than the plastic tuba mounted on the wall. "Hope I didn't leave a fingerprint."

"Don't do it again." He moved closer trying to look threatening, but the only threat was the possibility of his heart hammering right out of his chest like a cartoon character.

"A little possessive, are we?"

He narrowed his eyes.

She laughed and turned her attention to the bin of music books.

Was she flirting with him? Did he want her to be flirting?

He glanced over her shoulder. "You play guitar?"

"Thinking about it."

"Of course you are." Figured. Just another band member wannabe.

"What's that mean?" Annoyance equal to his own crept into the girl's voice, but curiosity clung to its edges.

"Everybody wants to play the guitar. Or the drums. Like they're the only instruments worth playing." He'd thought—hoped—she was different. But they were all the same. He walked off to find his drumhead.

"So says the drummer." She followed him into the next room hugging a guitar book to her chest. "You have a better suggestion?"

"Do you play any instrument?"

"Piano."

"Then why don't you stick with that?" Was he giving her advice? He should grab his drumhead and get out.

"Because it's not really a band instrument." She

clamped her mouth shut and gripped the book tighter, as if the confession embarrassed her.

"Everybody wants to be in a band."

"And that bothers you because...?"

"Because people think it's cool to be 'in a band.' But it's a lot of hard work." He studied the cubbies in the wall filled with drumsticks and slender boxes seeking the right drum head. Avoiding eye contact so he wouldn't self-combust. Or worse, say something to encourage her. As if anything encouraging ever popped out of his mouth. "Stick with the piano."

"Would you be in a band with a piano?"

"Depends." Sawyer looked at her. Was she really interested? Or just a flirty groupie? "You any good?"

"Of course I am." Her chin jutted up in the same defiant look she'd shown Thursday. She'd perfected that look. He liked that look. He wanted to memorize that look.

"Then I would." He finally glanced away and selected a flat, square box from the wall. "Plenty of bands have a piano or a keyboard."

"Good to know." She twirled around and returned to the music book bins.

Sawyer let the air out of his lungs. He hadn't realized he held his breath. Something about that girl... She wasn't like Felicia. She wasn't like Zoey. She wasn't like any girl he knew. Not that he'd be getting to know her.

Sawyer paid and headed for the door walking past the new girl again.

"So what did you buy?" she asked without looking up.

"New drum head."

"What's that?" She continued flipping through the

books.

"Like the cover of the drum—what you hit."

"You're replacing it because I touched it?" She snapped her head up staring as if he'd grown horns. "Seriously? Because I left a fingerprint or something? You're not possessive, you're obsessive."

"My drums. My *possession*." Her accusation punched him, and for some reason, he needed to defend his no-touching rule. A rule he had every right to enforce. "Anyway, different drumhead. It tore the other night."

"Oh. OK." The girl looked back at the piano books, but kept talking. "I'm hungry. Any good places to eat around here?"

"What do you want?"

"I don't know. Food?"

"There's a few restaurants around here—Thai, Greek, some coffee shops. Over where I live, there's an outdoor sandwich place and pizza."

"Pizza sounds good." She leaned against the music bin looking him straight in the eye. That orangey-brown color lit a fire again.

He swallowed to put out the flame. "It's over near the university, by the ice cream shack and a used bookstore."

"OK, yeah, I've seen the place." She hesitated a second. Waiting for him to say something? To invite himself?

He should probably keep his distance. After the mess with Zoey, he'd be crazy to attempt even a friendship with any other girl. And any other girl would be crazy to want him as a friend.

"I'll check it out. See ya." She stepped around him and toward the door, as if she couldn't care less. As if he'd imagined her hesitation.

He couldn't let her go. "I could meet you there."

She paused, hand on the doorknob. Silence stretched.

Of course she didn't want him to meet her. Who would? Only Justin. Only his best friend had ever wanted him around. And Sawyer had destroyed Justin.

Then she glanced back shrugging. "If you want."

His heart pounded in his throat like a beat on steroids. "I gotta take the car home and get my bike first."

She pulled open the door, and the guitar overhead strummed. "Be there in thirty minutes, or you're paying."

24

Walking Dead

Two days. Was that all the time that had passed since Zoey's confession?

Justin lay on his bed staring at the ceiling. Gloomy music filled the room. His hand rested on the speaker remote, ready to change songs the moment the music sounded too upbeat. What was he supposed to do? The question played through his mind on repeat, but he hadn't found an answer. His brain, his body, his soul felt numb and weighed down.

Someone knocked on the door.

He hit the pause button without raising his hand. "What?"

Mom peeked in. "Are you going to eat breakfast?"

"No."

"Justin, what's going on?" She pushed the door open wider and stepped into the room letting in a flood of sympathy. "There all that noise from the garage Thursday and Zoey in tears. Now you've barely left your room since then, and you haven't been out to practice at all. What happened?"

He didn't answer. Telling her would require putting into words something he couldn't even think about. Zoey and Sawyer...

He dug his fingernails into the fabric of his quilt.

But if he told Mom, could she help him understand? If anyone could explain why Zoey did what she did, it would be his mom. She had experience in cheating. But he couldn't say, Hey, Mom, why'd you cheat on Dad? So he stayed silent.

Mom sighed, but she didn't push him. "We're walking over to the Farmer's Market. Do you want to come with us?"

"No."

She hesitated a moment as though waiting for him say something more and then left.

He lay on his bed and listened to the chattering fade from the hall. His ignored thoughts grew louder in the silence. What exactly had Zoey said? He forced a replay of the conversation, every word a bullet to his heart.

I kissed Sawyer...It was a mistake.

A mistake. Had she meant that? Maybe it hadn't been her fault. He sat up and swung his feet over the side of the bed. She never would've kissed someone else. Besides, hadn't she apologized? He grabbed his phone. He'd invite her over, let her know he forgave her. She wasn't to blame for the kiss. His grip tightened. That was Sawyer's fault.

Can U come over and talk?

He stared at the phone for a few seconds and then headed to the bathroom. No text while he showered. No text while he dressed. No text until his mouth foamed with minty toothpaste.

He spit into the sink and opened the message.

Later. At band practice. I'll come after.

He wiped away the toothpaste at the corners of his mouth. He couldn't wait that long, even if he got in trouble with his parents for not asking permission.

~*~

Justin pulled up behind Zoey's car by the curb and parked. Walking through the overgrown grass, he could feel the faint vibrations of music. His heart pounded in time with the fast-paced beat.

He knocked, but it went unnoticed. Not surprising. Should he just let himself in like Zoey had? He needed to see her, to prove he'd forgiven her. So he grabbed the knob and, finding the door unlocked, stepped into the dark, cool Arctic entry.

Like the first time, the stale odors of ramen and old pizza filled the air. Those guys needed to change up their diet. His heart raced with the music drifting up from the basement. Retracing his path from the week before, he made his way downstairs. Then he hesitated.

Aurora Fire blasted the room. Bailee and some girl sat on the couch painting their nails. Zoey, focused on her singing, didn't notice him. He took the moment to watch her. She'd changed her hair to black and green—like his eyes. Had she chosen it for that reason?

She glanced up, and he offered a smile.

Her singing screeched to a halt. After an eternal second, she rushed across the room.

The rest of the band kept playing.

"What are you doing here?" She raised her voice above the noise.

"I came to see you." The song ended, and his

words echoed in the silence.

The attention of the entire room zoomed in on them. Interrupting practice was a major fail.

"What do you want?" Vance sounded accusing, but for what? Interrupting practice or breaking up with Zoey?

Justin opened his mouth but didn't know what to say. He wiped his sweaty palms against his jeans.

"Just give us a minute." Zoey gave Vance a tortured look. Her face was pale, and her eyes were red as if she hadn't slept. "Please?"

"Fine. One minute." Vance muttered something to himself.

"I said I'd come over after practice." Zoey pulled Justin closer to the recording equipment.

"I know, but I wanted to see you." He ran his fingers down her arm and wrapped her hand in his. "Let me stay and listen."

She slid her hand away and hugged herself with one arm. Staring at the ground, she twisted her necklace. "No. I...I don't want you here."

"Why?" Aching numbness spread through his chest. He needed to be in the same room with her so he could pretend nothing had happened. Didn't she need that too?

"I think we should break up." Her words, not much more than a whisper, slammed into him.

"What? Is this because of..." Justin struggled to breathe. It felt like an amp lay on his chest. "You said it was a mistake."

The band stopped talking, and their gazes locked on him and Zoey. He felt trapped in a bad reality show.

"It was, but..."

"Zoey, it's OK. Whatever happened, I forgive you." His voice rose with desperation, and he tried to rein in his emotions.

"I'm sorry." She turned away.

"No. Zoey, don't." Justin grabbed her arm yanking her back around.

"Please, leave." Tears pooled in her eyes.

"Come over later, like you said." The begging was pathetic, but he couldn't stop. "We'll talk."

"There's nothing to talk about." She eased out of his grasp.

"What do you mean? There's plenty to talk about."

She walked away.

"Zoey!"

"She said, leave." Vance moved back in front of him, arms crossed, chest puffed up like a protective big brother.

"Stay out of this." Justin's heart thumped, and every nerve twitched. Vance had known Zoey for what, two weeks? He didn't have a right to defend her. Not against Justin, who loved her.

"This is my house, so I'm in it." Vance wrapped his hand around Justin's bicep. "You need to get out."

Justin clenched his fist, his muscles tensing under Vance's grip. Then he jerked away.

On the other side of the room, the picture was all wrong. Zoey stood with her back toward him, Bailee's arm around her shoulders. The other band members stared, and judging from their hard eyes, they'd gang up on him if he didn't leave.

Bumping Vance's shoulder, Justin shoved past him and ran up the stairs.

Outside, the sun shone, but the warmth failed to pierce his chill. Had she really broken up with him?

He sped home barely aware of the traffic, the stop signs, the lights. His insides, his life, his everything was twisted up and knotted wrong. This wasn't supposed to happen. He loved Zoey. Why would she do this?

When he arrived home, he went straight into the garage. Music always calmed him and put things in perspective. He picked up his acoustic and ran his hands over the smooth wood. His fingers settled on the strings, ready to play. Nothing came. No melody. No songs. No music at all.

His grip tightened around the fingerboard, the strings biting the pads of his fingers. His other hand hovered, unable to move. He listened for the notes, a beginning chord, something. But all he heard was a pounding, building to a scream inside him. He raised his arm and then swung down slamming the guitar into the ground.

It splintered, like his heart.

He tried to catch his breath. What was he doing?

The guitar lay on the floor, fractured and cracked. A million memories shattered by a single blow.

He tore his gaze away from the fragmented wood. This wasn't right; it wasn't him. Destroying his guitar? How did his life get so messed up so fast?

Across the room, the red and silver drum set mocked him. Sawyer had caused all of this—the breakup with Zoey, the splintered guitar, the pain. So why was Justin taking his anger out on his own instruments?

He crossed the concrete floor to the shining pieces he wasn't supposed to touch.

25

Your Little Suburbia is in Ruins

Leaving his bike on the sidewalk, Sawyer entered the pizzeria.

The girl sipped soda through a straw and watched him.

He still didn't know her name. Why had he offered to hang out with a total stranger? She was just another flirty girl, fascinated by the band thing. She'd probably get the wrong idea, like Felicia and the movies. Except this girl wasn't quite like those others. He might not mind if she read too much into this.

"One more minute," she said as he slid into the chair across from her, "and I'd have my pizza paid for."

"I can pay anyway." The words came too fast, without thought. What had his mom said about paying and dating? This girl would think they were on a date for sure.

She stared at him with those strange orangey-brown eyes. Over the spicy tomato sauce and pepperoni smells, he caught a whiff of her heady orange and syrup scent. "No. I lost, so I'll pay for myself." She grabbed a menu and dropped her gaze.

Sawyer watched her trying to figure her out. One minute, she almost seemed to be flirting, but the next she acted not at all interested.

Plenty of girls flirted with him. Smiles, giggles, touches. He scared them off when they annoyed him usually after five minutes.

This girl had yet to smile, and she didn't act the least bit scared.

The waitress wearing the restaurant's red polo uniform walked up eyeing Sawyer. "You want something to drink?"

"Soda." He specified the soft drink, his gaze still on the girl.

She scribbled on her pad. "Ready to order?"

Sawyer opened his mouth, but the girl spoke first.

"A large pepperoni pizza." She didn't glance at Sawyer for agreement. "And can you split the check for us?"

"Sure, whatever." The waitress tucked the pad into her apron and walked off.

"What if I don't like pepperoni?" He leaned across the table. He didn't like Mom ordering for him and couldn't decide if this was the same thing.

"Sorry." She cocked an eyebrow, not looking the least bit apologetic. "Thought everyone liked pepperoni. But if you want something different, go order it."

He almost did, just to prove a point, but he usually ordered pepperoni pizza anyway. "I'll eat it, I guess."

Her mouth twitched, and she dropped her gaze to her drink. The waitress returned with Sawyer's drink and took off again.

"So, drummer boy." The girl raised her head stirring the straw in her glass. "What do you do around here besides practice with your band?"

The question stabbed his gut. What would he do

now if Justin didn't let him back into the garage? Hang out with this girl whose name he didn't know? "My name's Sawyer. You gotta name?"

"Yeah. Chey."

"Shy? Doesn't seem to describe you."

"It's spelled C, H, E, Y. It's short for Cheyenne. But no one better call me that."

"Oh, yeah? Well, no one touches my drums, Cheyenne." He stretched her name out like two words.

Chey's gaze didn't flicker, but a sharp pain jolted through Sawyer's shin. "Ow!" He rubbed his leg under the table.

"I warned you."

Laughter bubbled up inside him, but he shoved it down. No reason to let her think he found her funny. "Where you from?" he asked.

"Most recently, Portland, Oregon." The diamond stud under her lip wiggled. "But I've moved around a lot. This will be my third high school assuming I don't move again before school starts." She gave a short laugh but didn't sound amused.

"Sounds more exciting than my life. Why'd you move so much? Running from the law?"

"My dad's job. He's an engineer and moves from project to project. Right now he's doing something with the Trans-Alaska pipeline. I don't know what; he doesn't talk to me about that stuff much. Not anymore." She sipped her soda, and when she set it back down, the straw was flat, as if she'd bitten it. "Anyway, you didn't answer my question before. What do you do besides play the drums?"

"Bag groceries."

"At a grocery store?"

"Yeah. And Justin—" He glanced away cringing

inwardly. "He makes me go to all his church youth things."

"Makes you?"

"I usually don't have anything better to do."

The waitress interrupted with their food, and the next few minutes were filled with serving pizza and shaking parmesan over the slices.

"You a senior?" Sawyer asked between bites of tongue-burning cheese and pepperoni.

"I will be." Chey wrapped a string of mozzarella around her finger. "You?"

"Same."

She asked some questions about school, and he tried to answer, but he'd never paid attention to what classes were offered. The guidance counselor told him what he needed in order to graduate, and he didn't find any of the options all that interesting.

One slice of pizza remained on the silver tray. He reached for it.

"What do you think you're doing?" she asked.

"Uh, getting more pizza?"

"You've already eaten your half. That slice is mine."

"Really?" His hand froze in the air, the pizza slice dangling. Was she serious?

"Yes." Her voice didn't even hint at teasing. "I'm paying for half the pizza, so half the pizza is mine."

"What? You want me to pay you for this piece?"

"No." She took the slice from him. "I want to eat it."

"Fine." He clipped the word biting back another laugh. His phone vibrated. He wiped his greasy fingers on his jeans before checking the message. Justin's name showed on the screen. Sawyer's heart dropped to his stomach joining the four slices of pizza.

UR drums, out of my garage, @ transfer site.

He cursed.

"Don't say that." Chey interrupted Sawyer's torrent of thought. "Not around me."

He clenched his jaw and gave Chey a look Mom would ground him for. She couldn't tell him how to act. They'd just met.

She wiped her fingers on a napkin. Then she grabbed the phone from his hand.

"Hey!" Maybe this girl's boldness did annoy him.

"What's a transfer site?" She passed back his phone.

"It's a place with dumpsters where people take their trash."

"And someone took your drums there? Why?" The orange in her eyes flashed, as though offended for him.

He shook his head. He didn't want to get into the whole kissing Zoey thing. Especially not with Chey. The story couldn't be told without him looking bad. He rested his forehead against his palms.

"What are you waiting for?" she asked.

He raised his head.

"Aren't you going to go get them?"

"Yeah. I've gotta go get the car from my mom first." He clamped his lips shut to prevent another swear.

"Or I could help. I have a car."

He stared at her a second judging the sincerity in her eyes. With her, he'd get his drums back faster—before someone stole them. "OK."

She was already dropping a bill onto the table for her half of the pizza. Sawyer added his share and followed her out the door.

"Where's your bike?" She glanced around the parking lot.

"Right there." He pointed at the dull, red ten-speed leaning against a square column with flaking white paint. "I can come back for it later."

"That's your bike?" One corner of her mouth curved up.

"Yeah. So?"

"When you said bike, I thought you meant motorcycle, not bicycle." She said "bicycle" as if it was the funniest thing she'd ever heard and opened the door of a blue car.

"Well, I didn't." Sawyer yanked open the passenger door. The first time she cracked a smile, and it was to make fun of his bike? "Just because I don't have something like this..."

"This isn't what I want to be driving either." Chey backed out of the parking spot.

"You want a motorcycle?" He could totally picture her as a biker chick.

She shrugged. "Wouldn't turn it down. But what I really want is a classic. In Portland, I found a 1972 El Camino." Longing crept into her voice. "It needed a ton of work, but I used to help my dad restore old cars and trucks as a hobby, so I could do it." She stopped at the parking lot exit. "Which way?"

"Left." Sawyer pointed. "So why didn't you get the El Camino?"

"My dad said we moved too much, and a car like that would be unreliable." She sighed. "And he didn't have time to help me."

"He doesn't work on cars anymore?" Sawyer asked and added, "Right at the light."

"Nope. Not since Deanna."

"Deanna?"

"His wife."

Sawyer looked at her trying to read her emotion. She remained focused on the road. Was Deanna an evil stepmother? Or did Chey hate sharing her dad?

Sawyer glanced outside. "The transfer site's right there."

Chey turned down the short drive that opened to a dozen or more green dumpsters lined up in an L-shape.

His drums sat in front of one.

She parked next to them.

Sawyer jumped out and circled the car. Bending over, he examined the neatly stacked drums and the tangled metal stand pieces and swore again.

"What'd I tell you about that mouth, drummer boy?" Chey joined him. "I don't think this is some place you want to be stranded."

He glared at her.

She didn't act bothered by his look. "So what's wrong with them? Something broken? Torn up?"

"No." He crossed his arms. "It's all here, in near-perfect condition, except for the torn drumhead from the other night." He picked up a plastic bag off the top of the stack. "Even all the brackets are together, right here."

"And that bothers you because...?" Chey arched her eyebrow.

"Because they shouldn't be." He didn't deserve the care Justin had taken. "They should be scratched, dented, bent, destroyed. Anything but this."

"Well, we could leave and come back in a couple of hours. Maybe someone will run over them or steal them. Would that make you happy?"

"No."

"I'm having trouble understanding you, drummer boy."

Sawyer ran his fingers around the edges of the snare. She'd understand if he told her why his drums were here. Justin should've beat them up, like he'd tried to beat up Sawyer. That's what Sawyer deserved. But Justin was the good guy. The one who always took the freakin' high road. He felt worse than ever about that kiss.

"As much fun as I'm having hanging out at this dump, or transfer site, or whatever you call it," Chey said, "think we can load these up in my car and take them back to your house?"

"Yeah. Let's go."

"Am I allowed to touch them today?"

"Sure, whatever." He didn't care who touched them. Maybe he should take her suggestion and leave them here.

Without talking, they stacked everything in the car. Then he gave Chey directions to his house.

"What happened to get your drums thrown out?" Chey followed Sawyer into his house carrying the bass drum.

"Nothing." He set the armload of metal stand pieces on his unmade bed and took the drum from Chey.

"Nothing?" she echoed.

"Yep."

"Well, I'm sorry."

"You shouldn't be."

They finished unloading Chey's car, then faced each other in his tiny room.

He'd never cared how clean his room was or wasn't, but with Chey looking around the room noticing the clothes strewn about, the CDs scattered across his desk, the drumsticks on the floor, he had an urge to pick up.

"Impressive poster collection," she said. "And awesome bands."

"Thanks." Posters overlapped on his walls like wallpaper. "You wanna listen to music or something?"

"Your parents home?"

"No. It's just me and my mom, and she's at work."

"Then I should leave." Chey stepped around a pair of shoes and into the hall.

"Oh." He searched for a way to convince her to stay or to come back. "She's off tomorrow, if you wanted to come over and hang out."

"Maybe after church." She paused at the front door. "Can I see your phone?"

"OK." Sawyer handed it to her. "Why?"

"In case I don't show, and you want to know why." She punched a few buttons and passed back the phone. "See ya."

The door clicked shut, and she was gone.

He glanced down at his phone. Chey's name and number were on the screen. What did "maybe" mean? Did she want him to call her if he didn't see her again? Did he want to call her? He spent more time playing music on his phone than using it to talk to people. But he kind of wanted to call her right then.

He walked back to his room and cleaned it in case "maybe" meant "yes." And he needed space to set up his drums.

She stayed on his mind while he shoved the probably clean clothes into his closet and stacked CDs, but when he began assembling the drum stand, he forgot about Chey.

Each bracket he tightened on the stand felt like a screw twisting into his chest. No one could replace Justin or Zoey. And without them, he had no band and no need for his drums.

26

Change in the Making

"I'm sorry." Zoey straightened her shoulders and stepped away from Bailee's arm. "We can finish practice." She'd stood in Bailee's strangely comforting embrace since Justin had left struggling not to fall apart. Hadn't her confession Thursday night broken them up? Now she'd had to relive it. The need to cry burned her throat, but she swallowed against it. Aurora Fire didn't want to see her blubbering over her boyfriend. Her ex-boyfriend.

"Practicing after breaking up with your boyfriend? I don't think so." Bailee tugged Zoey to the couch.

Bailee acting like a friend? Her life really had turned upside down.

Zoey plopped onto a cushion, and Cherie settled on her other side.

"Excuse me?" Vance's eyebrows practically leaped off his forehead. "Who put you in charge?"

"Seriously, Vance? Look at her."

Zoey ducked her head. She'd prefer no one looked. Twisting her necklace around and around, she fought the rise of tears. Aurora Fire had enough problems with her; she couldn't lose it over a guy. The burn rose to her nose and her eyes, and she wrapped her fist around the necklace. She couldn't hold it together either.

"Get her something to drink." Bailee commanded the room. She slid her arm back around Zoey's shoulders. "So what happened? Why'd you break up?"

She pulled her feet onto the couch, resting her chin on her knees. Bailee and Vance already didn't like Justin. Maybe she could tell them the truth. Holding it in because everyone would side with Justin was about to kill her.

"Did he cheat on you?" Cherie asked.

She sniffled, but her nose was stuffy. "No, I—"

"Good." Vance's voice was hard—too hard. "But I wouldn't be surprised, since he has a family history of cheating."

Zoey clamped her mouth shut. Didn't Vance have a family history of that too?

"I hate cheaters." Vance glared at Cherie.

"Got it." Cherie spoke with the exasperated tone of having said the same thing too many times.

Goody. No telling them the truth.

Myles pressed a cold, open can into Zoey's hand.

"Thanks." She raised it and took a sip. Liquid the flavor of cat pee filled her mouth. She gagged spraying Myles.

"Hey." He jumped back.

"Problem?" Vance sounded like he was laughing at her, but he didn't smile.

She shook her head swiping her mouth with the back of one hand and raising the can with the other. Beer? She probably shouldn't be surprised.

"Don't tell me you've never had a beer before," Bailee said.

"I just didn't expect it." What was one more lie?

"What did you expect? Soda?" Bailee didn't say,

poor, pathetic little girl, but Zoey heard those words anyway. "How would that make you feel better?"

How would beer? But she held back the retort. For once, Bailee wasn't throwing out insults.

"So, if he didn't cheat on you, why'd you break up with him? Is there another guy?" Cherie's eyes sparkled, and her girlfriend-confidant tone begged for gossip.

Unfortunately, Zoey didn't have any gossip that wouldn't kill this E-string-thin thread of belonging. She sipped the beer. No gagging.

"Her break up is just as boring as her boyfriend." Shaking her head, Bailee shifted away. "It was probably something junior high, like he's always making gross noises."

"Justin Conrad? Not likely." Vance sat on the arm of the couch, and Cherie wrapped her arms around his waist. "He was always polite, even in junior high."

"Exactly!" Zoey took another sip. Really, it didn't taste so bad once she got used to it. "He's always polite."

"How's that a problem?" Bailee cocked her head to one side, her expression wavering between interested and yawning.

"He's always good. It's boring." Another sour sip slid down her throat. "He rarely gets upset with me over anything. Even when I told him I was singing with you guys for the summer. I could tell it bothered him, but he just smiled and said it was God's plan for me." Oops. She hadn't meant to share that much.

"God's plan?" Disgust dripped on Vance's words. "Sounds like him. You'd think he'd have grown up by now."

"Yeah." A strange combination of heaviness and

tingles snaked from her shoulders to her hands. Here she was betraying Justin and her faith in one little conversation. She took another drink. Throw in underage drinking, and today would go down as an epic fail. She needed something to redeem.

"He was a good boyfriend. Always nice to me." A lame compliment. Way to go.

"Nice?" Bailee's silver hoops jumped over her eyes. "Like you said, bor-ing. Where's the passion in 'nice'? What kind of sex do you have with a guy like that?"

Zoey gulped down more of the putrid beer so she couldn't answer, because she had no idea what the sex was like. But given the blah kissing, Bailee might be right. She shuddered. There was a thought she never expected.

"Now you can find someone interesting. Want me to fix you up?"

Bailee setting her up on a date? Only if Zoey wanted her life to go from horrible to...was there anything worse than right now? Her foggy head couldn't spit out an answer. She squeezed her eyes shut and opened them wide trying to wake up. This sluggish feeling reminded her of that day in her sophomore year after she'd stayed up all night texting with Justin. Come to think of it, he hadn't been so boring that night as he broke his parents' rules to make her laugh on the third anniversary of her mom's death. She'd forgotten about that until just now. Justin really was a great boyfriend, and she'd totally sucked as a girlfriend.

"If we're not practicing, I'm going home." She pushed off the couch ignoring the sleepiness in her limbs, and thrust the can at Bailee. "Don't think I can sing today, anyway."

The burn rose in her throat and nose again. She needed to be home before collapsing into tears. "I'll be here tomorrow."

"Next practice isn't until Monday. But you better be here." Vance's attitude about the missed practice reminded her so much of Sawyer that Zoey practically ran up the stairs. She didn't want to think about Sawyer, or Justin, or her ripping heart.

The nasty, cat-pee taste of the beer coated her mouth. Good thing she'd walked today, even if her trip home would take ten times as long. She dragged her heavy feet along the ground. Why had she kissed Sawyer? Why had she confessed to Justin? Why couldn't she answer those questions?

The walk worked out some of the weariness, and worrying about how she'd avoid Livvy or her dad finished waking her up. She drained her water bottle to dilute the scent of beer on her breath, but since it did little to erase the taste, she doubted it helped.

Rounding the corner onto her street, the sight of an empty driveway flooded her with relief. No one would ask her about practice or why she was crying again. She wiped the tears from her cheeks and hurried into the house. No one was around to find out what she did—about the betrayal, the breakup, the beer. The truth would stay cramped up inside.

If only there was someone she could talk to, someone who wouldn't hate her for breaking the heart of the best boyfriend in the world by kissing his best friend.

But there was nobody.

27

I So Hate Consequences

Justin looked around the garage. The drums—and Sawyer—were out of his life. Why didn't he feel better? The space where Sawyer's drums had been sat vacant like a black hole sucking away all the happiness. Justin shoved the couch into the corner and rearranged the rest of the furniture and the amps filling up the emptiness. It didn't work.

The splintered guitar was packed in its case, now a coffin. He'd learned all the chords on that guitar, most of them with Vance's help. Through months—years—of awkward noises, cumbersome chord changes, clunky strumming, that guitar had stuck by him until his playing turned smooth becoming an extension of himself. He'd carried the guitar into the house, to church camp, to Zoey's.

Justin sank onto the ottoman, staring at the closed casket. His heart felt ready for burial too. All that he loved, destroyed in a single day. If he hadn't gone to see Zoey, would things have turned out differently? Going to Aurora Fire practice had been like rushing through a song to the guitar solo, only to ruin the music.

The sound of voices drifted in from outside. His family walked up the driveway, Tristan sucking on a honey straw and Savannah drinking fresh lemonade.

"Feeling better?" Mom shifted bulging bags overflowing with leafy vegetables.

Would he ever? He forced a smile. "I guess."

"Good to hear."

"We got popcorn for tonight." Savannah raised a long, skinny bag stuffed with sugar corn.

"Yum." He attempted excitement, but his voice sounded dead.

Savannah's smile vanished.

He had more important things to worry about than his little sister's feelings. "Dad, I need to talk to you."

"OK." Dad stretched out the syllables, the unspoken "what's this about?" falling in between. "Let me put these bags in the kitchen first."

Everyone went inside, and the garage grew quiet again. Justin rubbed the back of his neck. Dad had to give him money for a new guitar. Justin baby-sat and helped Mom around the house without receiving an allowance because his parents said they'd give him money when he needed it. This definitely qualified as a need.

"What's up?" Dad stepped back into the garage.

"I need a new guitar."

"What happened to yours?" Dad glanced at the rack where the shiny blue and white electric stood alone.

"It's in there." He pointed at the case peeking from behind the chair. "It...broke."

"It did?" Dad frowned. "How?"

"It just did." He swallowed. How did he explain that he'd busted it? "It was getting old."

"Let's see." The lines in Dad's forehead deepened.

He wasn't buying it.

"It can't be fixed." Justin stalled. The sight of the splintered guitar would be as good as a guilty confession.

"Fine. I want to see it." Dad remained calm and unyielding.

Shoulders sagging, Justin slid the case into the open and unfastened the latches. Slowly, he raised the lid, revealing the jagged edges of wood, the loose strings, the snapped fingerboard.

"What happened?"

"Like I said, it just broke." Justin licked dry lips.

"I don't think so." Dad turned stern. "It looks run over by a car."

"I'd never do that."

"It didn't just break."

Justin glanced away. He should've blamed Tristan. Dad might've believed that. Too late now.

"I don't know why you destroyed your guitar, but you'll have to replace it yourself."

"Myself?" Heat boiled in his chest. Justin clenched and unclenched his fists. "How am I supposed to do that?"

Dad stared at the pieces of wood and released a long, sad sigh. "I guess you'll have to get a job."

"A job?" The pressure inside exploded. "I'm supposed to get a job now?"

"Justin, I'm not going to give you the money to replace an expensive piece of equipment that someone—you—clearly destroyed."

He hadn't meant to destroy it. It'd been an accident, a mistake. He almost laughed. Mistakes were ruining his life.

"What happened?" Dad studied his face. "And I

don't mean with the guitar. What happened with you? Did you have a fight with Zoey? Sawyer?"

"My guitar broke, and I need to replace it." Justin locked his jaw and ducked his head. His life wasn't available for discussion.

Dad was quiet a moment and when he spoke, he sounded tired. "I'm sorry, but you'll have to earn the money."

Staring at the ground, Justin let out one of Sawyer's words.

"What did you say?"

"Nothing." All his strength drained out of him leaving behind an aching emptiness. Nothing he did or said eased the pain.

"I don't know what's going on with you." Dad clamped a hand on his shoulder. "But if you're not careful, you'll end up grounded, unable to look for a job, and with no money to buy a new guitar."

He lifted his head. The sympathy flooding Dad's eyes only fueled the torment. He jerked away. "Whatever. It doesn't matter."

He slammed the guitar case shut with his foot and went into the house.

His relationship with Zoey, over.

His favorite guitar, destroyed.

His income, cut off.

What else was there to lose?

28

Losing The Lifeboat

"I don't feel so good." Zoey stood by the dining table and rubbed her head making her sleep-rumpled hair messier to emphasize her excuse to Livvy and Dad. Which wasn't really a lie. She felt terrible, even if it was guilt-terrible and not sick-terrible. "I probably shouldn't go to church today."

"You don't look so good either." Dad accepted Zoey's words at face value. And did nothing to help her feel better. "You haven't felt good for a few days, have you?"

"Nope." Another mostly truth. Zoey sniffed like she had a runny nose, but all the crying of the past few days had dried up everything, including the congestion, and left behind an aching head.

Livvy sat at the table and picked apart a muffin watching Zoey but not contributing.

"You should go back to bed." Dad slid a bookmark into the book he'd been reading. The cover was a dirty blue with scroll-y gold writing Zoey couldn't read, but probably gave some boring history title. "Want me to fix you a cup of tea or something?"

"No." Her stomach turned at the suggestion of anything, food or drink. She should be happy Dad was buying her excuse and not probing, but his sympathy only made her feel worse. She didn't deserve niceness. She deserved the misery reigning inside her head. "Thanks."

Zoey padded down the hall to her bedroom. Before she could push the door shut, Livvy was pushing the door open. Zoey tumbled onto the bed without making eye contact and hid under the sheets. *Go away. Just go away.*

"I know you're not sick." Livvy tugged the sheets off Zoey's face. "I know you don't feel good, but you're not sick."

Zoey rolled away, groaning and hoping Livvy took the sound as proof she *was* sick and not for what it really meant—annoyance.

"You don't want to see Justin, right?" The mattress sagged as Livvy sat. "I totally get that. Believe me, I get it."

With Livvy's dating history, yeah, she probably did. But losers breaking up with Livvy wasn't the same as what happened between Justin and Zoey. *Zoey* was the loser.

More groans. She buried her face in the pillow.

"But Zo, don't avoid God too." Livvy massaged Zoey's shoulder. Another show of sympathy she didn't deserve. "Trust me, He's the only one who will help you get through this."

No, He wouldn't. God knew what Zoey had done. If God was taking sides, He'd take Justin's. Justin was the good guy.

"If you want, you can come to the college class with me instead of the youth group. That way, you won't have to sit through an entire hour in the same room as Justin."

Couldn't Livvy just accept Zoey's sick excuse?

Apparently not. "The first time you see him will be hard—whether that's today, or next month, or next year. So you might as well get it over with so you can move on."

Why wouldn't *Livvy* move on? And why did she have to make so much sense?

"Fine." Zoey kicked the sheets to the end of the bed and sat up. "I'll go."

"Good." Livvy hugged her. "I promise, it'll start getting easier from here."

Zoey didn't deserve "easier" either.

~*~

Wrong, wrong, wrong. Justin sitting on a separate couch was wrong. Zoey being in the same room as him was wrong. Zoey being at church, in the presence of God, was wrong.

She tucked her feet up onto the couch. And Livvy was wrong. Nothing felt easier. Everything felt harder. Especially the pain, the guilt clawing at her chest, begging for release. But who could Zoey tell? Justin had been her best friend. She had other friends—girls at school, people she worked with at the ice cream shack—but they weren't confess-and-cry-on-the-shoulder friends. They were sit-together-at-the-movies friends or like-the-online-post friends. Sure, they'd listen to her confess the drama of the breakup, but for the entertainment.

Everyone knew her as Justin's girlfriend. That's who she'd been practically since she'd moved here in eighth grade. Everyone knew Justin too, and he was the good guy. The hurt boyfriend. Ex-boyfriend. She couldn't spin the story to make herself look good. She was the villain. Zoey didn't notice Chey until the girl sat next to her.

"Hey."

Zoey didn't respond to Chey's greeting.

"You OK?"

Zoey looked at Chey. The need to tell someone expanded inside her chest and pushed into her throat and out her mouth. "I broke up with Justin."

"I'm sorry." Chey glanced around the room sounding neutral rather than sympathetic. "How long were you together?"

"Three-and-a-half years."

"That's not a break up; it's a divorce." Chey's cheeks turned pink as soon as the words entered the air.

But Zoey felt a ghost of a smile tug her lips. Chey was a girl who wouldn't offer false sympathy to get the details. Weirdly comforting. "I guess you're kind of right."

"What happened?"

"I told him about Sawyer and me kissing."

Chey turned pale under her makeup, her black-lined eyes widening. "You and Sawyer kissed?"

Zoey nodded. Chey looked more shocked than Zoey expected. Chey barely knew Zoey, and she didn't know Sawyer at all, did she?

But the pain in Zoey's chest eased a little. Talking *did* help.

Zoey opened her mouth, ready to spill all the details and drama, whether Chey wanted to hear or not. But Brandon began to speak, so she closed her mouth. After class she'd confess everything. Maybe then the ache would ease even more. And she *could* talk to Chey because she was new and didn't have prejudices about Zoey or Justin.

Zoey rehearsed the conversation in her mind while Brandon spoke, and as soon as the dismissal bell rang and she and Chey walked out of the youth room, Zoey picked up the conversation as if class had never interrupted. "He said it was a mistake."

"Who did?" Chey gave Zoey a blank look, like their earlier conversation had been forgotten.

"Sawyer. After we kissed, he went home, and then he texted me and asked me to forget it had ever happened." Zoey kept her voice flat, like the words had no meaning, like she could fool herself into not hurting. "I should've listened."

"When was that?" Chey sounded breathless, almost scared. Which made no sense. Probably Zoey's imagination.

"A week ago. The night before my first concert with Aurora Fire."

"Oh."

"I told Justin because I felt so guilty. I thought I might feel better if I wasn't keeping secrets." Zoey's voice shook. So much for the words having no meaning. But these words meant everything. This part she needed to tell someone, but someone who didn't know Justin's perfection and wouldn't judge Zoey's stupidity. "Then I realized I'm not sure I love Justin anymore."

"Do you like Sawyer?"

"I don't know." Zoey stopped in the hall outside the almost empty foyer. Singing drifted from the sanctuary. "I'd never kissed any other guy before Justin." And she wasn't sure she regretted the kiss. The timing, yes. But the kiss? "Sorry to unload on you like that, but thanks for listening." Zoey glanced into the sanctuary. She didn't deserve to walk in there with all the holy people. Maybe she should go hide in the bathroom until the service ended.

Zoey looked back at Chey, trying to interpret the look on her face. Not quite sympathy. Definitely not judgment. More like she understood. And Zoey really needed someone who understood. "Want to come over to my house after church? I promise not to whine about breaking up with Justin all afternoon. But if you're busy, that's OK."

Chey snorted. "I'm not busy anymore."

"But you were?"

"Ironically, I was going over to Sawyer's. But that's not happening now."

"Wait." Zoey grabbed Chey's arm. Had Zoey just unloaded her cheating heart on Sawyer's new friend? So much for making Chey *her* new friend. "Sawyer invited you over?"

Chey nodded.

"How do you even know each other?"

"We met at that devo Thursday night, and yesterday we ran into each other at the music store downtown, and then we got pizza."

Was Chey telling the truth? Who had invited who? Sawyer didn't have any friends besides Justin. Not even like-the-online-post friends. And forget about a girlfriend. Of course, if Sawyer was into Chey, then he wasn't into Zoey.

Which in a weird way might un-complicate things. Or at least make it clear how Sawyer felt about the kiss. Zoey couldn't deny that the kiss was good. Really good. But she wasn't so sure about a relationship with Sawyer.

"You should go," Zoey blurted out before she

started second-guessing and decided to keep Sawyer to herself until she figured out her own feelings.

Chey returned Zoey's crazy stare. "You're kidding, right?"

"No. Sawyer doesn't like girls."

Chey frowned.

"That came out wrong. I mean, Sawyer scares girls off. He's never had a girlfriend. I think he only put up with me because of band practice. If he got pizza with you and invited you over...well, you have to go."

"I don't think so." Disgust hung heavily on Chey's tone.

"You have to." If Zoey's confession ruined whatever Sawyer wanted with Chey...Zoey couldn't handle more guilt.

"Two minutes ago you said you might like him. I don't want to get involved in that."

"But he doesn't like me." As Zoey spoke the words, she realized the truth. Sawyer could've talked to Zoey or invited her to hang out after the kiss. But he hadn't. "If I'd known you liked him—"

"I don't know the guy well enough to like him."

Zoey cocked her head and narrowed her eyes, not sure she believed Chey. "If I knew you two were hanging out, I wouldn't have said that. Seriously, Chey, promise me you'll go."

"I'm not interested in hanging out with some guy who doesn't know what—or who—he wants." The diamond stud under Chey's lip wiggled.

"Trust me, if he's asking you to hang out, he wants you. He's never invited me over or anywhere else." A new ache formed in Zoey's chest, but this one felt less like pain or guilt and more like regret.

Chey took a deep breath, and for a second, Zoey

was certain Chey would say no. "OK, I'll go."

"Good." Zoey forced excitement into her voice, but without much effort. If Sawyer had found a girl he wanted to hang out with, then Zoey wouldn't be tempted to jump from Justin to Sawyer. She could figure out what *she* really wanted. Or who.

Did she regret breaking up with Justin? Kissing Sawyer? Or did she regret what feelings she didn't have for either of them?

29

Caution, Dangerous Curves Ahead

Sawyer stepped out of the bathroom, his tee clinging to his still-damp skin.

"You got big plans today or something?" Mom asked. She sat cross-legged on the couch, scooping yogurt into her mouth.

"No." He headed into the kitchen to nuke a frozen breakfast burrito in the microwave.

"This is the second week in a row you've slept in on a Sunday." She raised her voice over the hum of the microwave. "And last week you cleaned the house, today you cleaned yourself. What happened to my son?"

"You make it sound like I never clean."

"Because you don't."

"But I do shower." The microwave beeped. He juggled the hot burrito onto a plate and carried it into the living room.

"Rarely before eating." She scraped the spoon along the sides of the plastic yogurt container.

"So? I wasn't hungry."

"Right." She nodded, a knowing pucker between her brows. "Something's up."

He bit into the burrito burning his tongue so he didn't have to answer. If he told her about Chey, then

Chey didn't show, Mom would tease him. Not that he cared, but he didn't want to spend the day listening to her.

"So what are your plans today?"

He shrugged and chewed. At least his drums were in his room. Playing would fill up his afternoon if Chey didn't show.

A knock interrupted his thoughts.

"Ah-ha! You do have plans." She poked him with her spoon. "Where are you going?"

"Nowhere." He gulped down the last of his breakfast, and leaving the plate on the kitchen counter, he opened the door.

"Hey." He held back a smile, a wise decision judging by the look on Chey's face.

"Hi." Her mouth formed a tight line, and flames flashed in her orange-brown eyes.

OK, he was good at annoying people, but how could she be angry with him before she even stepped into his house?

He moved aside, and Chey entered.

Mom twisted around on the couch. A slow grin spread across her face. "Hi, I'm Sawyer's mom, Lexi."

"This is Chey," he muttered.

Mom's smile stretched wide. Any moment she'd say something embarrassing probably on purpose.

"We're going to hang out in my room," he said.

"You invited a girl over." The wonder in Mom's voice lit a fire in his cheeks. "It's about time."

Sawyer hooked his head toward the hall. "C'mon."

"Nice to meet you, Chey."

"Yeah, you too." Chey's voice sounded clipped, and her smile was more of a twitch like she was being polite while anger seethed under the surface. He didn't get it. Why would she show up if she was ticked off with him? But he led her away from Mom.

Inside his room, they stood awkwardly. With his drums crowded between the desk and chest, there wasn't much floor space left. But at least it was clean today, though a jeans leg and shirt sleeve poked out under his closet door. The drumsticks were all together—how had he collected so many?—lined up on his desk next to the laptop Mom had bought him two Christmases ago.

He flipped up the edge of his blanket on his made-up bed and pulled out some shoeboxes. "We can listen to music, if you want."

"Wow, that's a lot of music." Chey's eyes turned as round as CDs as he set more boxes on the bed. "Do you buy everything on CD?"

"No. I've got more on my computer."

She removed the lid of one box and scanned the plastic cases. "You belong to those mail-order clubs? 'Cause they must love you."

"Yeah, but I only buy when the albums are like a penny each."

"My dad and I used to listen to this all the time." She held up a case featuring a horned skull. The angry look faded, replaced by sadness. "It was our road trip music."

"You don't listen to it anymore?"

She shook her head and dropped the CD into the box. "Deanna doesn't like that kind of music."

Ouch. A couple of guys Mom had dated brought with them their opinions on music, TV, food. He hated when Mom changed her interests for those men. "How long have they been married? Your dad and Deanna."

"Three years."

"What happened to your mom?" He didn't know why he was asking such personal questions. Maybe because he recognized the ache in her eyes whenever she talked about her dad and Deanna. He'd felt the same way.

"She ran off when I was two. I don't know where she is now."

"My dad disappeared when I was born." The words slipped out of his mouth. He'd never talked about his dad with anyone.

"Stinks, doesn't it?" Chey lifted her head and stared into his eyes. "They say it had nothing to do with you, but you always wonder if that's really true."

"Yeah." No one had ever admitted that before. Justin and Zoey definitely didn't get it. Justin's parents had stuck together even after his mom cheated, and Zoey's mom had died. They had no idea what it meant to be left behind by choice.

"OK, you've got every kind of music here, but this one really surprises me." Chey raised a CD and her eyebrow. "Country?"

"I went through a phase a few years ago."

"A few years ago?" Chey pulled out another case. "This album came out this year."

"But she's hot."

Chey's eyebrow went higher, and a smile tugged the corner of her mouth.

"I don't mean her, I meant her music."

Chey looked at him barely concealing laughter.

"Her music's hot," he finished lamely and swore under his breath.

The humor vanished from Chey's face, and she turned away from him. "The rule about your language still stands, drummer boy."

He scowled, ready to launch a defensive about his right to say whatever he wanted in his own house.

"Sawyer?" Mom called.

Relieved, he escaped his bedroom, but in the living room, his heart froze.

Mom held the door open for Felicia.

Good thing Chey couldn't hear what he muttered next.

Felicia grinned as if she'd won a grand prize, and Mom looked more amused than confused about his visitors.

He dragged his feet across the room.

"Hi." Felicia's brightness dimmed. "You said I could come over today, remember?"

"I did?" Why would he have done that?

"Yeah, on Thursday? After the devo?" She bit her lip.

Thursday? All he remembered about Thursday was the look in Justin's eyes when he confronted Sawyer. And Chey touching his drums.

"I asked you about your CDs?"

Oh, right. She'd said something about coming over to check out his CD collection. This couldn't be good. Was it too late to shove her out the door and pretend like no one was home? He glanced at Mom for help. But she only smiled and leaned against the door.

Didn't look as if he had any options.

"My room's down the hall, on the right." He pointed.

Felicia lit up again. "OK." She headed that direction.

Sawyer didn't move.

"You've become awfully popular." Mom pushed

the door shut. It clicked like the lock on a torture chamber.

"This isn't funny." He frowned.

"Oh, yes it is."

He raked his fingers through his hair. What was he supposed to do now? Join both girls in his room? They'd never agree on music. Felicia probably liked country. And she'd fill the air with her annoying giggles. He preferred the teasing gleam in Chey's eyes. Maybe he should escape, let the girls fight over the CDs alone.

Before he came anywhere close to a real solution, Chey stalked through the living room. The spark in her eye was far from teasing.

"I better go." Her nostrils flared.

He blocked her exit. "Don't."

"Why should I stay?" She crossed her arms and tapped a black-shoed foot radiating more heat than a wood-burning stove.

"Because I want you to?"

The air warmed a few more degrees.

"Look, I forgot about Felicia. And, anyway, she invited herself over. I agreed because her music knowledge is pathetic. She needs serious help."

"Excuse me?" Felicia stepped from the hall. "I'm pathetic?"

Things were getting worse. How was that even possible? "Well, yeah."

Felicia's jaw dropped, her face turned red.

Mom and Chey stared at him shaking their heads as if he was the pathetic one. They were probably right.

"You're a total jerk, Sawyer." Felicia shoved past him, yanked the door open, and slammed it shut rattling the windows.

"I agree." Chey's voice was low and hard. "Who do you think you are anyway?"

"What's that supposed to mean?"

"You're going after every girl who speaks to you."

"What do you know? You've known me, like, two days."

"I know why your band broke up." She lifted her chin. "It's because you kissed Zoey, isn't it?"

He heard Mom's sharp intake of breath behind him. His chest tightened, and his heart ached as the knife he'd stabbed himself with drove deeper. "Who told you about that?"

"Zoey."

Was she going around confessing to everybody? "That girl needs to keep her mouth shut."

"You're blaming her? Seriously?" Chey shook her head. "I don't know why I even came."

"Why did you?"

The diamond stud wiggled. "I guess I'm a slow learner." She reached around him, opened the front door, and marched down the steps.

Typical fail. Why'd he think he could keep a girl interested?

"That went well," Mom said.

"Why didn't you make some popcorn while you watched the show?"

"Hey." She lifted her hands in surrender. "Don't get mad at me."

He slumped against the door wishing he could disappear into it. The only person he was mad at was himself.

"Was that true, about you and Zoey?" she asked.

Actually, he was angry with Zoey too. "Yeah, so?"

"You kissed Zoey? Justin's girlfriend, Zoey?"

"Yes."

"How could you do that?"

"It was a mistake." He shoved away from the door. He needed to get behind his drums before he exploded.

"A mistake?" She grabbed his arm and forced him to face her. "You don't make mistakes that involve kissing, Sawyer."

"It didn't mean anything. It was an accident."

"No! You don't accidentally kiss someone."

"Mom, it was just a kiss." What was her problem?

"What if it had turned into something more?"

"More? We were behind the ice cream shack. What 'more' could happen?"

"A lot."

He stared at her, trying to follow her warped logic. "This isn't about me kissing Zoey, is it? It's about you." He yanked out of her grasp. "Don't worry, Mom, I'm not stupid enough to make a mistake that will leave me stuck with a kid."

His words hit their mark and hurt flickered across her face. He ignored the knife twisting in his heart and walked away.

~*~

Sawyer banged the drums in endless rhythms beating away the events of the day without success. So what if Chey knew about the kiss? He didn't care if she hated him. He hadn't done anything wrong. He and Chey weren't dating; he had every right to invite Felicia over too. And the kiss happened before he met Chey.

Movement in the doorway caught his eye, and he glanced up to see Mom. She shoved aside the shoeboxes still on his bed and sat.

He stopped playing.

"I'm sorry." Her eyes were red as if she'd been crying.

Was that his fault too?

"I don't want you to think I regret you," she continued. "Because I don't."

Sure she didn't. He lightly drummed his sticks against a tom. If it wasn't for him, maybe his dad would've stuck around. And even if his dad left anyway, she could've found someone else if she hadn't had a kid.

"I want you to know that the hard part was never what I had to give up when I became a mom." She raised her voice over his quiet rhythm. "It was knowing I was responsible for another human being. Someone I had to raise without messing up when my own life seemed to be a mess."

"You think I'm messed up?"

"I hope not."

He stilled his sticks. "If I am, it's not your fault."

"Are you sure? As far as I know, you've never had a girlfriend, but today you invite two girls over, and I find out you kissed another one. No offense, but that sounds a little messed up."

"Thanks."

"Sorry. Just trying to understand what's going on inside your head."

He was trying to do the same. "I don't know what happened with Zoey. She was crying, I was trying to make her feel better, and it just happened. I wish it hadn't." He'd do anything, promise anything, sell anything to take back that kiss. "And Felicia just won't leave me alone."

"She the movie girl from last week?"

"Yeah."

"But Chey's the one you really like?"

He shrugged. What was the point of admitting it? He'd never see Chey again.

"She is. You cleaned your room, showered, and practically begged her not to leave."

His face grew hot. "So?"

"So call her up and apologize."

"For what?" he demanded. "I didn't do anything."

She frowned that want-to-try-the-truth mom-frown.

"I didn't do anything on purpose."

"Whether you meant to or not, you hurt her. So apologize."

"Maybe I don't like her." He jutted out his chin sounding and acting like a ten-year-old. Why did he care if Mom knew he liked Chey? But he did care.

"If you want me to believe I haven't failed you, be a man who apologizes when he hurts a woman's feelings, got it?"

"Fine." He picked up his sticks again.

"Thank you." She started to leave but turned around at the door with that sad smile. "Guess I know now why your drums are in your room. I'm sorry."

And then he was alone.

He drummed. Apologize? He'd have to play all night to find that kind of courage.

But maybe Chey was worth an apology. Or a million apologies.

30

Welcome to Your Life

Justin walked into the kitchen Monday morning. A new week hadn't provided a fresh start or a new outlook. His guitar was still broken. His relationship with Zoey was still broken. His life was still broken. "I'm going to Rhythm and Notes to price guitars," he said.

Mom glanced up from the dishwasher, eyebrows raised in Mom-speak meaning, did you forget who you were talking to?

"If that's OK." Justin added the words of an obedient son and pulled a box of cereal from the cabinet.

"That's fine." Dirty dishes clinked into place on the top rack. "You should see if they're hiring. A music store would be a perfect place for you to work."

Justin scowled at the flakes and nut clusters cascading into his bowl. He'd hoped she'd forgotten about the job thing. "If I get a job, I won't be available to babysit whenever you want."

"I know, and I'll miss the free labor." Mom's voice was light teasing.

But Justin's insides felt heavy, weighed down by all these changes. No Zoey. No band. No guitar.

"You're seventeen. It's time you had a job."

"Fine." He shoved a spoon into the cereal splashing milk onto his hand. Now a job and no life.

"Speaking of babysitting, can you be home by three to watch Savannah and Tristan? I'm meeting someone for coffee."

Coffee? His heart seized, stopped for a beat, two beats, and then it raced. Coffee had been her excuse all those years ago, when that "someone" had been Vance's dad. Maybe he wouldn't make it home so she couldn't sneak off.

"I don't know."

"I'd really appreciate it." She rinsed a bowl in the sink and stuck it in the dishwasher. "But call me if you can't, and I'll ask Carrie next door if they can play at her house instead."

He hovered on the brink of confronting her, but she was still Mom. He couldn't accuse her of cheating on Dad without more proof than a random coffee date.

He carried his breakfast into the next room. Regardless of who she was meeting and why, she'd be sorry when he started working. Between a job and band practice...

He sank onto a dining table chair. No band, so no band practice. Just him, alone. Maybe he shouldn't even waste money replacing the acoustic.

"Justin!" Tristan burst into the dining room and scrambled into a chair. "What are you doing?"

Justin pulled his thoughts from the band. "Carving an elephant."

"No, you're not," Tristan giggled.

"I'm not?" Justin faked surprise. "What am I doing then?"

"You're eating, si-we."

"Oh, you're right." Justin grinned and took a bite.

His little brother had a way of cheering him up. Tristan was a reminder that his parents still loved each other, even after his mom cheated.

"Pway a game with me."

"Can't, buddy. I've gotta go find a job."

"Me too. I go with you."

"Sorry, you've gotta stay here."

"Pwease?"

"You can't."

"But I want to." Tristan's lower lip jutted out.

"I know. But you can't." Justin ruffled his little brother's hair. "I promise we'll play a game when I get home, OK?"

"O-tay." Tristan slid off his chair and ran out of the room. "Bye."

Justin finished eating and put his dishes in the dishwasher.

Now to find a job.

~*~

Justin parked in the empty gravel lot next to Rhythm and Notes and headed into the converted house. As he always did, he stopped inside the door to scan the flyers and business cards on a bulletin board.

Band looking for bassist.

Keyboard for sale.

Piano lessons.

Lessons? Why hadn't he thought of that? He'd taught guitar lessons before, but he hadn't charged much. If he raised his rates...

He did some quick math in his head. Might take a while to earn enough money, but guitar lessons beat flipping burgers.

He pushed open the second door, the strum of a guitar announcing his entrance. He passed the sheet music and lesson book section, the drumhead and drumstick replacements, and entered the room filled with guitars. Acoustics, electrics, and basses hung in parallel rows on the walls. Better than an amusement park.

"Hey, Justin." Zach, a tall, skinny guy with dirty blond dreadlocks, rounded the corner. "You here for new strings?"

"Uh, no. I'm looking at guitars."

"We still have that electric you've been eyeing." Zach gestured with his thumb.

"Actually, I need a new acoustic." *Don't ask why.* He didn't want to confess he'd smashed it like an immature rockstar. He lacked the rockstar fans and budget.

"You're probably as familiar with them as I am. Got a price range?"

"Anything for twenty bucks?"

"No." Zach laughed. "I don't think you're wanting cheap."

"Not really." He fingered the smooth edge of a guitar close to him. His heart twisted. Why had he been so stupid to destroy his? "I'll have to get a job before I can afford one. Can you help me with that too?"

"You know, I might be able to."

"Really?" He hadn't wanted to admit Mom's idea was a good one, but if he had to work, he'd rather work here, surrounded by instruments, music, and people who understood it all.

"Yeah. It'll only be part time—fifteen to twenty hours a week—but if you're interested, I'll get you an application."

"Great." Finally, something good. He followed Zach to the counter. "I was thinking I'd stick an advertisement up for guitar lessons on the board out there."

"I can help you with that too." Zach handed him the job application form. "Brian, who's been teaching here, has to scale back his load."

"Sweet. But all I have is an electric right now."

"We could probably work something out. A layaway deal where you could use the guitar here while paying it off."

Justin grinned and picked up a pen to fill out the form. Earlier, he never would've believed he'd feel excited about applying for a job.

"And I don't think you'll have any trouble getting hired," Zach said. "It's my decision."

Justin couldn't fill in the blanks fast enough.

After he'd provided the information and returned the application to Zach, Justin checked out the guitars again. He touched the dark and light woods, and music thrummed deep inside him.

"If you like one, go ahead and try it out," Zach said from across the room.

Justin lifted an acoustic-electric off the upper rack. He curled his hand around the neck and held his hand above the strings. Two days ago, he couldn't hear any music, much less play. What about now?

"Whatcha waiting for?" Zach walked over and stood in front of him.

Justin lightly strummed a chord, and then another, not playing anything in particular. But he kept going, until the chords combined into his unfinished song. "Zoey's Song." His chest ached at the notes, and the pain spread down his arms into his hands. Then it eased, as though flooding through his fingers and out the strings. Hurt and hope blending in harmony.

"That was good." Admiration shone in Zach's voice. "Really good."

"Thanks." He replaced the guitar gripping the neck a few seconds too long.

"About the job, can you start Thursday?"

"Sure."

The guitar-slash-doorbell strummed.

"Keep looking." Zach waved his hand and walked off.

But Justin didn't have to keep looking. He'd already chosen.

Inside, the hurt remained, raw like his fingers had been when first learning to play. But the alternating numbness and raging heat were gone, replaced by music.

Verse 2:

What can heal this ache
How much can I take
I'm losing her
But not refusing her
Please bring her back to me
I need her can't You see

31

Swimming Towards Propellers

Sawyer lay on his bed and stared at his phone. Chey's number glowed on the screen. Call. Apologize.

He raised a finger to the "call" button, then dropped his hand back to the quilt. Not so easy. What if she wasn't interested in listening? And why should she be?

But Mom had played the man card. And the single-mom card. Sawyer had ruined things with Justin and Zoey. They'd finally given up on him. But Mom told him how to redeem himself, at least in her eyes. And that started with apologizing to Chey.

He would. For Mom.

He stabbed the screen and listened to the rings.

"Hello?"

Her voice sent a jolt of heat through his stomach. He took a deep breath. "Hi."

Silence.

Sawyer opened and shut his mouth, his tongue too twisted to form words.

"Who is this?" she finally asked.

"Sawyer."

"Sawyer?" The shock in her voice proved she wasn't interested in listening.

But he was talking to her now. "About

yesterday..."

The apology wouldn't form. Saying "sorry" was harder than Sawyer imagined. *One word. Just say it!*

But he couldn't. He scrambled for a different excuse for calling, "Do you wanna go check out keyboards with me?"

"Why would I do that?" Her snappy attitude heated him, but didn't burn.

"Thought you might take my advice. Play the keyboard instead of a guitar."

"Yeah...I don't think so."

Silence. But she hadn't hung up. She still listened. Should he try again? Attempt that apology while he still had a chance?

Assuming he'd ever had a chance. "You don't want to because of yesterday?"

"Ding, ding, ding. Drummer boy wins."

"Look." His voice developed an edge. Enough with the jokes. Didn't she get that this was the hardest thing he'd ever done? The only thing harder would be apologizing to Justin. But he couldn't imagine ever telling Justin he was sorry. Even if he was sorrier about kissing Zoey than he'd been about anything else in his life. "That was a mistake."

"Another mistake? You make an awful lot of those, don't you?"

What did he say to that?

"Well, guess what?" Chey didn't wait him out this time. "I don't want to be one of your mistakes, got it?"

"Fine. Whatever." If she didn't want to listen, he wouldn't talk. He jabbed the "end" button.

His pulse thumped in his ears. She probably had a point. He'd probably mess things up with Chey too, if he could convince her to give him a chance to do something. But why should she? He couldn't carry on a conversation without sounding hostile. Justin and Zoey were the only people who had willingly put up with Sawyer's spikes—and he didn't mean the ones in his hair. Felicia had tried, for some unknown, insane reason. But he'd eventually stabbed her to death. And he was doing the same to Chey. Why did he want Chey to give him a chance?

Because she stabbed him back. She didn't put up with him like Justin and Zoey and even Mom. Chey didn't ignore his jabs like Felicia. Chey gave it right back. He needed someone willing to beat him with the same sticks he used on everyone else.

He hit the call button again.

"What?" She didn't bother with a greeting this time.

"I'm sorry." The words came quick, slurred into one.

Silence.

Sawyer checked the screen. Call still connected. A good sign. "So you wanna go look at keyboards now?"

"OK."

Her quick response caught him off guard. "Uh...can you pick me up? My mom's got the car."

"Is that why you really called me?" The sharpness returned to her voice, and he smiled to himself. "You just need a ride?"

"No." He repaid sharpness with sharpness. "I can walk and get the car."

Hesitation.

She was going to turn him down, and he had no clue how to talk her into agreeing. If she needed nice, he was in big trouble. He couldn't do nice.

"I have to ask my stepmom first." Chey's answer

brought a wave of relief. "If she's OK with it, I'll be there in about twenty minutes. If I don't show, she said no."

"OK."

Chey hung up on him this time, and he grinned. Yep, she was beating him with the same sticks.

Good thing black-and-blue were his favorite colors.

~*~

"Play something." Sawyer stood close to Chey peering over her shoulder. Her hands hovered over the keyboard. She'd touched every keyboard in Rhythm and Notes but hadn't played a single note.

Being surrounded by instruments without anyone playing left Sawyer twitchy. The keyboards were meant to be played. So were the drum kits in the basement, but they had big signs on them saying, "Do not play." Sawyer had been kicked out at least twice for ignoring those signs, and if Chey didn't start playing soon, he'd be getting kicked out again.

The name of the store was Rhythm and Notes. Music was supposed to happen.

"Play what?" She hesitated.

"Anything." He shrugged and shifted his weight from one foot to the other, his fingers tapping against his legs. "I don't play piano."

The muscles in Chey's neck stood out, tense and tight. Her shoulders remained rigid. She needed to play, that was obvious.

And she did. She started with what Sawyer recognized as scales, then she shifted into music vaguely familiar, blending songs Sawyer couldn't name. Her neck and shoulders relaxed. This was what made Chey different from Felicia and the other band groupie girls. She could play, and she needed to play.

"What was that?" Sawyer asked when she stopped.

She studied him for a second, but he didn't know what she was looking for. Judgment? Criticism? She wouldn't see any of those.

"A bunch of different things," she finally answered.

"Like you made it up?"

She shook her head. "I just mixed up different songs."

"Make something up."

"What?" She stared at him as if he'd suggested she stuff the keyboard under her black-and-white t-shirt and walk out of the store.

"Do your own thing. I want to know how the music sounds in your head."

"The music in my head?"

"Yeah."

If she needed to play, he knew she heard music in her head just like he heard rhythm and beats. And if she seriously wanted to play in a band as she'd claimed the last time they were here together, then she'd have to be brave enough to get that music out of her head and into people's ears.

Chey stared at the keyboard, and Sawyer watched Chey. Not her hands, but her face. She swallowed and then tightened her jaw. Fear. Insecurity. He could feel and practically smell those emotions pouring off her. Only one cure.

"Play." He spoke in a whisper, his breath fluttering her short blonde-and-red strands.

Her cheeks pinked, but her hands started moving, pressing keys, making music. Simple at first, then more complicated. Raw, but real.

Sawyer drummed his fingers against his legs hearing how he'd accompany her. If only this store would honor the "rhythm" part of their name and let him play along.

"Gold star," he said when the music stopped. "I'd play in a band with you."

"Too bad you don't have one right now."

Her comment felt like a stab with a broken drumstick. A splintered and jagged end. If he hadn't destroyed his band, could he have invited Chey to join?

Too late. He'd have to build a new band. "If you had a keyboard, we'd almost have a band."

"We would?" The eagerness in her tone matched that of the wannabes, but Sawyer didn't find Chey annoying. "Just a drummer and a keyboardist?"

"You gotta start somewhere."

Chey looked back at the keyboard, her fingers stroking the white keys. Was she considering his suggestion? Because he meant it. Completely.

He needed a band, and so did she. "What do you think?"

"Maybe." She glanced up, a practiced carelessness in the jut of her chin but a longing in her eyes that Sawyer recognized. He knew that need. That hunger.

Her "maybe" would turn into a "yes."

32

Casualties

Zoey washed the ice cream and waffle cone smell from her hair, and then she walked to band practice. The sun warmed her damp, messy ponytail. She couldn't get yesterday's conversation at church out of her mind. What had happened when Chey went over to Sawyer's? If Sawyer was into Chey, then did their kiss mean nothing to him? Because that made things easier. She'd know exactly where she stood and could move on. After all, she didn't like Sawyer. Not really.

She pulled her necklace out from under her shirt twisting it with an intensity that matched the wrenching of her heart. She'd felt something when they kissed. Even now, her toes curled against the soles of her shoes. Hadn't Sawyer felt the same thing? Maybe he didn't care.

Climbing the steps of Vance's house, she shoved those thoughts from her mind. Time to concentrate on her singing, her future. Maybe by the end of the summer, Aurora Fire would want to keep her as their vocalist, even after Halleigh came back. If not...

She'd be on her own, and she'd never wanted to go solo.

She entered the basement. Everyone was in their usual spots. Cherie and Bailee sat on the couch; Vance and Devin tuned their instruments; Myles and Travis talked and laughed in the back corner. Zoey moved to her spot among the speakers and amps squaring her shoulders. She'd nail practice today.

She placed her sheets in order and mouthed some of the lyrics waiting for the guys to be ready. Since she'd altered them, the words flowed more easily. She just had to focus.

"Let's start." Vance silenced the room for a second, and then he played the opening measure.

The hammered notes blended with the lyrics, the twisted pain of cheating and betrayal piercing Zoey's heart. This hurt and hate belonged to Justin, and it was all her fault. No, she couldn't think about that and sing. She had to concentrate on the beat, the notes, the intonation, not the emotions. But as she sang the next song and the next, the agony threaded through her chest mixing with her regret and confusion.

"One-second, you destroyed me, everything shredded, everything dead, one-second."

Maybe those words applied more to Justin, but she felt it too. Her life flipped upside-down and inside-out with that kiss. If it had never happened, nothing would've changed, and she, Justin, and Sawyer would be better off.

The final chord of the last song thrust her from her heartache and back into the basement.

"You did good today." Vance nudged her arm and slipped his guitar off.

"Thanks." The compliment failed to lift her mood. Maybe she sang well because she understood the lyrics too deeply.

"I gotta get to work." Myles crossed to the couch and kissed Bailee. "Later."

"Me too." Vance pulled Cherie to her feet and wrapped her in a slobbery kiss.

Zoey picked up her empty water bottle and papers ignoring all the coupling.

"You wanna stay and hang out?" Bailee spoke behind her.

Zoey moved toward the stairs.

"Hey! I'm talking to you."

Zoey spun around. Bailee wanted to hang out with her?

"You stayin' or not?" The demand rushed out of Bailee, and she crossed her arms looking at Zoey as though she'd better hurry up and answer.

"Yeah, sure." Zoey stuttered over the words. She had nothing else to do. And having Bailee on her side at the end of the summer might help her chances of staying with Aurora Fire.

"You too." Bailee linked arms with Cherie and led the way upstairs.

Zoey hadn't spent any time on the main level beyond walking from the front door to the basement stairs. Her nose twitched at the weird combination of over-microwaved Chinese food and stale pizza. The dim lighting cast shadows across the dirty-dish clutter on the kitchen counter and the overflowing garbage.

Bailee opened the fridge and passed out beers.

Goody, another can of cat pee. Her stomach churned, but before she could turn it down, Bailee slammed shut the fridge door and continued into the messy living room.

Bailee and Cherie plopped down on the tan couch.

Zoey perched on the edge of a matching chair. If she got too comfortable, she might discover more hidden grossness. The fluorescent lights muted the stains on the furniture and worn carpet. Video games and controls lay strewn across the floor surrounded by piles of clothes and trash. Good thing Alaska didn't breed cockroaches.

"You sounded awesome today." Cherie popped the tab on her beer. "Like at the concert."

"Yeah. Yesterday's practice was good too." Bailee tossed a dark T-shirt on the floor and pulled her feet onto the couch. Obviously, she was comfortable with the mess. "Maybe breaking up with your boyfriend is working."

"What d'you mean?" Zoey's throat went dry, and she opened the can in her hand.

"I think his lack of passion killed yours too. Now your singing shows more life."

Zoey raised the can to her mouth. Beer still tasted disgusting, like liquid punishment. Justin had always given her courage—and passion—when on stage. She downed almost half the can in one gulp.

"But speaking of you and boyfriends, I know a couple of single guys." Bailee almost sang the words. "Interested?"

Not if they were like Myles or Vance. She shrugged a shoulder. "I don't know. Maybe."

"You can meet them at Friday's concert."

"What about Travis and Devin?" Cherie kicked aside a stack of video games and propped her feet on the coffee table. "They don't have girlfriends, do they?"

Bailee shook her head. "But the guys have this stupid rule about no dating within the band. Which only applies to you." She tilted her beer can at Zoey. "At least, until Halleigh comes back. Then you'd be able to date them. You like Travis or Devin?"

She preferred drinking beer to dating either of

them. But maybe Halleigh wouldn't come back, and Zoey would stay in the band. She took another swig, only to discover the can was empty. How had that happened?

"I'll fix you up with someone." Bailee's confident offer hit like a threat rather than a help.

Zoey'd stay single.

"Throw that junk on the floor." Bailee waved at the shoes and clothes sharing Zoey's chair.

Zoey yawned. Her arms and legs felt heavy, and she cared less about the grossness. She cleared the chair, and then she relaxed and closed her eyes. Bailee and Cherie's conversation about some skanky girl they knew faded into the background.

~*~

A vibrating against her hip jolted Zoey awake. Where was she? Her muscles ached from being cramped. She stretched and her foggy vision took in an unfamiliar room.

"Hey, watch it!"

Blinking, she trained her gaze at the people sitting on a couch. Travis and Devin held video game controls and stared at the TV.

Now she remembered. Bailee invited her to stay after practice. Had she fallen asleep? Bailee and Cherie were gone, and she was alone with Travis and Devin.

Her phone vibrated again, and she pulled it out of her pocket. Four missed calls and eleven texts, all from Livvy. She squinted at the display. Two a.m.?

Her feet hit the floor. She was in so much trouble. She grabbed her lyrics and water bottle and hurried out the front door.

The sun had sunk below the horizon leaving a dusky hue to the world. Zoey practically ran down the sidewalk. She didn't have a curfew, but she always told Livvy or Dad where she was going and when she'd be home. Tonight she was only four hours late.

She scaled the porch steps and burst into the house pausing on the landing to catch her breath.

"Where have you been?" Livvy stared up from the lower level, hands on her hips, a frown between worried eyes.

"Sorry. I fell asleep." After drinking a beer. She watched her sister through the wooden railing. She'd better keep her distance.

"I was about to call Justin to see if he knew where you were."

"You didn't, did you?" The words burst out in a high pitched squeak. Her pulse beat at her temples. That would make things a whole lot worse.

"No. I figured since you broke up, he wouldn't know." Livvy started up the stairs. "But, Zo, I was really worried. Don't you dare do that again."

Zoey backed away. If her breath smelled as bad as it tasted, she didn't want Livvy too close. "What'd Dad say?"

"He went to bed, so I didn't tell him. Yet." The warning faded from her voice, replaced by suspicion. "You just fell asleep?"

"Yeah, that's all. I swear." Grabbing the handrail, Zoey stepped backwards up the stairs. "Bailee asked me to hang out after practice. We were talking, and I guess I fell asleep, until one of your texts woke me." Her stomach twisted into knots, but she was telling the truth. Most of the truth. OK, some of the truth. "I'm so sorry, Liv. I won't let that happen again."

"You better not. 'Cause, next time, I'll have to tell Dad." Livvy didn't say that like a warning. More like a regret.

"It won't. Thanks." Zoey pivoted on the next-to-the-top step and ran to her room. No matter what, she'd keep that promise. She wouldn't break Livvy's and Dad's hearts too.

33

Terra Firma

Sawyer had finally done something smart. Maybe the first smart thing he'd done ever. He'd apologized—to Chey. And after hanging out two days in a row, she still wanted him around.

Chey parked in front of Sawyer's house. "Your mom's home, right?"

"Yeah. There's her car." Sawyer pointed to the dirty white compact car. "What's the deal with wanting my mom here? You afraid of what I might do?" He almost laughed. He snapped *at* people. He'd walk away before he actually snapped.

She glanced at him. "I'm not worried about anything you might do."

"Really?" His heart pounded in his stomach. Or maybe he felt the pulsing bass of the radio. Chey had a sweet stereo system. "So you're worried about what you might do? Like what?"

Chey's cheeks turned as dark as the cinnamon-red hair at the back of her neck. She switched off the car and climbed out.

So she didn't want to answer. The pulsing in his stomach picked up tempo. Whatever she might do to him if they were alone couldn't be all bad.

Inside his house, they loaded their arms with bags

of chips, cookies, and sodas, and carried them to his room.

"What d'you wanna listen to?" Sawyer dropped the food on his bed.

"I don't know." Chey scanned the posters on the wall and pointed. "Them."

Their two albums were on his mp3 player, so he didn't have to dig through a dozen shoeboxes for the album. He hit play and connected it to the speakers.

Chey plopped on his bed and ripped the cookie package open.

"Hi, Chey." Mom walked into Sawyer's room resting her chin on a pile of laundry. She met Sawyer's gaze with a look half-apologetic, half-it's-your-own-fault. "You left clothes in the dryer."

Was she trying to embarrass him by dumping an armload of his underwear in front of Chey?

"Sorry." Mom didn't sound sorry. "I gotta do my laundry too."

Chey smirked and bit into a cookie.

"Thanks, Mom." Sawyer shoved the clothing off the foot of his bed and sat on the laundry-free space.

Mom left them alone.

"About my hypothetical keyboard." Chey popped open a can of cola. "If I played with you here, where would it go?"

"There." Sawyer waved his hand at the empty space in front of his closet. Shoes spilled out the cracked door. As long as he kept the door closed—both the closet door and the bedroom door—the keyboard would fit.

"Wouldn't it be a little crowded?"

"Yeah. So?" He crunched on a sour-cream-and-onion chip. Probably a bad food choice around Chey after their earlier conversation. His pulse sped up thinking about what she might do if they were completely alone. "It'd be a good crowded."

She stared at the space as if imagining how a keyboard would look.

"You really should get the keyboard. You're really good."

"You think so?" Her voice turned shy, and she ducked her head.

"Yeah." He meant it one-hundred-percent. No matter how much Chey excited him, he'd never lie about music.

"I'll think about it." He thought he caught a glimpse of smile, but when she looked up, it was gone. "How long have you been playing the drums?"

"I've had 'em about a year and a half. Freshman year I played in the school band."

"You were only in band for a year?"

"Yeah. Too many people, and I didn't like the band director."

"Didn't like him because he wasn't a nice guy? Or didn't like him because he told you what and how to play?" One corner of her mouth inched up.

"The second reason."

"That's what I thought." She gave him one of her rare half-smiles. "So how did it work in your band? Who decided what you played?"

"We all did. Justin—" He swallowed against the twisting in his chest. "Justin usually wrote the melody. Then he and Zoey worked out the lyrics, and she'd come up with the bass part. I did drums. Sometimes I'd play something, and Justin would add in the guitar. It just depended on the song."

Chey stared at him with those strange, orangey-brown eyes, as if she was trying to read his thoughts. No, his soul. "Do you miss it?"

"Miss what? Playing?" He glanced over at the red and silver drum set. "I've got 'em here and can play all the time now."

"But what about creating songs with Justin and Zoey? Do you miss that?"

"No." He avoided her gaze. This he was lying about. He missed playing with Justin and Zoey more than he'd ever missed anything including his dad.

"Liar."

Enough about his band or ex-band. He stood and grabbed a pair of sticks off the desk.

"You gonna play for me, drummer boy?"

"You want to play?" He twirled the sticks through his fingers.

Chey's brows sprang upward. "Me?"

"Yeah." He held out the sticks. What was he doing? No one played his drums except him. But his hands seemed possessed.

She scooted off the bed and tried to take them from his hands, but he tightened his grip.

"You've got to promise you'll play exactly what I tell you," he said.

"OK." She tugged on the drumsticks.

"Promise. You won't just hit them; you'll play only what I say."

"I promise." She gave another tug and laughed. "You want me to swear it in blood?"

"That's not a bad idea."

Chey yanked the sticks out of his hands. "You need to relax a little. I won't break them or anything. Girl Scout promise."

"Like I believe you were ever a Girl Scout."

"There's a lot you don't know about me, drummer boy."

Would he learn everything about her or chase her away?

Chey slid onto a chair from Sawyer's dining room table. The stool was probably still in Justin's garage. "OK, what do I play?"

He stared at the drum set. He was on the wrong side, and everything was backward. He switched off the music so he could concentrate. Then he slowly pointed to the different drums, and Chey followed his directions.

"Was that a song?" she asked.

"Not really."

"Do I get to play some more? Or have I had my five-seconds-for-life with your drums?" She sat behind them as if she belonged. Her eyes sparkled with a challenge daring him to let her play again, as though she knew that was hard for him. And if it were anybody else, he never would've handed over his sticks.

"You can play the same thing again. Remember how it went?"

"No." She stated that fact without a silly giggle or an attempt that was all wrong sticking to her promise.

He pointed her through the beats again and then faster, until the simple rhythm sounded interesting, and Chey got tangled up.

"Sorry." She winced. "It's not easy, is it?"

"No." He couldn't help smiling at her remark. How many times had he heard the phrase "How hard can it be?" about the drums? He'd thought it himself before learning how complicated finding a rhythm could be.

"Hey." Mom rapped on the doorframe behind him. She had changed into black slacks and a white shirt. Her waitressing uniform. "I'm leaving. Working until close."

"Bye," he told her.

"I should go too." Chey stood and handed him the sticks.

"Do you have to go home?" Suddenly an evening alone, banging his drums, didn't sound fun. "'Cause we could go somewhere else."

She shrugged. "Why not? It's better than going home."

They carried the food from his room to the kitchen counter and walked out to Chey's car.

"So what d'you wanna do?" she asked.

"I don't know." He drummed his fingers on the arm rest. "Not much to do around here."

"Isn't there an ice cream place a couple of blocks that way?" Chey jerked her thumb over her shoulder.

"Yeah." But Zoey worked there. "You still hungry? There's another ice cream place on the other side of town."

"I've seen it. And eaten at a million of those. I want to go some place that belongs only in Fairbanks. And it's close."

Sawyer drummed his fingers faster. Maybe Zoey wouldn't be working. Maybe the ice cream shack would be busy. Maybe he'd be lucky.

The universe owed him some luck.

A few minutes later, Chey parked and they climbed out of the car. Sawyer scanned the tiny parking lot for Zoey's car. He didn't see it, but that didn't mean anything. He walked up to the salmon-colored building as if it were a house of horrors, not a stand of sweets.

"Alaska cranberry. Deadhorse blueberry." Chey read some of the flavors off the chalkboard. "Spiced grapenut? Does that have anything to do with the cereal?"

"I don't think so." He glanced inside.

Zoey was scooping ice cream in the back laughing with another girl.

He shifted out of her view. The overly sweet scent of waffle cones turned his stomach. Zoey always smelled like waffle cones.

The universe was determined to crush him.

"Vanilla Shower in a sugar cone," Chey ordered. She squinted and looked over the cashier's shoulder. "Is that Zoey?"

"Yeah." The cashier glanced back. "Hey, Zoey!"

Sawyer flattened himself against the wall, next to the window, clamping his mouth shut. He still wasn't sure how serious to take Chey's threat about his cursing.

Chey waved.

"Chey!" Zoey's voice drifted through the open window.

Sawyer pressed against the building, out of Zoey's sight. Sweat rolled down his temples and plastered his shirt to his skin. The edges of the siding dug into his arms, his back, his shoulder blades.

"What are you doing here?" Zoey asked Chey.

"Getting ice cream."

"Right." Zoey laughed.

"I didn't know you worked here."

"All the time, seems like. I'm either here or at band practice. But in a few minutes, I'll have a couple of hours free all for me."

"Want to hang out with us?" Chey glanced at Sawyer, cocked her head, studied him.

His heart felt like a ball of fire lodged in his throat. He wanted to hang out with Chey, not Zoey. He didn't know how to hang out with Zoey anymore.

Chey narrowed her eyes, but not like she was angry. More like she was trying to figure him out.

Did Chey want to hang out with him or with Zoey? After last Sunday, Chey should've figured out he failed at hanging out with two girls. He failed at hanging out with people.

Chey looked back inside the building.

"Us?" Zoey asked.

"Sawyer and me."

"Oh." Was that hesitance in Zoey's voice? Maybe she didn't want to hang out with him either. But then she added, "Sure."

Chey received her change and faced him. "You don't want Zoey around?"

"No."

"Why?" Chey lifted her chin, her gaze unwavering. "Because you kissed her?"

Why else? "No, because the band broke up."

"The band broke up because you kissed her." Chey spun on her heels, walked over to a red metal bench, and plopped down.

He swore under his breath and marched after her. "You don't know that."

"So that's not why the band broke up?"

He slammed onto the opposite end of the bench.

"That's what I thought," she said.

"Why does it matter to you?"

"It doesn't." She shrugged a shoulder and watched the order pick-up window.

Sure it didn't. "Then why'd you ask?"

"I wanted to know if you'd be honest."

Fail. Weird since he usually had no trouble being honest. But he didn't want to be honest with Chey. Not when honesty made him look so bad. For Chey, he wanted to look good. Or better, to actually be good. He wanted the impossible.

Zoey called Chey's number from the window. Then her gaze locked on Sawyer.

He looked away feeling nauseous.

Chey stood at the counter for a few seconds, both girls glanced at Sawyer. Probably talking about him. He should leave.

Chey returned licking around her ice cream. "Zoey's meeting us at the park." She headed for the opening in the short picket fence. "Coming?"

She still wanted to hang out with him? He hurried to catch up.

"Living close to a playground must've been fun when you were a kid," Chey said between licks.

"Yeah, my mom used to bring me here. I fell off that slide probably a dozen times. Had to get stitches once."

"Really?"

"That's how I got this scar on my chin." He pointed to the dimpled scar on his jaw.

"Did you fall on your head every time? Because that would explain a lot."

"Ha-ha. Funny."

"I wasn't trying to be funny."

Sawyer glanced sideways at her. She did look serious. But that kind of comment was always a joke, right? "Are you this mean to everyone, or am I special?"

Chey ran her tongue around the edge of her ice cream cone. Clockwise. Counterclockwise.

Sawyer watched her pink tongue flicking in and out.

"The last guy I dated was using me to make his girlfriend jealous." Chey spoke to her ice cream cone, not looking at Sawyer.

"Huh?" Sawyer snapped out of his Chey's-tongue trance. "I'm not...I don't like Zoey."

"You go around kissing girls you don't like?"

"No, I..." He put his hands on his head, gripped the stiff, gelled spikes. If Chey couldn't see past the kiss, if she couldn't believe he wasn't interested in Zoey, if she couldn't like him, then... "Forget it." He started to walk away.

"Sawyer...I..." Chey touched him, her fingers icy against his arm.

But jolts of heat shot through him.

"Hey." Zoey walked up behind Chey carrying a red shaved ice, her lips already stained dark. "What are you guys doing?"

Chey held Sawyer's gaze a second longer, a warm glow in her eyes.

The warmth traveled straight to his stomach.

Why did Zoey have to show up now? Why did Zoey always show up at the wrong time?

34

Bury Your Heart

Zoey interrupted something between Sawyer and Chey. Awkward silence followed her greeting, and Sawyer glared. Not his usual grumpy glare. This was a why-did-you-show-up-now glare.

Of course, Sawyer may not have wanted Zoey to show up at all. Which was why she had. When Chey asked if Zoey wanted to hang out with them, Zoey saw the chance to figure out what was going on between Sawyer and Chey. And between Zoey and Sawyer. And between Zoey and Chey. Could Zoey and Chey be friends? Especially if Chey and Sawyer had a thing?

Chey set the pace, walking across the grass, and cracked through the awkwardness. "Sawyer was telling me how many times he fell off the slide as a kid and landed on his head."

"As a kid? He fell off several times last summer." Zoey stuck a spoonful of flavored ice into her mouth, relaxing into the conversation. Even though they'd just met talking to Chey felt like talking to an old friend.

Like talking to Justin. Zoey wouldn't think about him. Not today.

"Is he clumsy?" Chey asked pulling Zoey off the achy Justin path.

"Hey!" Sawyer waved his hands in front of their

faces. "I'm right here."

"Not clumsy," Zoey answered as if he hadn't spoken. They walked over to a picnic table. Zoey stepped onto the bench and sat on the tabletop. "He seemed to think he could walk on the poles surrounding the platforms. He couldn't."

"Does he do stuff like that often?" Chey sat next to her.

"He jumped off his roof last summer too."

"Really?" Chey looked up at him. "You got a death wish?"

"No." He crossed his arms, and the glare he gave now was probably meant to be threatening, but Zoey only wanted to laugh. "I'm going home."

"Bye." Chey sounded indifferent. His glare didn't seem to bother her either. But was that the tone of a girl who liked a guy?

"Bye." Sawyer marched off toward the chain-link fence.

"He was in a hurry to leave." Chey's tone was light, as if she didn't care Sawyer had left. Maybe she didn't. Maybe Chey was hanging out with Sawyer because she didn't know anyone else.

"Yeah." Zoey sipped her melting shaved ice. How could she find out what—if anything—was happening between Sawyer and Chey? And why did she care? Because she couldn't get the kiss out of her head. Because if Sawyer had a thing for Chey, he didn't like Zoey. Because if Chey had a thing for Sawyer, Zoey would have to choose between friendship with Chey or finding out if the kiss meant anything to Sawyer.

Zoey needed a friend more than a boyfriend. "You two been hanging out a lot?"

"Not really." Chey shrugged and licked ice cream

off the edges of her cone. "He asked me to look at keyboards with him."

"Keyboards?" Zoey scrunched up her face. If Sawyer initiated a date, figured it would take place in a music store. "Why?"

"He thinks I should get one and play with him."

"Are you going to?"

"I don't know. Maybe." Chey's indifference sounded faked, as if she was fighting not to feel something. "He was teaching me to play his drums today."

Zoey coughed, splattering her hand with pink spit. She grabbed a napkin. "He did what?"

"Taught me some beats on his drums."

"Taught, as in let you hold his sticks and hit his drums?" Zoey's heart thrummed. Sawyer didn't just have a thing for Chey. He was making a commitment. Shopping for a ring. Buying a tux—or at least one of those tuxedo-printed T-shirts. Did Chey have any idea how serious Sawyer was?

"Uh, yeah. How else would he teach me?"

"I don't know. It's just that Sawyer doesn't let anyone touch his drums—not me, not Justin, not anyone." Zoey swirled the straw in her raspberry slush. Sawyer had absolutely no interest in her whatsoever. That kiss really *had* meant nothing. To him. "Wow. He's really into you. Do you like him?"

"I don't know."

"Why not?"

"I don't know if I trust him." She looked Zoey right in the eye.

Zoey gulped, nearly choking again. Confessing to Chey had been a mistake. But Chey knew about the kiss now, so no point in hiding. "Because of what happened between us?"

"That, and Sunday, he'd invited over another girl too. Felicia?"

"Felicia? Oh, right." Sawyer, who never seemed interested in any girl, had Felicia chasing him, had kissed Zoey, and was teaching Chey to play his drums. That guy had suddenly become all kinds of girl drama. Zoey would've laughed if she didn't feel so confused.

"What do you know about Felicia?"

"She's had a thing for him since the end of the school year, and I think they went to the movies once. But that was before he met you."

"Yeah, well, apparently Sawyer did a lot of things with other girls in the week or so before we met."

Heat rushed to Zoey's face. She probably matched her red slush.

"I'm OK with being friends." Chey sounded sincere, despite all the other clues she'd given about being into Sawyer. "Like I told you, I don't want to get involved with a guy who doesn't know what he wants."

"I think it's just really bad timing. Sawyer's never shown interest in a girl before."

"But I arrive when he develops an interest in every girl?" Chey arched an eyebrow. "No, thank you."

"He's not interested in me." Zoey's voice was firm but thick, the heaviness pressing against her lungs a surprise.

"I don't want to get hurt again." Chey's stud jiggled. "The last guy I dated—the only guy I've dated—just wanted to make his ex-girlfriend jealous. I really thought he liked me and I...anyway, we dated about a month, and his plan worked. His ex-girlfriend broke up with the guy she was dating, and they got back together."

"I'm sorry." Zoey stared at her for a long moment. What was Chey's story? Was she good enough for Sawyer? Silly question. Sawyer wasn't some good guy who deserved the best girl. He wasn't Justin. But Zoey felt protective of him anyway. Sawyer might act as bitter as a stalk of rhubarb, but even rhubarb was good in the right recipe. "But you know, I don't think Sawyer's that...smart or manipulative. Maybe you take it slow, but don't write him off altogether."

"I haven't yet."

"You gonna get that keyboard?"

Chey ducked her head. "If my dad says yes."

35

Internal Illumination

Sawyer munched on his toaster-cooked breakfast in the kitchen staring at the front door. The washer rumbled behind him with a load of his clothes. Chey had texted earlier about wanting to bring over her new keyboard, so he'd cleaned his room. Again. At this rate, Mom would start raising her expectations.

"It's so cute how you keep trying to impress that girl." Mom carried a crumb-covered plate to the dishwasher.

"I'm not trying to impress anyone."

"Uh-huh." Her eyebrows danced.

"I'm not." He just didn't know Chey well enough to let it all hang out—like his dirty underwear.

Someone knocked on the door. He shoved the last chunk of strawberry-frosted, toaster pastry into his mouth, dusted the crumbs from his hands, and hurried to answer.

"Hi." He held the door open for Chey, who tilted a long, rectangular case through the doorway.

"Hey." She followed him to his room, set the keyboard on his wrinkled-but-passing-for-made bed, and unzipped the nylon case.

Sawyer moved to help.

"Hold on, drummer boy." Chey angled herself to

block the keyboard. "I didn't say you could touch it."

"What?" He backed up.

"This is my instrument. Don't touch."

"Are you serious?"

"You bet." The corner of her mouth twitched slightly, as if she was teasing him. "Keep your hands off."

"Fine. I'll watch." He sat on the chair behind his drums.

Chey assembled the stand pieces and set the long, gray keyboard on top.

"Gold star." Sawyer clapped. "Now, do you plan to take it home with you, since I can't touch it?"

"I don't know." She sat on the edge of his bed. "If I leave it here, can I trust you?"

"Probably not."

"Then I guess I'll have to take it with me." She ran a hand over the side of the keyboard, pride crossing her face. "You coming to the youth devo tonight?"

"Uh, no." Was it Thursday? All the days ran together in the summer.

"Why not?" She tilted her head staring at him in that intense way she had, as if she was trying to see all his secrets.

He wanted desperately to hide every single one.

"Because Justin isn't making you?" she asked.

"No." He leaned back in the chair and rocked the front legs off the floor crossing his arms. "No one makes me do anything."

"Really?" She stretched out the word. "You told me that the only reason you went was because Justin made you."

He had said that. The chair legs thudded against the ground. "I'm working tonight."

"If you weren't, would you go?"

"Are you going to start making me?"

"No."

"Then why are you asking?"

"Because I'm trying to understand you." She glanced around the room, the stud under her lip wiggling. "A lot of the bands on your wall put a strong faith message in their music, but you don't seem to care about having one in your life."

"And that matters to you?" He could probably trade shifts tonight.

"Yeah, I guess it does." She flicked the zipper on the canvas case. "But I'm not going to make you."

"Then it must not matter that much."

"You've got to want to go. Making you...wouldn't change anything."

"What do you want to change? Me?" He pounded out the last word. Everybody seemed to want him to change, but why should he?

"No, not exactly. You're a pretty good guy."

"Yeah, you don't know me very well." Sawyer pretended to laugh. He was anything but the good guy. Had Chey forgotten?

"Maybe you don't know yourself."

This was too intense. Sawyer grabbed a pair of sticks from his desk. "I thought you came over to play."

"Can I ask one more question?"

"About my religion?"

"No."

Her wiggling diamond stud reflected a ray of sunlight, distracting him. "OK."

"Do you like Zoey?"

The question punched him in the gut. "Why?

What do you care?"

"Because I thought the last guy I dated was a good guy too. And he went to church with me." She dropped her gaze to the keyboard case pulling the zipper a few inches shut and then open. Shut. Open. Shut. "Didn't change him. Didn't stop him from using me. Didn't keep me from making mistakes."

Sawyer's hands tightened around the drumsticks. He wanted to smash that jerk's face in.

"I don't want to end up there again." She lifted her head looking him square in the eye. "And I don't have time to waste guessing at the truth."

"What are you accusing me of?"

Chey shrugged holding her gaze steady.

His heart slammed against his ribs. He had no clue what to say. Did she think he was like her ex-boyfriend, just using her? He clenched his jaw. "Did you come over to grill me or to play?"

"I don't have a chair."

"You'll have to get one from the table." He tapped a beat on the drums. He should probably offer to get the chair for her, but he didn't care. She shouldn't go around accusing people of stuff. He didn't want to make Zoey jealous; he wanted nothing to do with Zoey. He'd never liked her...had he?

He banged the drums in rhythm with his pounding heart. Faster and faster. Zoey might've been Justin's girlfriend, but she was the only girl Sawyer hadn't hated hanging out with. Until Chey.

Chey returned with a chair, and he slowed to a quiet beat on one drumhead.

"Maybe I did like her." His lungs constricted with the confession. "She's the only girl who's ever held an intelligent conversation about music with me. And she's talented. But Justin loves her, and I'm still ticked off with her for confessing. What happened between us was a stupid mistake. Definitely not worth breaking up the band over."

Chey stared. Did she believe him? He held his breath waiting for her response. Now that he'd said it, he realized every word was true. Even the part about liking her. But he didn't want Chey believing he still had a thing for Zoey.

"OK." Chey spoke quietly, a gentleness in her voice that Sawyer hadn't heard before. "So what are we going to play?"

That was it? He'd better get with it. "Play that song you made up at Rhythm and Notes the other day."

"If I can remember." She leaned over the keyboard running her fingers over the keys before she started playing.

Sawyer joined in, the heady rush of creating music allowing him to breathe again. This wasn't like playing with Justin and Zoey, but in some ways it was better. In this moment, he understood that extra chemistry Justin and Zoey had, beyond what the three of them had shared as a band. The chemistry he'd destroyed.

His high crashed.

No girl was worth breaking up a band.

Across the room, Chey lifted her head. Her face reflected the same rush he felt at hearing the blend of instruments becoming music. He wanted to play with her forever—whether the music sounded good or not.

Maybe he was wrong. Some things might be worth giving up for a girl. Not just any girl. But definitely the right girl.

36

My Own Enemy

Justin wanted to be somewhere else.

He stepped out of his car and onto the Newmans' front lawn. They were hosting this week's youth devo. He glanced at the cars spilling from the driveway and along the curb. Zoey's car wasn't there. She probably had band practice. His heart clenched. What hurt more—knowing she was playing somewhere else or being in the same room with her?

A car he didn't recognize parked behind his, and Chey climbed out.

"That was nice of you." She raised her voice so it carried through the sun and mosquito-filled air.

"Huh?" He slapped a blood-sucker and looked around trying to figure out what he'd done.

"You waited for me." Chey walked to his side.

"No, I didn't."

"I wasn't serious."

"Oh." His voice fell flat. He really wasn't in a joking mood.

"Zoey and Sawyer aren't coming tonight, if that's why you're scared to go inside."

"I'm not scared." But was he relieved they wouldn't be here? He wasn't sure. He was annoyed this stranger was telling him about his friends'—

former friends'—plans. "How do you know?"

"They told me." She studied him.

What had they told her about him? Acid burned Justin's throat. He'd been a good friend, a great boyfriend. He'd done nothing to deserve Zoey breaking up with him or Sawyer's betrayal.

"Are you coming? Or staying out here and having alone time?" She waited a moment, and then she turned toward the house. "OK. See you later."

"I'm coming." He quickstepped to catch up. This seemed weird acting all friendly with Chey. Did he want to be friends with Sawyer's new friend? Then again, she'd also been hanging out with Zoey. Maybe Chey could explain what was going on with Zoey. Then he could fix things.

They stepped inside the Arctic entry and heard singing. They were late. Justin followed Chey around a corner to the living room. A couple girls scooted over to make room on the floor.

As Justin joined in the blend of voices, he felt the stares, and his insides churned. They all knew what happened between him and Zoey and between Zoey and Sawyer.

After the song ended, Brandon led a prayer and began speaking.

"Last week, we talked about our responses to our own mistakes, and we discussed two extremes—Judas's suicide and Peter's remorse. But how should we respond when someone has wronged us?" Brandon glanced around the room.

"Forgive them," a sophomore girl said.

"Exactly. Good job." Brandon slapped his Bible shut. "And, since that's so easy, we can be done now. Let's go eat."

A few people chuckled, but Justin scowled at the carpet. Had Brandon chosen this topic because he'd heard about the breakup? Even if Sawyer apologized — not likely — Justin couldn't forgive him.

"But it's not that easy, is it?" Brandon continued. "Sure, if someone accidentally stomps on your foot and says, 'Sorry,' you don't have any problem saying, 'That's OK.' But what about when someone stomps on you? And what if they don't apologize? Can you forgive them? And should you?"

"Yes, you should, because it heals you too." Chey's voice rang strong with experience. "Sometimes forgiving someone isn't about accepting an apology, it's about letting go of your hurt or anger."

Letting go. Justin stared back at the floor. Right. As if he could just forget the pain in his chest, his silent cellphone, his empty and lonely hands. No. He didn't have anything left to hold on to, so how could he let go?

~*~

Later, after Brandon wrapped up the lesson Justin tried to ignore, he sat on a couch eating a slice of pepperoni pizza. Everyone avoided him, like they had avoided Jenny Stewart after her dad died last year. Which kind of made sense. Justin certainly felt as if someone had died.

"I've got a question." Chey plopped down on the couch next to him. Apparently she wasn't concerned about his mourning.

"OK."

"What's your story about the breakup?"

"What?" Justin stared at her. Was she seriously

asking him about breaking up with Zoey? They were practically strangers.

"Everybody's talking about it. I've heard Zoey's side. But Sawyer's not saying much."

"Like he could say anything." Justin couldn't have hidden his anger if he'd wanted to. It leaked out in every word, every thought, every breath.

"It was his band too," she said.

"You're talking about the band?" Some of the ache in his shoulders lessened.

"What else would I be talking about?"

"I don't know." He wasn't about to mention Zoey. But how else could he explain the breakup? His and Zoey's breakup. The band's breakup. They shared the same cause: Sawyer. "You can't keep playing with people you don't trust."

"OK, I get that." She peeled a pepperoni off a slice of pizza and ate it. "Do you miss it though?"

His fingers tingled at the question, and he didn't have to think about the answer. "Yes."

"Do you think I should join a band?"

Justin stared at her for a long second. Her expression was unreadable. "Not one that includes Sawyer."

"Hmm." Chey's mouth twisted to one side which pushed out the diamond stud below her lip, and stared at him, as though trying to read his mind.

He shifted away.

"You know, I've never had a best friend," she said. "I moved too much to keep one friend like that. You're blessed."

"Blessed?" The word sprang from his mouth high and loud. Had the girl been paying attention to anything?

"Yeah. You're blessed to have friends who care about you like that."

"Friends who care?" This girl didn't have a clue. "Sawyer cares about only one thing—his drums."

"He's teaching me to play them."

"What?" He'd heard her, but it didn't make sense. "Sawyer's teaching you to play his drums?"

"Yep."

"And he's letting you touch them?"

"Uh-huh."

"His drums?"

"Yes, his drums." She repeated each word slowly, like playing individual notes. "You hard of hearing? Maybe you need to turn the volume down when you play."

Sawyer, who got angry when anyone looked at his drums, was teaching Chey how to play them? Why would he do that? Unless he actually liked this girl. Justin stared at her. She looked like Sawyer's type, if he had one, with her blonde-and-red hair, the piercings under her lip and along her earlobes, and her odd clothing combinations of tulle, lace, and denim. But why now? What made this girl special?

"Are you busy tomorrow?" he asked.

"No, why?"

"We could hang out. Go to a movie or something."

"Hang out?" Her voice dropped, hardened. "Just you and me?"

"Sure, why not?"

"Why not?" Her amber eyes lit like flames. "Because you're still in love with your ex-girlfriend, whom your best friend kissed, that's why. Been there. Done that. And I deserve something better." She stood and glared down at him. "I'm not a pawn for someone's revenge game."

The people sitting nearby stared, mouths dangling open like Chey's words had triggered some sort of jaw-hinge switch.

Chey marched off in a quiet symphony of scratchy, rustle-y tulle.

The accusations hung in the air and grated against Justin's skin leaving him raw and exposed. He hadn't been trying to ask her out; he only wanted to find out why Sawyer liked her. He pushed off the couch walking in the opposite direction of Chey. He had to get out of there. How would Zoey react when she heard about this? If Chey didn't tell her, someone else would, and he'd never fix things with Zoey.

He tossed his empty plate in the trash and headed outside to his car. Why should he feel guilty? He hadn't cheated on Zoey. They'd broken up. He could ask out anyone he wanted. Those were the rules. The only persons off limits would be your friends' interests or exes or girlfriends.

And he and Sawyer weren't friends anymore.

Justin turned on the engine and scrolled through his playlists for something to take his mind off Zoey and Sawyer.

But not even the most upbeat song could unknot his twisted spirit.

37

Whatever It Takes

At the knock, Sawyer practically vaulted over the couch.

"Careful!" Mom's warning didn't slow him down, but knowing Chey waited on the other side of the door, he paused. Took a deep breath. Transformed his posture into indifference. Squashed all eagerness. Then he opened the door and stepped out of the way so Chey could enter. "Hey."

"Hi, Chey." Mom twisted around smiling over the back of the couch. The TV blasted a cooking show on cakes.

Chey lifted her hand in a wave, her nose wrinkling.

Sawyer sniffed. The acidic smell of nail polish hung in the air.

"Would you like a manicure?" Mom asked.

"Mom." He stretched the word into three syllables, each one carrying warning.

"Most girls would appreciate a guy who can paint nails."

Sawyer groaned.

"Aren't I right, Chey?" Mom raised her right hand showing off fuchsia nails. "He does a great job—no streaks, no paint on the skin."

Chey admired Mom's nails then looked at Sawyer, her face pinched like she fought not to laugh, but was losing the battle. "You did a good job."

"Never again." He practically pushed Chey into the hallway.

"I'm seeing you in a whole new light—drummer boy manicurist." Her shoulders shook. "That's what you should name your nail salon."

"Yeah, yeah." He shoved her into his room. Mom could paint her own nails in the future. "Let's play."

Chey squeezed between his bed and the keyboard. Sawyer kicked a shoe into a corner and dug through a box of CDs.

"I found this." Sawyer held up a case.

"What is it?"

"Justin made it." Sawyer paused, as if saying Justin's name required a moment of silence. Felt wrong playing Justin's music with someone else. But time to move on. Justin wasn't giving him a choice. "It's his guitar part in our songs. He recorded it for me and Zoey so we could practice at home. During school, we can't play together as often. Anyway, I thought we could use it to practice."

"OK." Chey turned the word into a question, as if she didn't understand what Sawyer meant.

"Just listen to it first." Sawyer placed the disc in the machine and hit play. The song was slow. Automatically, Sawyer moved his hands as though beating the drums.

Behind her keyboard, Chey closed her eyes. Sawyer watched her, the way she bobbed her head, the way she swayed, the way she sat on her hands as if to keep them still. Sawyer was certain she heard more than Justin's playing. She heard her music too.

The song ended, and Chey opened her eyes.

"Do you want to listen again or try playing?" Sawyer held a hand over the CD player.

"Playing?" Chey's voice squeaked. Panic flooded her orange-brown eyes. "What am I supposed to play?"

"Whatever fits the song."

"I can't do that. It's one thing to make stuff completely up like we did yesterday, but I can't come up with something that sounds good with other music."

"Yes, you can."

"No, Sawyer, I—"

"Do you want to play with me or not?"

"Are you saying you won't hang out with me if I refuse to play with that CD?"

"You said you wouldn't hang out with me unless I stopped cussing."

"That's hardly the same thing." Her laughter was high pitched, almost hysterical.

He just shrugged letting his eyes challenge her. If she wanted—no, needed—the music as badly as he did, she'd try.

"Fine." She sat a little straighter, as if physically rising to the challenge. "But let me listen again."

Sawyer played the track again. Then replayed the first thirty-seconds a dozen times before realizing Chey needed another push. Or a shove. "This time, play."

Chey opened her mouth to argue.

"Play," he demanded.

She scowled, narrowing eyes that tried to look angry, but still held panic. Fear.

He didn't know what to say to make her feel safe. But he knew what not to. He wouldn't say anything about her first attempt, which wouldn't be her best. Even if that was the point. They called it "band practice" for a reason. No one's first run through sounded great. Few sounded even decent. But she'd get better, just as he always did.

Chey twisted a knob on the keyboard and pressed down keys. Silent keys.

"It doesn't count if no one can hear it."

Chey glared and eased up the volume, changing the silent notes into a whisper.

He hit the pause button. "What's wrong with you?"

"Nothing."

"You tell me off practically every time we're together, but you're playing like you're scared."

"OK, first you compare my playing with your cussing, now you're comparing it to telling you off. That doesn't make sense."

"Yes, it does."

"No. It doesn't."

"Yes. It. Does." Couldn't she see how playing a few notes, good or bad, wasn't any scarier than being bold to someone's face?

Chey pressed her lips together as if she might give him the silent treatment—with both her mouth and her hands—indefinitely. But then she spoke. "Fine."

He hit play, and she began, grimacing when the notes clashed. But he didn't say a word. After thirty-seconds, he restarted the song. Over and over it played, and Chey grew bolder.

She found her harmony.

As Sawyer saw her confidence grow, a pride swelled inside him stronger than any he'd ever felt when playing his drums. "Gold star." Sawyer paused the CD. Sometime between the tenth play and the hundredth, he'd gotten comfortable on his bed. "Get it now?"

"Get what? How this is like cussing or telling you off? No."

"Just don't be scared about it." He leaned forward, hands outstretched wishing she could see and hear what he did. "Whatever you start with will probably not be good, but it'll get better."

"That would've been nice to know earlier. Can we take a break now?"

"Yes, please, take a break," Mom called from the living room. "An hour and a half of the same thing and I'm losing my mind."

"Did we really work on that for an hour and a half?" Chey asked.

"You worked on it. I just hit the back button."

"And that wasn't even a whole song."

"Told you being in a band was hard."

"This isn't a band. It's you, me, and a CD."

"Did you have fun?"

"Fun?" She sounded as if he'd asked if Algebra class had been fun. Then her face softened. "Yeah, it kind of was."

He grinned. She got it. He knew she would.

"So is this what it's really like to be a band? Playing the same thing over and over until you get it right?"

"Sometimes." His smile faded. "Though you're right—you, me, and a CD isn't a band."

"Might make a decent album title."

"Yeah, maybe."

"So we'd need an actual guitarist in the room to be a band?"

"It would help. And a name." Sawyer relaxed against the wall. He, Justin, and Zoey never had agreed on the name thing. Now they never would. "But what you really need to do is perform."

"Really?"

"Yeah. What good is playing in a tiny room like this where no one can ever hear you?"

"I can hear you," Mom called.

"Someone other than my crazy mother." His voice grew louder with each word.

"You think we could perform?" Chey didn't act bothered by Mom's eavesdropping. "Just you and me?"

"Maybe. If you ever learn an entire song." He didn't put any meanness in his tone. Besides a name and a venue, a band needed a song. Or a dozen songs.

"When does your mom leave for work?"

"It's my day off," Mom answered.

"Enough with the eavesdropping," Sawyer yelled.

"Let's play again," Chey said. "But with you on drums."

"Finally." Sawyer slid off the bed and sat behind his drums. "Now it'll be music."

38

Cross the Line

Zoey stared into her closet, her cell smooshed against her ear. "What should I wear tonight? Something glittery?"

"Definitely." Livvy sounded firm over the phone. Then her voice softened. "Sorry I won't be there."

"It's OK." Livvy's regret warmed Zoey's heart but put her out of a sparkly mood. She shoved a few shirts aside. "You couldn't skip out on wedding shopping with Karmen. You're maid of honor."

"I'll be home tomorrow morning to hear all about it."

"OK, but I might crash with Aurora Fire tonight. It'll be late, and if I help them unload the gear after, I might as well just stay." A long silence followed her words. "Liv? You still there?"

"Uh, yeah. Just...distracted. Are you sure you wouldn't want to sleep in your own bed?"

"At 2 or 3 a.m., I won't care. And I already told Dad. He's OK with it."

More hesitation. What was Livvy's problem? Zoey hadn't hung out with Bailee or Cherie or the band after another practice, even though Livvy was out of town and Dad would never notice. And Bailee had asked. If Zoey kept putting her off, Bailee would slip back into her snarky self, ready to replace Zoey at the first false note. She couldn't risk that. Things were finally good.

"If Dad's fine with it...be careful and stay out of trouble, OK?"

"Yeah, yeah." Zoey let her annoyance bleed through. Livvy was acting way too parental for a big sister. "You don't have to worry about me."

"Good to know. See you tomorrow."

"Bye." She disconnected and tossed her cell onto the bed. Now to choose an outfit.

~*~

Zoey paced in tiny circles in the back of the club. Aurora Fire went on in an hour, and while Zoey knew she'd be fine as soon as she stepped on stage, right now her nerves were about to jump right through her skin.

"Stop moving around." Bailee didn't even glance up from her phone. "You're making me crazy."

Zoey tried to be still, but her muscles twitched.

"Do you want to meet Max and Xavier before or after?"

"Huh?" Zoey glanced around, but she and Bailee were the only ones in the room.

"They guys I told you about?" Bailee looked up and slowed the words with exaggerated patience. "You wanna meet them now or later?"

"Uh, later." She paced again. Movement kept her knees from feeling as if they'd give out.

"OK. Later...at the...bar." Bailee spoke and texted.

"At the bar?" Zoey halted. "I can't."

"That's why I got you that I.D., remember?" Bailee wasn't bothering with fake patience now. "Makes life easier?"

"Right." The shiny, new, fake driver's license tucked in her sparkly black shorts pocket nearly singed her butt cheek. She didn't need to be over-eighteen to perform, only to hang out in the bar. And apparently, to meet guys. Looked as if that I.D. was just complicating things.

"Sit down." Bailee set aside her phone. "You need to relax. I'm feeling all jittery from watching you."

Zoey sat but couldn't keep her legs from jiggling in the fishnet stockings.

"Here. Maybe this will help." Bailee thrust a brown bottle at her.

"I don't think my stomach can handle it."

"Just try it. It's better than that cheap stuff the guys have at the house."

Zoey took a tiny sip. The liquid burned, but at least it didn't taste like cat pee.

"What's up? You seem more nervous than last time."

Nervous wasn't quite the right word. Anxious. Tense. Terrified. That's what she felt.

Zoey rested her elbows on the rough stockings, staring at her black and purple shoes. No one in the audience would be cheering just because she was on stage. No one would show up tonight just for her. No one out there would care about Zoey Harris. But, most importantly, Justin wouldn't be out there encouraging her with his grin.

How could she sing about cheaters and heartbreak when she was the worst?

The door creaked open, and Vance walked in.

"Hey." Bailee looked past him. "Where's Cherie? She was supposed to meet me here."

Vance's lip curled back, his nostrils flared, and he released several comments about his girlfriend—probably now his ex.

"Don't tell me, she failed your little test?" Bailee crossed her arms and flopped back. "Seriously, Vance? Why? She was nice. You've gotta stop being so suspicious."

"I've got a right to be, if they keep failing."

"What test?" Zoey glanced back and forth at the two of them, the argument a calming distraction.

"Vance can't trust his girlfriends, so he arranges these stupid setups where some guy hits on her. Basically, the guy pushes himself on Vance's girlfriend until she gives him her number or lets him kiss her or something."

"Why?" She stared at him. What kind of guy forced his girlfriend to cheat on him?

"Because I expect faithfulness, no matter what."

"But if you're setting her up, making a guy flirt with her, it's not her fault." Poor Cherie. Zoey hadn't known her very well, but she didn't deserve that.

"So?" Vance glared, hate mixing with the hurt in his narrowed eyes. "That's not an excuse to kiss some other guy."

"But if she was caught up in some moment, and he was standing close to her...maybe she didn't mean for it to happen." A burbling started in Zoey's chest and rose into her throat. "Maybe the kiss upset and confused her most of all."

"Wait, is that why you broke up with your boyfriend?" Bailee's jaw dropped, but she sounded impressed. "Wow, I didn't think you were capable of cheating."

"You cheated on him?" Vance's face glowed like a

red spotlight shone on him, his eyes bugging out.

Zoey shrank back, swallowing hard. Best not to answer a guy who looked like that.

"I don't believe it. All girls are alike. Eventually, they cheat on you or they use you to cheat on someone else." Vance jabbed a finger at her. A spear aimed at her heart. "No matter what Justin was like, he didn't deserve that. No one does."

Tears streamed down her cheeks. Strange, but Vance's conviction hurt more than anyone else's.

Vance stormed out of the room. The slam of the door broke what little hold Zoey had on her emotions. She buried her face in her hands, sobbing like the night she'd told Justin about the kiss.

"OK, you've gotta get a grip, girl." Bailee patted her back. "You can't walk out there looking scarier than a zombie with bad makeup."

"He wants me out of the band now." Zoey thought the worst had happened—she and Justin had broken up. But greater tragedies waited. She should've listened to Sawyer and forgot about the kiss.

"Who, Vance? Doesn't matter, they still need you, at least until Halleigh gets back."

As if that made things better. She coughed on the choking tears.

"Stop it." Bailee gripped her shoulders, forcing Zoey to look at her. "You can cry later."

"I can't sing tonight." She hiccuped. "I can't."

"Yes, you can." Bailee grabbed her purse off the floor and dug through it. "I'll fix your makeup. You take this." She held out a tiny, blue pill.

"What is it?"

"Something to calm you down and cheer you up. It won't hurt you." Bailee shoved her hand under

Zoey's nose. "Look, you gotta get it together and perform tonight. Don't mess it up for the guys. Then they'll all want to kick you out of the band."

Before she could talk herself out of it, Zoey popped the pill in her mouth and swallowed.

"Vance'll get over it." Bailee piled powder, eye shadow, mascara, and other tubes and cases on the couch between them. She scrubbed at Zoey's face with a tissue.

"You think so?" Zoey closed her eyes, and Bailee swiped the tissue around them.

"Sure. Maybe. At least you didn't cheat on him. I don't know what his hang up is with cheating—something to do with his parents—but it really ticks him off." Bailee tossed aside the pink and black stained tissue and attacked Zoey's cheeks with powder. "Close your eyes."

Zoey did, and Bailee rubbed eye shadow over her lids.

"How'd you end up kissing another guy?"

"It was stupid." Tears welled up in her eyes.

"Don't tell me if you're going to start that again. Look up."

Zoey raised her gaze to the ceiling, her head swimming. The couch started rocking, and she braced her hands on the cushion.

"OK, not so scary. I'm going out front." Bailee dumped the makeup back in her purse and stood. "Don't fail us."

Zoey nodded and giggled to herself. She'd never felt her brain slosh around before. Bailee was right, she felt less jittery and scared. She could do this. She'd give her best performance ever.

She wiggled her head and tried to stand but

slipped as though the concrete floor was made of ice. Her hip hit the ground, pain jolting through her leg, and another laugh bubbled out. Maybe she'd lie down for a minute and think calming thoughts. Who'd installed those sick, swirling light fixtures? There were one...two...three...four, no, had she counted that one already? Start over.

~*~

Groaning, Zoey forced her eyes open and then squeezed them shut. Who would use 200-watt bulbs? And why could she feel every bone and muscle in her body while her head felt stuffed with rocks that scratched her skull? She pushed herself upright and peeked through her eyelashes.

"You conscious?" Vance's voice seared her sensitive ears.

"What? Yeah, I guess." What was going on? Someone kicked her foot. She lifted her rock-filled head and stared at Vance. The anger on his face looked etched in granite.

"You messed up big time."

What was he talking about? She squeezed her eyes shut, trying to remember where she was and why her head hurt so much. Fragments flashed through her mind. Vance's girlfriend setups. Crying. Bailee fixing her makeup. That pill. Bile rose into her throat. What had she done? She tried to stand, but her legs wouldn't support her. She settled onto the cold, concrete floor, her knees pulled to her chest.

"We had to perform without you." Vance's words drilled her ears, and his face swam in and out of focus. "You know how pathetic that was?"

"I'm sorry," she whispered.

"Sorry? Yeah, like that fixes tonight." Vance leaned right in front of Zoey. She could smell his sour breath. "You're done. We'll find somebody else, someone reliable. Someone who doesn't cheat on her boyfriend."

Zoey's soul shattered. A million broken pieces.

"You better call someone to come get you. They're ready to lock this place up." The door slammed shut behind him.

Zoey wanted to cry, but she was too empty. Empty of tears. Empty of hope. Empty of life. She tried to get her eyes to focus. Everything was blurry, but she recognized her cellphone. She blinked, opening her eyes wide to read the time. Two a.m. Who could she call in the middle of the night? Livvy was in Anchorage, and she couldn't call Dad to come get her. Not looking drugged. She scrolled through her contacts until she found the name of someone who wouldn't need the answers to any questions about this mess.

She hit the call button.

39

Dirty Scene

Ringing punched through Sawyer's sleep-fog, and he groaned. Where was his phone? What time was it? The glow behind his blinds meant nothing. Could be three in the afternoon, and he'd been asleep for over twelve hours, or could be three in the morning and he'd been asleep for a measly two. Felt like three a.m. though.

He found his phone under a T-shirt and answered the call without checking the time or the I.D.

"Huh?" His attempt at a "hey" came off as a grunt.

"Sawyer?" Hesitant, girl voice.

"Who's this?" He scrubbed a fist over his eyes trying to wake up.

"It's me. Zoey."

"Why?" Sawyer sat up. She better not have woken him to talk about what-never-should've-happened again.

"I need...I need a ride, and I didn't know who else to call. It's the middle of the night, and I didn't want to wake up my dad and Livvy's in Anchorage. I really messed up, Sawyer. Really, really messed up."

Was she crying? Not again. That's what had destroyed everything to begin with. How could whatever she'd done now be worse than what had happened the last time he'd helped her?

"Please, Sawyer? I can't—I can't—"

Definitely sobbing.

He shouldn't get involved again. He should run the other way. But it was—he checked the time on his phone—two-twenty-two a.m. And if Zoey had called him to rescue her, she had to be in huge trouble.

"Where are you?" He swung his feet off the bed and kicked around laundry until he uncovered his shoes.

She named a club outside of Fairbanks. What was she doing there? Explained why she didn't want her dad or sister knowing.

Sawyer tugged the T-shirt that had hidden his phone over his head. "I'll be there in fifteen minutes." He shoved his phone in his pocket, grabbed the keys out of the bowl on the table, and stepped outside into the midnight—or two-in-the-morning—sun, then doubled back to scribble Mom a message on the fridge's white board. Just in case. He'd probably be home and asleep before she woke up and would never know he'd left.

There were no cars on the roads in town or out of town and very few in the parking lot of the dingy, brown-sided club. Zoey's car was one of them. He recognized the license plate. If Zoey had a car, why did she need a ride?

He walked to the club door and tugged the handle. Locked. This was getting complicated. He pulled out his phone to text Zoey, but a side door opened and a guy with brown hair pulled into a ponytail, with tats down his arm, stepped outside.

"Hey!" Sawyer jogged over. "A—my friend—called me to pick her up. Know where I can find her?"

"You mean Zoey?" The way he spat her name showed he wasn't a fan. Or a friend. He jerked his thumb behind him. "In there."

Sawyer moved to open the door.

"She blew it, man." The guy threw in a few words that stiffened Sawyer.

Sawyer's grip tightened, fist-like, around the door handle. Sure, he tossed out the occasional cuss word, but these were aimed at Zoey. He got why she needed rescuing.

Sawyer yanked the door open, letting it bang against the outside wall, and stormed into a dark hallway. His insides steamed like an overheated, microwaved burrito. Where did the guy get off saying things like that about Zoey? Blinking as his eyes adjusted to the lack of lighting, he peeked into doorways and found Zoey in the third room.

She sat on the stained, concrete floor, hugging her knees to her chest, face pressed against legs, rocking.

"Hey, Zo." Sawyer knelt next to her. "You OK?"

She raised her head. Gray streaks discolored her cheeks. Puffy pink skin pushed her eyes into slits. Her mouth opened. Shut. No sound. She shook her head.

Upset, crying girl in the back of a dingy club. Sitting on the floor. A wreck.

"Did something…what happened?" The possibilities and the sour smell in the room—or maybe the scent came off Zoey—sickened Sawyer. He glanced out the open doorway. Did he need to track down that guy outside and punch him for something other than the names he'd called Zoey? Or had someone else hurt her?

"I don't. I can't. Not now. Please?" Zoey struggled to her feet swaying.

Sawyer grabbed her arm and helped her balance. Placing his mouth close to her ear, he kept his voice low. "If someone did something to you, then…" He couldn't finish his thought. Didn't know what he would or could or should do. But walking Zoey out of here and doing nothing felt wrong.

"I'm the one who did something. Or didn't do something." Zoey sniffled, the sound echoing off the dingy concrete block walls. "Or both. It's my fault."

"No. It wouldn't be your fault if someone—"

"No one did anything, Sawyer." Strength blasted into Zoey's voice, behind the trembling. "Not like you're asking. And I called you because I thought you wouldn't do any asking. You'd just give me a ride. Can you do that? Please?"

"Sorry." He couldn't keep the bite out of that word, even if Zoey looked a mess. But if she was only looking for a ride, he'd only give her a ride.

"Could I also, maybe, go back to your house and crash?" The lost, aching sound returned, and Zoey turned her stained face toward Sawyer. "I can't go home yet."

"Sure." So a little more than a ride. Not that he minded. Mom wouldn't either. Zoey needed somebody tonight, and she'd called him. Not because of the kiss—at least, he didn't think so—but because she knew he'd be available at two in the morning for a ride and a place to crash. He didn't offer much to his friends, all two or three of them, but he could offer that. "Let's go." Supporting Zoey with one arm, he led her out the back way.

~*~

Knocking rattled Sawyer's head. He twisted, rough fabric scratching his cheeks and shoulders. What? Where? He forced his eyes open and oriented himself. He'd passed out. On the couch. After taking off his shirt. But the TV was off, so why'd he fallen asleep here?

Zoey.

The knocking sounded again. Someone else waking him up. Was it still the middle of the night? He glanced around for his phone. Missing again.

More knocking.

"Coming." He groaned and stumbled toward the door. Opening it, he was slammed with a blast of sunlight and Chey's face. What was she—

Right, they'd planned to play today.

"Are you early?" He yawned, not bothering to cover his gaping mouth.

"It's after ten." Chey peered behind him. "We're practicing, aren't we?"

"Yeah. Sure." Sawyer turned and headed for his room. Where practice would happen. And where his clothes were.

Chey's footsteps echoed behind his, all the way to his bedroom.

"Get up." Sawyer aimed his demand to the lump in his bed. He'd given Zoey his bed last night, and a clean T-shirt, before crashing on the couch. She'd needed a mattress and blankets and pillow more than he had.

Groaning came from the bed.

Sawyer tugged a shirt over his head, going blind to the room for a few seconds. When his head popped through, he yawned and glanced around. Room was more of a mess than usual, with Zoey's shoes and tights and shirt on his floor.

Chey stood frozen in the doorway, her face pale, eyes wide, mouth parted.

The lump on the bed shifted, Sawyer's worn navy blanket falling out of the way. Black and green streaked hair hid Zoey's face and muffled her voice, words that sounded like "my head."

Chey spun around and ran for the front door.

"Chey?" A jolt hit Sawyer, like an energy shot had hit his blood. He darted after her, stumbling over one of Zoey's shoes. Where was she going? Weren't they supposed to practice? "Chey!" His legs were still weak with sleep, and the door slammed before Sawyer could catch her. He opened it in time to see her car speeding away.

That couldn't be good.

40

Useless Alibis

Zoey rubbed her head. The rocks from last night had softened to packing peanuts, a slight improvement. She'd been so stupid. Groaning, she rested her forehead against the rough blanket over her bent knees.

"Why'd she leave?" Sawyer's words drummed like shots from a nail gun.

"Probably because of what she saw." Yuck, her mouth tasted like packing peanuts too.

"I look that bad without a shirt?"

Was he serious? Zoey squinted at him trying to clear her fuzzy vision. "I think it was me in your bed that made her leave."

A full second passed before the confusion cleared from his face. Then he swore. "Sorry," he added.

Whoa. Had Sawyer just apologized for cussing? Her head ached from trying to process that. The world really had flipped upside-down; she'd taken drugs, and Sawyer was apologizing for his language. No, forget an upside-down world; she'd entered a parallel universe.

Sawyer dove for the window, sending the bed swaying and rocking. He peeked through the blinds. "She's gone." The words traveled on a dejected sigh.

He collapsed onto the end of the bed.

Zoey's stomach lurched. "Please stop bouncing."

He wiggled back and forth on the mattress.

At least some things hadn't changed.

"Thanks for coming last night." Her gratitude sounded lame after running off Chey.

"You sounded pretty messed up. What happened anyway?"

"Aurora Fire kicked me out after I..." She stared at the blanket, accordion folding it over her legs. She felt like throwing up but didn't think the beer or pill were to blame. "I passed out and couldn't sing."

"Why'd you pass out?" His eyes narrowed, as if he suspected the answer, but wanted to hear her say it.

She'd rather keep the truth to herself. "I was really nervous, and Bailee gave me something to calm me down."

"What kind of something?"

"I don't know." Her voice came out in a scared little whisper. "Some sort of pill."

"You took drugs from someone without knowing what it was?" Sawyer blasted her. "How could you be so stupid?"

Tears spilled onto her cheeks.

"Even I'm smart enough to know better."

"I know." Shame knotted her stomach. First Vance chewed her out for cheating on Justin, now Sawyer was laying into her over taking drugs. Would the devil lecture her for her sins next?

"Stop crying." He lightly backhanded her leg. "That's what started this mess—you crying, me trying to make you feel better. I'm not doing that again."

She giggled through the tears. His attitude was so comfortably Sawyer that it cheered her. Or maybe she was still a little high.

"Is that keyboard Chey's?" She touched the gray side, only inches from the bed.

"Yeah. She's really good." A compliment wrapped in a tone of sadness. Two things rarely heard from him.

"I'm sorry about Chey. But explaining things—"

"Why should I?" Sawyer shifted back into his normal grumpy. "I didn't do anything."

"I know, but if you like her, you'll have to tell her what she saw wasn't what she thinks she saw."

"No matter how many times I've said that what happened between us meant nothing, she doesn't believe me. Why would she believe me about this?"

An awkward silence settled on the room. Zoey tugged out her necklace. "Did it really mean nothing to you?"

Sawyer turned toward her, but she kept her gaze focused on the beads of the necklace.

"You're Justin's girlfriend."

"We broke up." She lifted her chin, staring into his eyes and feeling exposed and vulnerable. Goose bumps tingled down her legs. "Doesn't that mean I can date whoever I want?"

He stared back for a long moment. She tried to read the emotions on his face, but all she saw was regret.

"Yeah, I guess. And I can date whoever I want. That'll never be you." Despite the cruelty of the words, Sawyer's voice wasn't cruel. More like firm. Certain. Definite. He pushed off the bed and left the room. A door in the hall clicked shut.

Zoey stared into space, emptiness crowding her soul. Only three weeks ago, she'd believed all her dreams were coming true. But she'd thrown it all away last night. No, she'd lost her dreams the day she ditched Justin and Sawyer for Aurora Fire. She climbed off the bed anchoring her feet to the floor until her head stopped swimming. If this was the after effects of drugs, she'd never make that mistake again. Feeling as if she had the flu wasn't her type of recreational fun.

After closing the door, she eased on her black denim shorts and her shoes. She balled up the stockings and her shirt, vowing to return Sawyer's tee later. Then she crept into the hall.

The crashing water of the shower echoed through the bathroom door. Zoey leaned against the wall. Her house was a ten-minute walk, but she doubted she could stay upright that long. Livvy might be home, but her car was still at the club so she couldn't come get Zoey. Closing her eyes, Zoey groaned. How would she explain?

A door creaked. Her eyes popped open, and she straightened trying to look alert.

Sawyer's mom stepped into the hall. Her gaze traveled down, and her eyebrows inched up.

Heat climbed her neck. Zoey hugged her arms around Sawyer's shirt trying to hide it. This had to look bad. Really bad. Worse-than-what-Chey-thought bad. As if Lexi could think anything worse. But she was a mom. It was worse.

"Zoey. I didn't know you were here."

"Uh, yeah." Goody, that sounded intelligent. But she couldn't exactly say, yeah, been here since about two a.m. That would only support the thoughts registering on Lexi's face.

"So..." Awkward silence swallowed Lexi's word. "You hanging out here for a while?"

"No. Actually, I need a ride home."

"I'm heading for work, but I can drop you off on my way."

"Thanks."

Lexi knocked on the bathroom door. "I'm leaving for work and giving Zoey a ride home."

Zoey walked into the living room missing Sawyer's response, but it must have satisfied Lexi.

"C'mon." Lexi waved her hand toward the door and breezed past.

Dragging her feet, Zoey followed. Lexi was cool and probably wouldn't ask any questions, which was why Zoey called Sawyer last night—not that she had any other decent options. But Lexi was still a mom who had just found a girl hanging around her son's room wearing his clothes.

Maybe she should've attempted walking home.

In the car, Zoey fastened her seatbelt and waited for Lexi to start driving. But after the engine roared to life, Lexi gripped the steering wheel staring through the windshield for several seconds.

"OK, what happened?" Lexi twisted to face Zoey, the demand in her voice and eyes. "I know about the kiss, but Sawyer's been hanging out with Chey and you're Justin's girlfriend, so what's going on?"

Something blazed inside Zoey's chest. Had someone tattooed "Justin's girlfriend" on her forehead? They'd broken up! She was just Zoey. "Nothing happened. I got into trouble last night and needed someone to...rescue me."

"What kind of trouble?"

She ducked to avoid Lexi's hard stare.

"Look, I can see it in your face, and the fact you came here last night instead of going home." Lexi let out a sigh. "Drinking, drugs, whatever it was, I've lived it."

She peeked around her curtain of hair. A parent admitting to those things?

"I wasn't in a band—Sawyer got his talent from his dad—but I met Toby Sawyer at a club where his band was playing. I know what that culture can be like." Lexi's voice faded and then returned stronger. "But you and Justin, you've always been good kids and a good influence on Sawyer. I don't want him—or you—to lose that by getting into trouble. My kind of trouble. Understand?"

She nodded. Yeah, she understood all right, but it was a little too late. She'd already lost Justin and her "good kid" status. Her heart shattered again. How many times could a heart break?

"But if you do need rescuing again, don't hesitate to call Sawyer or me, OK?" Lexi pulled away from the curb.

What would she need rescuing from? No band. No friends. No future. Her dreams were destroyed.

For once, she was glad Mama wasn't around.

41

Collapsing

Sawyer picked up his phone for the millionth time, stared at the blank screen for a few seconds, and tossed it back on his bed. If he called Chey, what would he say? He shouldn't need to apologize for rescuing a wasted friend. Chey should apologize to him for jumping to conclusions.

But judging from the look on her face right before she fled, she wouldn't be speaking to him anytime soon.

He grabbed his sticks and started drumming. The rhythm usually helped straighten his tangled thoughts. But today, more than just his thoughts were tangled. His life was tangled.

Across the room, Chey's keyboard, still shiny-new, sat silent and accusing. If they'd been playing at her house, would she react like Justin and dump his drums at a transfer site?

His hands froze. Why was he bothering to play anyway? He'd destroyed his band this summer—not once, but twice. Even if what he and Chey had wasn't really a band, it was close enough. And what good was being a drummer without a band? Worthless.

His chest cracked open and whatever hope he'd had oozed out. He was worthless.

Sawyer stood and paced down the hall and back to his room, twisting the sticks in his hands. Now that Zoey was done with Aurora Fire, she'd be back with Justin in a week, two weeks tops. Because Justin was the good guy, the honest guy, the worthy guy. He'd forgive Zoey, and they'd play together again.

But Sawyer was finished. When Justin and Zoey reformed their band, Sawyer wouldn't be invited. And Chey hated him, but she'd probably end up joining Justin and Zoey's band.

He walked back into his room and picked up his laptop. He no longer needed his drums.

~*~

When he heard the front door open later, Sawyer grabbed the flier and met Mom. "I'm taking the car."

"OK." She closed the door and dropped her purse on the table. "Where are you going?"

"Rhythm and Notes. They close in half an hour."

She arched her back stretching out the kinks of delivering plates of food for eight hours. Then she spied the paper in his hand. "Wait. What's that?"

"Nothing." He turned the flier so she couldn't see.

"It's something."

"I'll be back in an hour." Sawyer stepped around her, and she snatched the flier out of his hand.

"You're selling your drums?" She sounded disconnected, as if she didn't understand what she was saying. "Why? What happened?"

"Nothing." He grabbed for the flier.

"Not nothing." She held it out of his reach and blocked the door. "You're not going anywhere until you explain this."

"They're my drums. I can sell them if I want."

"Yeah, you're right. But you selling your drums is like..." Her head twitched back and forth searching for the right words. "Like me selling you."

"Huh?"

"You love those drums more than anything. So why are you selling them? Do you need the money?" Her eyes widened, and her voice raced higher. "You accepted one of those credit cards that comes in the mail, and now you owe hundreds of dollars."

"No."

"Thousands of dollars?"

"Mom, stop it. I don't owe any money."

"That's a relief." The horror faded from her face. "Then why do you need the money?"

"I don't need the money. I just...don't need the drums." The confession tore a hole inside, and he avoided meeting her gaze.

"That's a lie."

"C'mon, Mom, let me go before the store closes."

"Not until you tell me the truth."

He groaned. Didn't she see how hard this was without the third degree? "They're my drums. I can do whatever I want with them."

"Yes, you can." She hid the flier behind her back clearly not caring about his privacy. "And I let you do a lot more than most mothers would. Those gauges in your ears? I still think you'll regret them in about ten years, but I let you get them. You remember why?"

"Because I asked?" What did that have to do with selling his drums?

"No. I let you because when I asked you why you wanted them, you told me the truth. You thought it was cool. Not a great reason, but an honest one. And you're not leaving this house tonight unless you tell me the truth. Why are you selling your drums?"

"Because I don't have a band, so what's the point?" Saying it out loud ripped the hole bigger.

"What about Chey? You two sounded good yesterday."

"She came over this morning, but when she saw Zoey..." The hole filled with pain. He swallowed and stared at the floor. This hurt. "Anyway, Zoey will get back with Justin, and Chey will probably join them. So why do I need drums?"

"But—"

"Don't."

The sympathy in her voice tugged at the pain-filled hole threatening to pull it to the surface and spill its ugly guts.

She sighed, a sound long and sorrowful. "I'm sorry."

"Yeah, whatever." His voice was gruff trying to hide any hint of hurt. He yanked back his flier and walked out the door.

When had everything fallen apart anyway? The night he'd kissed Zoey or the night she'd confessed? Sawyer glanced at the price he'd listed for the drums. Six hundred dollars or best offer—that's what his betraying kiss was worth.

But it cost him everything.

42

What I've Overcome

Relief mingled with Zoey's guilt. The house was empty. Maybe she should've asked Sawyer's mom to take her to Livvy's car. If she drove it home, she might get away with no one else finding out about last night. But she still wasn't in any condition to drive, since climbing the stairs left her light-headed and exhausted. Maybe she'd come up with a plan after a nap.

She crawled onto her bed and passed out until a knock woke her.

"Huh, what?" She pushed up on her elbows and stared at the door.

"Hey, you're home." Livvy stepped into the room, wearing a frown like a question mark. A gray streak—Tiger—darted through the open door. "Where's my car?"

A chill rolled over Zoey, waking her up completely. Did they have to talk about that before she was coherent? "It's at the club."

"At the club? Why?"

Zoey sat all the way up staring at the swirl of colors on her quilt. She needed some excuse, some explanation that wouldn't get her into trouble.

"Zoey, baby." Livvy joined Zoey, and the mattress sagged. "What happened?"

Maybe it was the fear in her sister's voice or maybe it was how much like Mama she sounded, but suddenly, sobs exploded from Zoey. After all the tears she'd shed in the past two weeks, she'd expected to be all dried out. But these came from somewhere deep inside, the place where she'd locked up her deepest fear—failing Mama. Last night, she had.

Livvy cradled her until the shaking and bawling slowed. She brushed back the hair clinging to Zoey's tear-streaked cheeks. "Can you tell me now?"

She sucked in an uneasy breath. "Vance kicked me out of Aurora Fire."

"Why would he do that?"

"Because..." She didn't have the strength to say anything but the truth. "I couldn't perform last night."

"Why not?"

Zoey raised her head. Sad lines were etched around Livvy's eyes. Like Lexi and Sawyer, she seemed to already know. "Because I took something...and it made me pass out."

"Took something?" Livvy's voice jumped an octave. "Like what?"

"I don't know," she whispered.

"You don't know? How could you?" Livvy jerked back, face red, eyes on fire. "That's how people die, Zoey. Die! As in dead. Gone forever."

"I know, I know." The tears started again, and she buried her face in her bent knees.

"Oh, Zo." Livvy sagged against her. "I didn't want you to make the same mistakes I did."

"What?" Had she understood that? Zoey's tears dried up. First Lexi admitted to drinking and drugs, now Livvy? What next? Would Justin call her up and confess to getting high on the weekends?

"After you came home late this week, I got suspicious, but I didn't know what to do." Livvy twisted her hands in her lap. "I didn't want to rat you out to Dad, and I really hoped you were telling the truth about falling asleep."

Goody, now she felt a million times worse. How was that even possible? "It was the truth."

"Really?" Livvy's tone held no belief. "You just fell asleep?"

"After having a beer," she added in a small voice. Instead of feeling a weight lifted, the confession seemed to push Zoey down.

"Oh, Zoey." Livvy groaned.

"Well, if you knew I was doing that, why didn't you stop me?" Maybe if her big sister had stepped in sooner, she wouldn't have been kicked out of the band.

"I didn't know how! No one was able to stop me." Shame gripped Livvy's words. "All I could think to do was pray God would intervene in some way before you ended up messing up in a way you couldn't undo, like I did."

Seemed like God intervened about five minutes too late. But she was more curious about Livvy's mistake than talking about her own. "How did you mess up? You've always been the responsible, grown-up one."

"Don't you remember?"

Zoey shook her head, not knowing what she was supposed to be remembering.

"I wasn't there the night Mama died. I was at a party, drinking and doing other...stuff. The cops raided it, and four hours after Mama passed, Dad was bailing me out of jail."

Zoey's mouth hung open. This whole parallel

universe thing was freaking her out. Was no one who they seemed to be? She searched the dusty corners of her memories. "I remember you and Dad fighting and lots of crying, but I thought it was just because of Mama and what was going on."

"It was more than that." Now Livvy was crying. "While you couldn't spend enough time with Mama, I couldn't deal with watching her die. I missed out on her last few months of life, and I can never get those days back."

Suddenly, getting kicked out of Aurora Fire didn't sound so terrible.

"But her death sobered me up, and along with that grief counselor Dad made us see, I realized that while I couldn't relive those months, I could learn something from it and live my life better because of it."

"I sort of remember you not being there, but Mama just said that you had friends and a life outside of the hospital. And we shouldn't hold that against you because she didn't."

"It took a lot of visits with that counselor before I didn't hold it against me." Livvy wiped the tears from her cheeks.

Zoey shifted backward on her bed to lean against the pillows along the headboard.

Livvy scooted next to her.

"You think Mama's disappointed in us?" Zoey stared at the aurora painted on her ceiling, too scared of the emotions on Livvy's face to look at her.

"Right after she died, I thought so. But later, I started thinking that if she knew her death was what straightened me out, she was probably pleased to know some good came from the timing."

"I failed her though. She always said I'd become

famous with my singing, but I couldn't survive in a real band."

"What do you mean 'a real band'? What about with Justin and Sawyer? You did fine with them."

"But we weren't really a band. Not yet. Aurora Fire had fans and venues. Justin, Sawyer, and I only had our friends and families and a church fellowship hall. How would we ever get famous with that?" Zoey sank into the pillows. "I blew it."

"Let me ask you something." Livvy faced her. "Did you have fun singing and playing bass with Justin and Sawyer?"

"Yeah."

"And what about with Aurora Fire? Did you have fun singing with them?"

Fun? The lyrics that threatened to choke her? "No."

"You are an amazing singer, Zoey."

She struggled to believe that. Amazing didn't seem to be the right adjective today.

"Mama had faith that one day others would see that too." Livvy's conviction stirred up hope inside Zoey. "But she never intended for you to force it to happen by doing something that makes you miserable."

"Well, it doesn't matter now." If hope were a candle flame, reality was the wind blowing it out. "I don't have anyone to sing with."

"What about Justin and Sawyer? I know you and Justin broke up, but don't they still need you?"

"We broke up because Sawyer and I kissed."

"Oh." So many unsaid thoughts weighted Livvy's simple word that it practically sank into the middle of the bed.

She chanced a glance at Livvy out the corner of her eye. No disappointment, no sadness, no judgment. Some of her guilt eased.

"Why'd you and Sawyer..."

Zoey let the unfinished question fade before answering. "I don't know. I was crying—big surprise, huh? I don't think I've cried this much since Mama died." Her mouth twitched with an almost-smile. "Anyway, he was being nice, hugging me and trying to reassure me, and...I kissed him, he kissed me. Then he turned all Sawyer on me swearing and running off."

"So are the two of you together now?"

"No. He says it was a mistake." She twisted to face Livvy. Now she'd admitted the kiss, she could finally pour out all her questions. "But I don't know if I agree with him. I felt something when we kissed—something that was missing when Justin kissed me."

"Like what?"

"Like excited." Heat crept up her neck. "Like my toes curled, and I didn't want him to leave. That has to mean something, doesn't it?"

Livvy sat quiet a moment, her mouth knotting to one side. "You know what Mama told me about boys when I started dating?"

"No." Zoey snapped the word, a little hurt by the reminder of mother-daughter moments she'd missed. "How could I?"

"Good point. I probably should've shared this with you before. But she told me that I shouldn't base falling in love on how attracted I was to his looks or how my heart fluttered when he spoke to me or the way my stomach flipped when he kissed me. Love is more than that. She told me to read I Corinthians 13 so I'd know what love really was."

"That's the love chapter, isn't it?"

"Yep. And it says nothing about curling toes or fluttering hearts. It's all about love being patient and kind, not being jealous or bragging or rude or crabby."

"In other words, love is everything Justin is and Sawyer is not." Zoey flopped back against the pillows. "I really messed it up, didn't I?"

Livvy slipped her arm around Zoey's shoulders. "Not necessarily. After all, if you're not willing or able to show that kind of love to Justin, then maybe you should've broken up with him."

"Not helping." Zoey frowned at the wall.

"I know." Livvy sighed, as if she didn't really know. "Maybe I'm not trying to. Justin's a nice guy. He doesn't deserve to be cheated on."

Zoey jerked away. "I didn't mean for it to happen!"

"I know." Livvy forced her back into a hug. "Love is complicated. Especially in high school."

"You're telling me."

"But I don't think you should start dating Sawyer just because you enjoyed one kiss."

"Don't worry, he's not interested in me. He likes this new girl, Chey." They both acted so tough and rough, but she remembered how Chey's face lit up when talking about Sawyer and the disappointment on Sawyer's face when Chey ran out of the room that morning. "They're perfect for each other."

"I'm sorry."

For a long time, they sat on Zoey's bed, Livvy's arms wrapped around Zoey, Zoey leaning against her big sister. The world was beginning to look normal again. Joining Aurora Fire had been wrong for so many reasons, but now that she'd confessed all the horrible, ugly, embarrassing truths of the last few weeks, life felt a little less complicated. She fingered the beads on her necklace. *I'm sorry, Mama.*

Then she heard Mama's voice as if it spoke directly in her heart. *It's OK, baby. But I'm not the one you should be talking to.*

What did that mean? She needed to apologize to Justin? Probably. And Sawyer and Chey. But could she bring herself to do that? Eventually. Maybe. Then it hit her. It wasn't just them she'd wronged. *God, I'm sorry. I should've talked to you about my dreams. Not Mama or Justin or Livvy.*

A peace she'd never experienced—not even while singing—settled over her soul. Maybe getting kicked out of Aurora Fire wasn't all bad.

After a few more minutes of quiet, Livvy squeezed her shoulders and then pulled away. "Since my car's been abandoned, I'll need Dad to give me a ride. But I think I'll let you explain why it's still at the club."

Zoey groaned. This was what repentance got her? "Can't you do it? Please?"

"Nope." Grinning, Livvy pranced to the door. "I think I've protected you from Dad enough lately."

She stuck out her tongue at Livvy's back. "Fine. In a few minutes."

First she had some reading to do. She pulled her Bible from under a pile of CDs. She'd start with the love chapter.

43

I Never Said I Was Through With You

Sawyer lay on his bed staring at the ceiling. He could probably map out every bump up there now, but he had no reason to get up. He had nothing to do, nowhere to go, no one to see.

Screams and pounding bass blasted from his speakers. Mom was at work, so no one was bothered by the deafening music. He crossed his arms and imagined lines connected the ceiling bumps into shapes. Monsters, horned demons, writhing spirits. What would Mom say if he used a pen to trace those pictures?

A banging rattled his windows, and he sat straight up.

What the—?

He peeked through the blinds. Zoey wiggled her fingers at him, an I'm-not-leaving-until-you-talk-to-me look on her face.

Sawyer pulled back from the window. What was she doing here? And did he really want to know? Zoey had caused enough problems over the last few weeks. But he swung his feet over the side of the bed and grabbed a shirt. He had nothing to lose. After switching off the music, he headed for the front door.

Zoey and Chey were on the steps.

He rubbed his eyes. Maybe he'd fallen back asleep and was dreaming. Or maybe they were here to jump him and beat him up.

"Hi." Zoey's smile downgraded from determined to uncertain.

Chey hung back avoiding his gaze as if she didn't quite want to be there.

A lump filled his throat. It felt like the word sorry. But he couldn't bring himself to let the word out. Instead, he swallowed it back into the pit of things-he-should've-said-but-didn't. "Hey." He stretched the word into a question.

"Chey and I talked. I told her what happened Friday night. Everything. And she's forgiven me," Zoey said.

"OK." He twisted the doorknob behind his back to make sure the door was unlocked before pulling it closed. Mosquitoes buzzed around, and nothing was worse than a rogue mosquito in the house sucking blood while people slept.

"Chey and I are good now." Zoey glanced over her shoulder at Chey as if to double-check.

Chey nodded, but her expression didn't exactly look as if all was good. Then again, maybe things were good between Chey and Zoey but not between Chey and Sawyer.

Sawyer scrubbed a hand over his face. Where was Zoey going with this anyway?

"But we've still got a problem." Zoey swept her finger around at all of them. "The three of us, we're all without a band, and we need one." Why were they telling him? He knew that better than anybody.

"Do you have the flier?" Zoey asked Chey.

Chey handed her a folded paper. Zoey flipped it

open and passed it to Sawyer.

He glanced down. "Poor and Loud." A free concert this coming weekend featuring local artists. Why were they showing him? Were they inviting him? "Yeah, I remember this. We went last year."

Zoey nodded. "And Chey volunteered you to play this year."

"Me?" He looked at Chey, but she avoided eye contact. If she was still mad at him, why'd she come?

"Not just you." Zoey stabbed out the last word as if Sawyer was being stupid. "The two of you. Your band. And I thought you might let me join."

"We have a band?" Sawyer rubbed his eyes again. This was insane. Had to be a dream. He slapped a mosquito. "The concert is this Saturday. There's no way."

Zoey looked at Chey, and some sort of silent communication passed between them. Chey climbed to the step right below him.

"Why not?" She raised her chin and made dead-on, right-in-the-eyes contact. Whatever anger or embarrassment or insecurity she'd felt before had been erased.

"A drummer, a bassist, and a keyboardist who doesn't know what she's doing? No offense," he added at the flicker of hurt in Chey's eyes. "But we're not a band. And we can't be one by Saturday."

"So you were lying when you said that you and me could be a band if we performed?" Her chin rose higher, her eyes flashed.

"No. I also said you needed to know more than one song. How are we going to do that in five days? And I said you needed a name. I bet whoever you talked to didn't even take you seriously."

"I gave them a name."

"You did? What?"

"You, Me, and a CD." She spoke barely loud enough for him to hear.

She had to be joking, but the embarrassment written on her face said she was serious. He burst out laughing. "I can't believe you used that. It's got to be the lamest name."

"Yeah, well at least I'm doing something." Chey stepped onto the top step crowding him on the narrow, concrete rectangle. "Are you too scared to try?"

"I'm not scared. I'm being realistic."

"Yeah, right." She crossed her arms, and her diamond stud wiggled.

What would that feel like if he kissed her? Would it get in the way? Cut his lip? This was probably not the time to find out.

"What do we have to lose by trying?" Chey's demand included a slight tremble.

"Our reputation?" Standing so close, her scent of oranges and maple syrup overwhelmed him. The temperature rose by ten degrees. He was in no hurry to escape.

"As You, Me, and a CD?" She cocked an eyebrow. "If we sound terrible, we'll change our name and reinvent ourselves."

"We're changing the name period."

"So you're in?"

Right now, she could probably talk him into anything. Agreeing to be a drummer in a band—even the worst band in history—was easy. "We'll have to spend every waking moment practicing."

"I've got nothing better to do."

Nothing better to do than practice. That had to be

the best thing a girl had ever said.

"But with my mom's job, we won't be able to practice that much."

"My house." Zoey's interruption cut through the heat between Sawyer and Chey like a northern wind on a steamy hot day. He'd forgotten Zoey was here. He wished she wasn't.

"We have to practice at my house." She continued talking as if she couldn't tell Sawyer wanted to push her away from the steps. Maybe he'd lost his edge. "I'm kind of grounded because of yesterday." She blushed. "Anyway, my dad says if we set up at my house, I can play with you."

"Guess we can't do this without you." He spoke half under his breath. Hanging out alone with Chey would be better. But he and Chey didn't make much of a band.

"Told you he'd only agree if you asked." Zoey flashed Chey a grin.

Chey glanced away, her stud jiggling crazily as if it might fall out.

"I'll go take apart the drums." He opened the door. "You coming to get the keyboard? Unless you've decided I can touch it now."

"I don't think so." Chey entered the house behind him. "I'll pack it up."

Five minutes ago, he'd had no band. Now he had a band and a show. Sure, he'd probably mess everything up again by tomorrow, but at least he knew things wouldn't stay messed up forever.

44

Busted Heart (Hold On To Me)

Justin paused inside the Rhythm and Notes entry. The same fliers and business cards decorated the bulletin board. Piano lessons. Guitar for sale. But a for-sale ad with a picture of drums was new. Justin scanned the description stopping on the phone number.

Sawyer was selling his drums?

Justin ripped the flyer from its red thumb tack. That couldn't be right. Sawyer would sell a kidney first. He wasn't selling them because he needed a kidney or something, was he?

No, that was crazy. But not as crazy as Sawyer selling his drums. Justin crumpled the paper in his fist, shoved it into his pocket, and entered the store. He'd ask around and find out what was going on.

"Morning, Justin." Zach walked out from a back room where the violins, violas, and other stringed instruments were kept. He gave Justin a wicked smile. "I've got something fun for you to do."

"O-kay."

Zach disappeared into the back again for a moment and returned with a box. "The pick trays need refilling."

Justin took the box. Inside, dozens of plastic bags

were filled with colorful guitar picks of every width. A guitar-related chore. Not bad.

"I'm restringing a cello, so you've got the register."

"No problem." Justin walked over to the counter separating the guitar room from a smaller room with keyboards, drum sticks, and drum head replacements. A large rectangular box divided into dozens of squares, each holding a different size or brand of pick, sat on the counter. Another vertical box with drawers held even more. Grabbing a bag of picks, he got to work.

Justin refilled the plastic trays, the guitar picks clinking against each other. Having a job wasn't so bad. At least he was surrounded by music. And he never had to ask, "Do you want hot sauce with that?"

The entrance guitar strummed. Glancing up from his chore, he saw Vance walk through the doorway. Justin clenched his fists, the picks digging into his palm.

"What are you doing here?" Vance stopped on the other side of the counter.

"Working." Justin spoke as if he'd seen a Slow, Proceed with Caution sign.

"Really?" Vance laughed, not as if he found Justin working funny, but as if Justin had fallen and *that* was funny. "You had to get a job? Things falling apart in the Conrad family again?"

Justin shoved the picks into the case and shut the lid. "What do you want?"

"Is that how you greet customers?" Vance mocked. He circled around to the rack with guitar strings. "Need a new D-string."

Keeping an eye on Vance, Justin moved to the register.

"How's Zoey?"

Hearing her name sent a tremor through Justin. But why would Vance ask him about Zoey? "Fine, I guess."

"You haven't heard, have you?" Vance walked over looking a little too excited about a new string. "That's right, you weren't the one she called to rescue her. It was some other dude. Guy with spiky hair, gauges in his ears."

"Sawyer?" Nausea grabbed hold of Justin's stomach. Why would Zoey call Sawyer? Unless there actually was something going on between them. Justin's hands tightened on the edge of the glass counter.

"That's his name?"

Justin ignored the question and tried to keep his voice casual. "What happened?"

"Your girlfriend—ex-girlfriend—got totally wasted. She couldn't even perform Friday night. So we kicked her out."

Was Vance messing with him? "Zoey wouldn't do that."

"She did. Totally flaked out on us." Vance muttered something under his breath.

"Don't call her that." Justin's voice was as tight as his clenched fists. Punching a customer would probably get him fired, and except for that night with Sawyer, he'd never gotten into a fight. But keeping the counter between him and Vance was necessary.

"You're defending her?" Vance laughed as if this was better than Justin having a job. "Man, you're pathetic. She ditches your band, hooks up with another guy, dumps you, and you're still in love with her."

Justin snatched the guitar string off the counter

and rang it up. Love didn't disappear just because someone messed up.

"I guess in your perfect little world, couples can pretend everyone's happy. No one ever cheats." Vance pulled out his wallet and slapped down a bill.

Justin wished. If he really could pretend, he wouldn't be wondering about all the times Mom asked him to baby-sit or questioning if Zoey—and Mom—really deserved to be forgiven. And he'd be able to call Sawyer to ask why he was selling his drums. Not that he cared about that anymore. Sawyer could do whatever he wanted.

Justin made change and handed Vance the bag.

"You need to grow up, kid." Vance narrowed his eyes, not letting the conversation die. "In the real world, life's unfair. Parents divorce, friends stab you in the back, and girlfriends sleep around."

"Hey! It was just a kiss."

"Yeah, but in your G-rated world, that's the same as sex."

Justin should be angry, insulted by everything Vance had said, but instead he felt cold, numb, and as if every word was true.

"But you always did want to play songs about love and forgiveness and that church junk." Vance's gaze rolled over Justin, and his mouth twisted into a smile. "Though you don't look like you believe it all now."

Justin tried to open his mouth to deny it, but his jaw had wired shut.

"Hard to stay innocent when the world keeps biting you in the butt, isn't it?" Smirking, Vance took his guitar string and left.

Rooted behind the counter, Justin stared into

space. Just because he was angry with Sawyer didn't mean he'd lost his faith. He still believed in God and definitely love. His breakup with Zoey hadn't changed his beliefs. But what about the other things Vance had mentioned? About Zoey and Sawyer and Friday night? The crushing ache returned. His cell rang and he pulled the phone from his pocket. Mom? He answered and returned to the guitar picks.

"Sorry to bother you at work." Mom's apology sounded more polite than regretful. "But what time do you get off tonight?"

"I'm working until close. Six." He dropped blue picks into the right slot. "But Zach's showing me how to close, so I'll be home later."

"Can you pick up Tristan from Carrie's house next door when you get home? I've got this chick flick night with some ladies from church at Nina Walters' house that I'd forgotten about. And since your dad's in Anchorage, I need you to watch Tristan."

She'd forgotten? So Dad didn't know about it either? "Told you that if I got a job you'd lose your free babysitting."

"I guess it's a good thing the store closes early. Savannah's at Allie's house, so you won't need to worry about her, but don't forget to get Tristan from Carrie's, OK?"

"OK." He disconnected and dropped the phone back into his pocket. Was she really going to a chick flick night? Maybe it was time to find out if forgiveness after cheating did work.

~*~

"Shooom, shooom." Tristan bolted into the house,

his arms spread wide. "I'm a bomber," he explained, darting into the kitchen, around the island, and into the living room.

"Be careful, buddy." Justin avoided a mid-air collision and headed for Dad's study. "I'm going to look at something on the computer. Then we might go out."

Bomber-Tristan paused. "Go where?"

"For a drive."

Justin hadn't been able to drop his suspicions about Mom. If she'd known about the movie night, why hadn't she marked the calendar or asked him to babysit earlier? Maybe she was taking advantage of Dad's absence.

Several minutes of searching the Internet brought up Nina Walters' address north of town. He also checked the church's online events calendar. No mention of a chick flick night or anything at Nina Walters' house.

A lump like a porcupine—big and prickly—settled into his gut. He shut off the computer and tracked down Tristan. "Wanna go for a drive, buddy?"

"No, I wanna fly. Shooom, shooom." Tristan buzzed around Justin.

"How about you fly out to my car?" He picked up Bomber-Tristan, flew him to his car, and unlocked the doors.

"Hey!" Tristan squirmed and kicked like swimming in air. "No car seat! I can't go."

Right, the car seat. "Sure you can, buddy. It's just a short ride. It'll be OK." He helped his little brother into the car and buckled the too-big seatbelt over him. He'd drive real careful, and no one would find out. Justin backed out of the driveway and drove north, away from the University and town. Nina Walters lived on one of the many roads leading up the hills outside of Fairbanks. He watched the green street signs.

"Gotta go potty!"

"Tristan." Justin groaned. "Can you wait? There's nowhere to stop."

"O-tay."

Crisis averted. A steady thumping of kicks hit the back of Justin's seat. There was his turn. He slowed and turned onto an uphill dirt road. A half-dozen switchbacks later, he found the right number posted on a spruce tree. He crept past the property, searching for Mom's van, but the house and any cars were sheltered by spruce and birch. He did a U-turn and stopped at the base of the drive. Now what? Did he dare turn into the driveway, hoping no one saw him or recognized his car? He hadn't come all this way to leave without an answer.

"Gotta go potty!"

"Tristan, seriously? Can't you hold it a little longer?"

"No! Now."

Justin glanced over his shoulder.

Tristan bent over rocking back and forth, his face twisted in desperation. "Potty right now."

A three-year-old did not make a good covert ops partner. Only one solution: the hundreds of trees surrounding them. He put the car in park and opened the door. He might as well check out the driveway on foot anyway. Maybe that would be less noticeable.

"OK, buddy, see that tree?" He pointed at a birch tree that looked like all the other birch trees with its curling white, paper-thin pieces of trunk. "That's where you can go potty."

"Outside?" Tristan stared up with round eyes. "Doggies go outside."

"So do people who have to go potty right now where there aren't any." He led his brother to the other side of the driveway. "Just aim at that plant, OK? I'll be right over here."

After scanning the hill and trees for signs of moose or dogs, he moved a few feet up the driveway looking for the cars, but the driveway snaked behind the house.

"All done!" Tristan shuffled up the hill, his pants around his ankles.

This was insane. "C'mon, buddy, pull up your pants." He bent to help his brother.

"Justin!"

The voice startled him, and he nearly gave Tristan a wedgie.

"Mommy!" Tristan, fully clothed, ripped past him and up the driveway.

"You're here." He didn't know whether to feel relief or embarrassment at the sight of Mom's red, pinched face.

"Of course, I'm here." She patted Tristan's head, and he wrapped his arms around her legs. "But why are you?"

"Um..." Should've thought of an excuse just in case, because seeing her, the truth sounded awfully stupid.

"I really want to know, Justin." Mom's mouth tightened until her lips almost disappeared. "I want to know why, when Natalie cried, 'Some kid is running naked out there,' that I discovered it was my kid running naked. My kid who is supposed to be home, getting ready for bed." She paused again staring at him for an answer.

The prickly porcupine was back in his gut shooting poisonous quills through him. What right did she have to be angry with him? Sure, he'd been spying on her, but it wasn't like he didn't have a good reason. She expected him to baby-sit nearly every day, even after he'd gotten a job. How was he not supposed to be suspicious?

"I'm serious, Justin. I don't understand what's gotten into you lately. First a fight with your friends in the garage, then you destroy your guitar, now you can't even handle putting your brother to bed?"

He remained frozen staring at Mom, the quills digging deeper and deeper. He just wanted to know how much more of his life was about to be destroyed. And he wanted a chance to stop it or fix it or at least understand it. Because none of it made any sense. But he couldn't put all that into words.

"Explain to me what you are doing here before you find yourself grounded for a very long time."

"I thought you were cheating on him again!" The words exploded from him, stronger and louder than he'd expected.

Mom's face shifted to colors like a turnip—from white to almost purple. "Get in your car."

He trudged back down the driveway. That had come out wrong. Or maybe it had come out right. Even with the certain grounding about to follow—like he had anything to be grounded from—the tension melted from his shoulders. He'd said it. Now she'd have to talk to him about it.

Or maybe not.

He slid into the driver's seat. Mom helped Tristan in the back before sitting in the passenger seat.

"How dare you." Her voice was quiet.

Dangerously quiet. Calm before the storm-of-the-century quiet. "You don't have the right to spy on me and accuse me of that."

He stared at the steering wheel. Didn't he have a right to know if his life was about to be destroyed? Even hurricanes and tornados came with warnings. But he had experienced an earthquake. An unexpected shaking of his world bringing everything crashing to the ground. Followed by endless aftershocks.

"Why...why would you even think that?"

"Because you're going out all the time lately to meet people, like before." He turned his hot stare on her. Those questions he'd bottled up inside all these years suddenly burst forth. "When you told Dad that you'd been cheating on him, you said it started with coffee dates."

"You heard that?" Her voice dropped to a whisper.

He nodded.

"I'm sorry." She sank against the seat. "I didn't know."

"Well, what about now? Who are you meeting on your coffee dates?"

"Friends, Justin." The irritation in her voice returned. "Not that it's any of your business, but I've been spending time with girl friends, talking, shopping, and drinking coffee. Satisfied?"

No. She still hadn't explained why it happened in the first place. What had led her to sleeping with some man other than Dad? Why had she risked their family and ruined their friendships?

"Have I been asking you to babysit too often? Is that why you've suddenly become suspicious? And, by the way, your dad knows where I am tonight. I'm not hiding anything from him."

He pulled a pick from his pocket and twisted it through his fingers concentrating on something other than the never-ending ache. So forgiveness had worked for them. Why wasn't it working for him? "Zoey broke up with me."

"I thought so." The anger faded from her voice, and she rubbed his shoulder. "Hon, I'm sorry."

"She kissed Sawyer."

"Oh." Mom withdrew her hand.

"Why'd she do it?" He stared at the shiny blue plastic flashing between his fingers. "Why'd you do it? Why would anyone cheat on the person who loves them?"

She stared out the window for a few minutes. In the back seat, Tristan had curled up and fallen asleep. A truck passed them on the road kicking up a cloud of dirt.

"Even if I could explain that to you, it wouldn't answer your question about Zoey. There are so many factors and reasons, and none of them may have anything to do with you."

Yeah, right. He could've done something different. "How do I convince her I've forgiven her? How did you and Dad stay together?"

"It's not the same thing." She shook her head. "Your dad and I are married. We had you and Savannah and a commitment to do everything we could to stay together. And it wasn't easy. It's still not easy." She brushed a tear from her cheek with a knuckle. "For you, it might be better not to get back together. Because it's hard when you can't trust someone." She grabbed a fast-food napkin from a cup holder. "Even harder when you're the one who can't be trusted."

A heavy silence settled around them. He'd never expected the answers to his questions would make her cry. But even if that's how she felt, it wouldn't be the same with Zoey. Sawyer was the one who couldn't be trusted.

He looked at Mom and the tears rolling down her cheeks. "I'm sorry."

"Well." Mom wiped her eyes and gave him a tight, sad smile. "I'm blocked in or I'd follow you home. I'm not in much of a movie mood anymore."

"Sorry," he repeated. He should've stayed home or picked his timing better. Like somewhere private and secluded twenty years from now.

"It's OK." She tucked the makeup-stained napkin back into the cup holder. "But come with me and get the car seat out of the van first. And never take Tristan without his car seat again, unless it's an absolute emergency, which"—she jabbed a finger at him—"for the record, this was not."

"I know." He followed her up the driveway again. She continued into the house, and he wrestled the car seat loose from the van.

Mom might have experience, but she was wrong about Zoey. He loved her, and now that she was out of Aurora Fire, they'd get back together. They could even reform their band, just the two of them, like it should be.

After all, they didn't really need a drummer.

45

Circus, Circus

The acoustics in Zoey's family room were terrible. She'd never noticed until she, Sawyer, and Chey took over with their instruments, but their playing sounded like loud noise instead of music. Then again, maybe they were just bad. Not a comforting thought.

She and Sawyer eyed each other.

"We sound horrible." He crossed his arms. His words carried the conviction of a guilty verdict.

Zoey sighed and glanced down at her bass. Its weight felt good in her hands. And singing songs she helped write healed the sore spot on her heart from breaking up with Justin and failing with Aurora Fire. She was lucky Dad understood her need for music, but she was grounded in pretty much every other area of her life for a while.

"Is it that bad?" Chey asked.

Poor Chey. She really was trying.

"Yep." Sawyer delivered his gut-kicking honesty. "But it's not you."

Sawyer's reassurances to Chey were so cute, but they reminded Zoey of Justin. He'd done the same for her. She missed that. She missed him.

"It just doesn't sound quite right," he added.

"We need Justin." She whispered the statement to

her bass, but everyone heard her.

"Yeah." Sawyer started drumming. Even if no one else was playing, Sawyer was drumming. Tiger seemed to appreciate it. The cat who hid from everybody, even his own family, curled up underneath Sawyer's drums during practice. Maybe he found the vibrations soothing.

"Then what do you suggest?" Chey raised her voice over Sawyer's playing.

He stopped and looked at Zoey. "Guess we could ask him."

Him. Justin.

The scab ripped right off that sore spot, and her heart felt raw again.

Justin was the most logical solution—possibly the only solution. Sawyer didn't look any happier about the idea than she was, but Justin was the missing piece in every song. After everything that had happened, why would Justin ever agree? Then again, maybe he needed their band again as much as she and Sawyer.

One of them would have to ask him, and she was the one most likely to earn a yes.

"I'll go over to his house tonight." The thought shook her knees. She hadn't seen him in over a week, not including church, and after dumping him in front of Aurora Fire, he might not want to see her either. But she had to try. The band depended on her. And on Justin.

After practicing another half-hour on one song, Sawyer had to go to work. Chey followed him, and Zoey was left alone.

She couldn't leave until Dad came home from teaching at the University and gave her permission— he never had his cellphone on, so she couldn't text him.

She waited on the couch in the family-room-turned-practice-studio, strumming the bass to her favorite song she'd written with Justin—"Forever Having Yesterday." From underneath Sawyer's drums, Tiger watched and listened to her sing along.

> "Wherever life takes you
> On this road to tomorrow
> We will forever have
> Memories of yesterday."

A tear dripped onto her hand. Were memories all she and Justin had anymore? She'd read I Corinthians 13 a half-dozen times since her conversation with Livvy on Saturday. That was the kind of love she wanted, not kisses that sent tingles all over. Sawyer might not be the mean, rude guy everyone else saw, but he wasn't the guy for her. He was the guy for Chey. And Zoey wouldn't risk her new friendship with Chey by hanging on to something with Sawyer that would probably always be nothing.

But Justin...he'd been the perfect boyfriend. He understood love. He understood friendship. He understood Zoey. If only things could go back to normal—playing in Justin's garage as if Aurora Fire and the kiss had never happened.

A door squeaked and interrupted her thoughts. She glanced through the stair rails and saw Livvy step onto the landing.

"Hey." Livvy walked down the stairs and joined her on the couch. "Practice over?"

"Yeah. Sawyer had to work." She set aside her bass.

"How's it going? Think you'll be ready by

Saturday?"

Zoey flopped back against the cushions and groaned. "I don't know. If we still had Justin, we'd be great. But without him..." The hopelessness in her voice finished her sentence.

"I'm sorry, Zo."

"When Dad gets home, I'm gonna ask if I can go to Justin's and ask him to play with us." She twisted her necklace. "Do you think that's OK?"

"To go to Justin's?" Livvy arched her brows. "You'll have to ask Dad. I'm not allowed to give you permission for anything right now."

"I meant, do you think it's OK to ask him to play with us?"

"Oh." Livvy shrugged. "Why couldn't you ask? You've been playing together for almost three years."

"Yeah." She concentrated on her necklace. Silver bead, rosette, green glass oval. "What if I got back together with him?"

"Well, I don't think Dad's going to let you go out on a date anytime soon."

"Justin wouldn't care if we couldn't go anywhere."

"You're probably right about that." Livvy spoke slowly, as if she didn't want to say what she was thinking. "You still love him?"

"Yeah, I mean, I hate that I hurt him, and I still care about him. A lot. I really miss him."

Livvy was quiet. Zoey looked at her, trying to read her thoughts. Sadness? Worry? Did Livvy not believe her? Because Zoey did care, and she missed Justin. She wanted to hear his music blend with hers, feel his hand wrapped around hers, see that grin aimed only at her.

"I guess that's really between you and Justin then." Livvy smiled in a way that wasn't encouraging but more like it's-your-decision.

Zoey jumped to her feet. "Thanks, Liv."

Clutching her bass in one hand, she ran upstairs to wait for Dad. The heaviness inside was gone, and she felt bouncy inside and out. In a few hours, everything would be back to normal.

46

Falling On Deaf Ears

Sawyer scanned the bulletin board in the Rhythm and Notes entry for the flier he'd tacked up Saturday night. It was gone. Who would remove it? Sure, he was there to do just that, but still. Wasn't worth worrying about. But he was here, so he should pick up some sticks. He'd broken a couple and already lost half the ones he'd found in his room last week. How did he do that? He entered the store and went straight to the room with drumheads and sticks.

Someone entered from the opposite door.

Justin.

Sawyer froze, his heart pounding like a hyperactive kid on the drums.

Justin's mouth opened and shut without a sound.

When it came to being a band, they'd almost developed a telepathic communication, but today, there was a power outage. They stared at each other, a local rock station filling the awkward silence.

"Hey." Sawyer choked out the word.

Justin stiffened and glared before walking off.

Sawyer heard that loud and clear.

Justin hated him.

He moved in front of the drum stick cubbyholes looking at the round ends without seeing them. Should he leave? Wasn't like he needed new sticks today. And being in the same building as Justin could be dangerous. But before the glare, Sawyer had caught a flicker of emotion in Justin's eyes he'd seen a long time ago—on the day in seventh grade when Justin's dad had moved out.

Breaking up with Zoey had destroyed Justin's life again. And he blamed Sawyer.

Sawyer swore under his breath, and then he clamped his mouth shut. He really was trying to stop. Cussing was probably on Chey's list of reasons why she wouldn't go out with him yet. He snatched a couple of sticks from a cubby. Drumsticks weren't the only thing he'd broken. Maybe he should do something or say something or just be something. Something instead of his angry, can't-fix-it-so-forget-it self. Taking a deep breath, he carried the sticks to the counter.

Justin stared down at the register and punched the keys.

"I'm sorry." Sawyer forced out the words.

Justin glanced up, long enough for Sawyer to see the flicker of surprise, and then he shoved the sticks into a plastic bag. "Sixteen seventy-five."

Sawyer pulled money from his wallet. "Look, what happened with...with Zoey..." The words clawed his throat on their way out. Saying this out loud to Justin was harder than he expected. "I'm sorry. It never should've happened."

"But it did." Justin yanked the bills from his hand and made change.

"I'm sorry." Those words were getting easier to say.

"What does that mean?" Justin thrust the change

at him, every muscle in his face tense. "You're sorry. So what?"

"It didn't mean anything—kissing her."

"So I should forgive you for kissing my girlfriend because it didn't mean anything to you?"

Each word landed like a punch in the gut, and Sawyer felt pain. Physical pain. He looked away from Justin's heated gaze.

"Then why'd you kiss her? Huh? Why'd you do that if it didn't mean anything?"

"I don't know." The truth came sharp, every word distinct. "It just happened."

"Yeah, right." The anger on Justin's face didn't overpower the hurt in his eyes. "But it doesn't matter now, does it? She broke up with me, and now you two have a band together."

"That's not my fault." Sawyer hadn't expected Zoey to break up with Justin or for her to ask him to reform their band. She belonged with Justin—as a girlfriend and as a band.

"Yes, it is. So if you're here to talk me into playing with you, forget it and get out."

"Whatever." Sawyer grabbed the bagged sticks off the glass counter and left.

47

Breaking Me Again

Playing the electric guitar didn't quite soothe Justin. Never had. But he kept playing.

In the corner, almost hidden, his acoustic lay inside its coffin. Every reminder of Zoey brought on a new wave of pain, and any fading of the ache since her confession seemed only temporary. He still loved her. How long until she realized she still loved him too?

The music flowed slow and sad. He'd left the garage door mostly closed making the room hot and stuffy, because the bright sunlight felt too happy. But twilight wouldn't fall until close to midnight, and it was barely eight now.

Had he heard a knock? He stopped playing and ducked to peek through the two-inch opening. All he saw were purple and black shoes, but that was enough.

He stood, catching his guitar before it fell to the floor, and hurried to open the garage bay door.

It couldn't rise fast enough.

"Hi." Zoey lifted one hand and twisted a necklace bead with the other.

"Hi." His heart thudded rattling his rib cage. They stood in the opening staring at each other for an awkward moment.

"Can I, uh..." Zoey waved at the inside of the

garage.

"Yeah, sure. Come in." He stepped out of her way and put his guitar on the rack. His movements felt jerky and unsure. He felt unsure. Why was Zoey here?

But the why didn't really matter.

"You've rearranged." She looked where Sawyer's drums had been. Now the couch angled through the corner.

"Yeah, I moved things around."

Zoey bobbed her head, as if she didn't know what to say.

He didn't have a clue either.

Finally, she faced him. Her eyes held the aching look that had made him fall in love with her. All he'd ever wanted was to be the one who erased the sadness. He had with music.

"Did you want to play together?" he asked. Dumb question, since she didn't have her bass. But she could always sing while he played. That often cheered her up.

"Not tonight." The corner of her mouth tipped upward. "I wanted to talk to you."

"OK." He kept his voice calm. She'd already broken his heart. No other news could be that bad. But how did he know what she had to say would be bad? Maybe this was good. His racing pulse sent vibrations through his body.

"I messed up Friday night, and Aurora Fire kicked me out."

"I know."

"You do?" She sounded surprised and also as if he'd interrupted her planned speech.

"Yeah. Vance came into Rhythm and Notes yesterday and told me about it."

"He did?" She glanced away, cheeks pink. "What happened...it was really stupid."

"Hey." He reached for her hand. "It's over now."

"Yeah. It's all over with them." She gave him another almost-smile and curled her fingers over his. "And I'm playing my bass again. With that new girl, Chey Michaels...and Sawyer."

"Oh." Justin jerked his hand away.

Hurt rose in Zoey's eyes, but she babbled on as if to hide it. "Chey heard that Poor and Loud this weekend had a cancellation, so she volunteered her and Sawyer, and then they asked me to play with them."

He couldn't look at her. This was what she came to tell him? That she'd started a new band with Sawyer? His heart hardened like baked clay and sank to his stomach.

"But we really need you."

She couldn't be serious. "No. I won't play with him."

"I know you're mad at us for what happened—"

"No, I'm not. I'm not mad at you." He grabbed her hand again squeezing her fingers between his. He had to forget about Sawyer and focus on Zoey. This was his chance to fix everything. He couldn't blow it. "I'm really not. I don't blame you for what happened. I love you, Zoey."

"But you should be mad at me. It's as much my fault as it was Sawyer's." Tears shone in her eyes.

"No, it wasn't."

She wore the sad, forlorn look she'd had when they'd met in eighth grade. Back then, he hadn't known how to cheer her up, but he'd wanted to. Now he did know, and it wasn't working.

"Zoey." Justin wrapped his arms around her shoulders pulling her close and breathing in the scent of waffle cones that never quite washed out. She melted against him fitting where she always had. "I forgive you. It's over. Now everything can go back to the way it was."

She stiffened against him. "Justin, I'm sorry."

"I know. Like I said, it's OK."

"No, no it's not." She sniffled and pulled away. "I've made a lot of mistakes this summer—ditching you and Sawyer to sing with Aurora Fire, drinking with Bailee...other stuff." Her voice broke and tears overflowed again. "But breaking up with you...I don't think that was a mistake."

"Zoey, don't say that." The clay ball that was his heart cracked and crumbled.

"I care about you, I really do, and you're like my best friend, but I don't think that's enough."

"Of course, it is." He reached for her again, but she moved away. "Couples are always saying how they married their best friend."

"I'm so sorry." Her cheeks were wet, tears dripping from her jaw.

Justin couldn't look at her. He'd been wrong—there was worse news than breaking up. He faced his guitar fingering the tuning pegs and fighting the sting in his eyes.

"There's one more thing." Zoey's voice shook. "The music we're playing, it's all your stuff and if you're not playing with us..."

He twisted the peg. Did she think he'd sue her for the rights to the music they'd written together? "It's yours too."

"Thanks." A few seconds later, her footsteps faded

out the door.

Justin kept twisting the peg, around and around, tighter and tighter, until the string snapped and curled into the air.

48

One Thousand Apologies

Sawyer rang Zoey's bell and waited a few seconds. Practicing at Zoey's was still weird. Should he walk inside? Walking into Justin's garage had always felt easy, natural. And not like he was invading someone's house. But playing in Zoey's basement *was* invading a house, and he couldn't bring himself to just enter. Not yet.

"Hey." Zoey flung open the door and sucked in a breath that took the oxygen out of the Arctic entry before bursting out with, "Justin said no."

"He did?" Sawyer shouldn't be surprised. Not after his conversation with Justin yesterday. He knew Justin wouldn't want to be anywhere near him. But he'd hoped anyway. Especially if Zoey did the asking.

"Actually, he said he'd play with me, but not you."

"Oh." That sounded right.

Sawyer followed Zoey downstairs.

"I told him that wasn't happening." Zoey spun to face him, and Sawyer nearly knocked her off the last step. "He can't blame you and not me."

"Sure he can." Sawyer blamed himself more than Zoey. Never should've crossed that line.

Zoey squinted her eyes as if she wanted to argue.

But then she shrugged tossing her black and green hair and her thoughts aside. "Anyway, I'm not getting back together with him, which he thinks will happen. So I guess it's just the three of us."

"We should quit." Sawyer moved to his spot behind the drums. *The three of us* wasn't making music.

"Quit?" Chey spoke from the stairs. Sawyer hadn't even heard the door open. Guess Chey felt comfortable enough to let herself in.

"Justin refused." Zoey plucked mournful notes on her bass.

"So we're giving up?" Chey walked over to her keyboard and glanced at them, her expression fighting between disappointment and determination.

"There's not much point." Sawyer wanted to offer something more, something that would erase the disappointment completely. But he had nothing.

"Is my playing that bad?" Chey said this as if she was joking, but a hint of a tremble gave away her worry.

"No." Sawyer played a rhythm on one of the drums. All he had was rhythm. Someone else had to find the melody. "But without Justin, we're missing something. Something important."

"Didn't you tell me you performed without Zoey?"

"Yeah."

"She's the vocalist—isn't that an important part too?"

"Yeah, and we weren't all that great." Truth.

Zoey's mouth knotted, and she ducked her head.

"We can't give up now." A spark ignited in Chey's voice. "Let's keep practicing and praying. God can help us fill in the missing parts—with or without

Justin."

The spark caught hold inside Sawyer too. And another, familiar feeling. He looked at Zoey. "She sounds like him, doesn't she?"

"You're right, she kind of does."

"I sound like who?"

"Justin." Sawyer had missed that insane optimism. Living inside his negative head got depressing. "That's the kind of thing he'd say."

Chey gave him a funny look, then shook it off her face. "So are we going to keep practicing for Saturday?"

Sawyer beat his sticks in the air for a few seconds. A concert guaranteed band practice. And band practice guaranteed Chey would stay in his life. "Why not?"

"If he's in, I'm in." Zoey sounded confident, a complete change from her attitude two minutes ago.

"Good." Chey let out a sigh, as if she needed their band as much as any of them. "Then let's practice."

"But—" Sawyer stabbed a drumstick toward her. He finally knew what he had to offer—a challenge. "If we're going to play without Justin, you'll have to learn the melody."

"Me?" Her voice squeaked. "Why?"

"Because despite our awesome—and still not official—name, playing with a CD won't work so well. And I can't play the melody on the drums."

"What about Zoey?" Her panic fanned the flame ignited earlier inside Sawyer. It wasn't her fear so much as the challenge of pushing her to prove herself. Chey was talented, and if she needed their band, she'd have to put her talent on display, for success or failure.

He wouldn't let her back down. Or fail. "You'll have to do it if you want us to play."

She narrowed her eyes and jutted her chin in that way he was becoming familiar with. A way that said she would rise to his challenge, whether he challenged her to never touch his drums or to play the music she heard inside her head. "Fine. I'll learn it."

For five hours, they worked on two different songs. Chey struggled to match the melody on the CD, and Sawyer threw out encouragement and criticism. Couldn't let her get too confident if they wanted people to like what they heard on Saturday.

Finally, they had to quit so Sawyer and Zoey could get to work.

Sawyer followed Chey outside.

"You coming to the devo tonight?" Chey asked.

"No. Work." He let the screen door slam shut.

"Right. Think you'll ever be man enough to face Justin again?"

Where did that come from? "I don't make the work schedule."

"But you used to ask for Thursdays off, didn't you?" She spoke in that odd way she had of sounding curious and accusing. But not offensive. At least, not to him. But he was the most offensive person in the world, so maybe he was immune.

"Sometimes."

"So when will you ask again?"

"I don't know." He scowled. She was right. He didn't want to face Justin. "I talked to him yesterday."

"You did?" Chey straightened and her voice went high as if she was shocked. "You asked him to play with us?"

"Not exactly." He tapped his foot on the edge of the concrete driveway. The hairs on his arm prickled. "I tried to apologize for...things."

"By things, you mean kissing Zoey."

Why was she always saying it? It was as if she didn't want to forget.

"That's probably hard to get over."

"Yeah, I guess." His insides swirled around. Was it hard for Chey to get over too? "I better go."

"I'd offer you a ride, but I saw your bike," Chey said.

"I don't have to be to the store for a couple of hours." He wasn't ready to say good-bye to Chey. Never was. Which was a strange feeling. One he wanted to explore. Like maybe as a date. An official date. Assuming Chey was interested in *him* beyond his band connections. Big assumption. "If you wanted to hang out, I could come back for it later."

"Hang out? Where?"

"I don't know." He drummed his fingers against his jeans. "We could get something to eat."

"We could. Are you hungry?"

"I can always eat, if I'm not playing." Why did this feel so hard? He glanced around looking everywhere but at Chey, his fingers drumming faster and faster.

"Would we be getting food because we're hungry or would it be like a date?"

From that question, he couldn't tell what her interest was. And he couldn't bring himself to be direct about his own. Not if she threatened rejection. Look where that had gotten Justin and Zoey. Dating relationships destroyed a band.

But that wasn't enough to stop him from pushing Chey a little to find out what she thought. "You could call it that, if you wanted."

"And what would you call it?"

"Whatever you called it."

Chey crossed her arms. "Well, this is a fun conversation."

He grinned. She didn't really mean it, but he did. This was kind of fun.

"I like you, but I'm not ready to date you, Sawyer."

"You're the one who brought up dating." His grin slipped slightly, but he forced it not to fall off completely. Couldn't let her see he cared. "I just asked if you wanted to get food."

"Yeah, I'm not all that hungry." She smiled, but it didn't look quite sincere, before turning away toward her car. "See ya later."

She was leaving. But she hadn't turned him down, had she? Not exactly.

"Will you let me know when you are?"

Chey froze, her hand on the car door. She kept her back to him. "You want me to let you know when I'm hungry?"

"No." The car window reflected Sawyer's head above her shoulder. His heart felt ready to explode. What was he doing? Was he actually asking a girl—Chey—out? But one thing he'd figured out about Chey, she liked honesty. Upfrontness. Truth. "When you're ready to date me."

She faced him leaning against the car door. "I think we need to be friends and get past all the crazy stuff that's happened this summer."

"You mean Zoey and me kissing."

Chey swallowed, as if buying time before responding. "That and other things. Besides, there's a lot about me you don't know."

"Like what?"

"Like pretty much everything."

"I know a lot about you."

"OK, drummer boy, then what is it about me you like?"

"I like..." Several seconds of silence followed. Should be an easy question. But he couldn't put into words what it was about Chey that set his pulse racing and his blood on fire. Something about the way she refused to let him get away with anything. How she forced him to speak up or risk her walking away. How she stuck to her convictions. How she gave him a second and third and fourth chance to mess up, as long as he was willing to apologize.

"Exactly." Chey pronounced the final judgment on the silence. "I don't think we should date until there's something more than lust between us."

"Lust?" He laughed. "You think awful highly about yourself."

"Bye." She opened the car door.

He had to tell her something. Put his feelings into words. "That's it, right there. That's what drives me crazy about you."

She paused, one foot in the car, one still in the grass.

"You're always walking away. Most people I'm trying to run off after five-seconds of being around them, but you leave before I'm ready."

Chey hesitated and then put her other foot in the car and pulled the door closed. She didn't answer, but she wasn't rejecting him.

Sawyer finally recognized her actions. She was running.

And he'd finally found a relationship he wanted to chase.

49

Unraveling of a Tragedy

After the devo Thursday night, Justin piled a plate with food and found a spot on a brown couch. Alone. The only reason he'd bothered coming was because his parents insisted. Even after confronting Mom the other day, he couldn't get grounded from youth group. Not that she'd grounded him at all, which had been a surprise.

Chey crossed the room, heading straight toward him. But after last week, she couldn't possibly want to sit by him.

He was wrong.

"So it's just you and me again." Chey plopped down sounding as if she wanted to be his new best friend.

Justin wasn't ready to fill the vacancy, but when he was, it wouldn't be with Sawyer's girlfriend.

"How's it going?" She crunched into a carrot.

"Fine, I guess." He put no energy in his voice and shifted into the arm of the couch. Maybe if he was quiet, she'd get bored and find someone else.

"Good. I'm doing OK too." Chey kept talking, upbeat and happy. "A little freaked out about Saturday. This band thing is fun, but scary."

A chill climbed up his back. If he had to listen to

her talk, it wouldn't be about the new band. He searched for a safer topic. "You like living here?"

"It's not so bad. I think I've met people faster here than anywhere else I've moved. But maybe playing the keyboard with people instead of trying to talk helps. Common interests instead of saying something stupid."

"Doing all the touristy stuff with your family?" He couldn't risk the conversation drifting back to music.

"Not really. Turns out band practice is time consuming. But you know all about that, don't you?"

"Yeah, I guess." Justin gave up trying to steer the conversation and stared at his food.

"I'm thinking I shouldn't have pushed them to follow through with this festival thing."

He grunted. Take the hint. No such luck. She had no concept of boundaries.

"Sawyer and Zoey say we'd be fine if you joined us."

"Look." He snapped toward her. Heat replaced the earlier chill. "I don't know what you're trying to do here. But normal people realize it's rude to push someone to talk when they don't want to."

"Yeah, well, I think it saves time, skipping all the politeness stuff." All the upbeat-happy in her voice was gone. Now she sounded as cold as he was hot.

"Maybe that's why you have trouble making friends."

She flinched, and he felt a tremor of guilt. What was wrong with him lately? He wasn't a guy who went around hurting people. He took a slow breath to cool the heat and tried to soften his insult. "I'm just not interested in talking about any band."

"Because of what happened between Sawyer and

Zoey?"

"Seriously, what is the matter with you?" He barely kept himself from yelling. Forget about being nice. If she couldn't be polite, he wouldn't bother either. "That's none of your business."

"Well, it kind of is. They're my friends too."

"Friends? You just met them."

"Chill." She leaned away. "What's the matter with you?"

He didn't answer. Maybe that would be enough to shut her up. He crammed a couple of chips into his mouth.

"You know, both Zoey and Sawyer have said I'm like you, and I'm starting to think that's an insult."

"What's that supposed to mean?"

"It means, I thought I'd worked hard to get rid of my hate and my grudges and my need for revenge. But clearly I must not have if they think I'm like you."

"And what do you know about me?"

"Not much, I guess." The words were flippant but delivered like a slap. "You had a band with your girlfriend and best friend. Then they made the dumbest mistake ever, and now all three of you are miserable because you won't forgive them."

"That's not true." He'd forgiven Zoey. It wasn't his fault she wouldn't accept. "Besides, I have a right to be angry."

"Angry? Or a right to hate Sawyer?"

"Both." The word popped out before Justin thought, and he gave the wrong answer. The true answer, but wrong.

"No one has a right to hate."

"Yeah? Maybe no one's ever betrayed you."

"And what do you know about me?"

"Nothing."

"Then let me tell you." Chey twisted to look him straight in the eye. "My mom ran off when I was two, and, yeah, I get that she's messed up in the head, but who abandons their kid and never looks back? After that, it was just me and my dad. But he moves us around all the time, so what's the point of making friends when you're just going to leave? Then my dad met a woman, not even ten years older than me, got married and started having babies with her. Now he has a new family, and I'm just a boarder until graduation. And don't forget my first boyfriend last year. Turns out he was just using me to get back at his ex for cheating on him. So don't tell me I don't understand wanting to hate someone." The heat in her voice lit up her amber eyes.

"Sorry." Lame, but he didn't know what else to say. She was right, and compared to that, Justin's life sounded like an energetic, happy pop song.

"Yeah, well, I'm over it. Mostly." She took a deep breath and flopped back against the cushions. "I know my dad and stepmom care about me, and they won't kick me out of the house the day I graduate. But it's only because of God's grace that I can let go of everyone else's mistakes. It's not like I haven't made any of my own."

He cringed at the mention of God and grace. "But all that, it's not the same thing."

"Yes, it is. All Sawyer cares about is music, and you're trying to take it away because of how he spent a very stupid five-seconds."

"He kissed my girlfriend, and she broke up with me!" Didn't she see how his entire life fell apart because of those "five-seconds?"

"And you won't even accept his apology." She fired an accusing shot like she didn't care about how much pain he was already in.

"Like he even meant it."

"How do you know?"

"Because I know Sawyer. I've known him most of my life. Sawyer never feels sorry for anything he does."

"I think you're wrong."

"But I'm not." His voice sounded firm and sure, but inside, question marks floated like bubbles. Then they popped. Even if Sawyer did regret the kiss, it didn't undo what he'd done. Nothing would.

Chey pushed off the couch. "I gotta get home. But if you change your mind, you know where to find us on Saturday."

His mind was made up.

He left the devo soon after Chey. When he got home and walked into his garage, he glanced around the practice space. Despite the rearranged furniture, the holes remained obvious. The corner without Sawyer's drums, the two empty spaces on the guitar rack, all missing pieces.

Missing pieces inside him.

How much truth was there in Chey's accusations? And what about Zoey saying breaking up with him was the only decision she didn't see as a mistake? Remembering her words splintered his heart all over again. If she'd never kissed Sawyer, would she have questioned whether she loved him?

And that was why he couldn't forgive Sawyer.

Fire flowed through his veins. Chey was right. He was holding a grudge. He wanted revenge.

How had that happened? He was the one who

smoothed out the conflicts between Zoey and Sawyer. He pointed out God's role in their music and their lives.

So where had God gone in his life? Holding on to faith seemed impossible when everything fell apart. Did that mean he'd become bitter and hateful like Vance?

That thought rolled over him like a bucket of ice.

The black guitar case caught his eye. He couldn't quite bring himself to get rid of his first guitar, even if it was destroyed beyond repair. So he kept it, broken and splintered like his heart and his friendships.

But unlike the guitar, relationships could be fixed.

Bridge:

Is there too much brokenness
For any of us to survive this
Oh God, help us find
Forgiveness
Before heartbreak
Manages to take
Away our dream

50

Born for This

"We're here." Livvy wedged the car between a maroon hatchback and a white suburban in the dirt parking lot. "You nervous?"

"No." Zoey's answer was clipped. If she said she wasn't nervous, would that make it true? She leaned forward gazing through the windshield. Trees and park equipment blocked her view of the soccer fields where the stage and booths were set up. It was almost twelve o'clock. She, Sawyer, and Chey didn't go on for more than an hour, and the festival was just getting started.

Glancing around, Zoey found Chey's car.

"I'm going to find Chey and Sawyer." Seizing her water bottle, she opened the door.

"OK. I see Karmen and Greg." Livvy grabbed her arm. "Hey, you'll be great. Just have fun."

Could Livvy see the psychotic moths swooping around her insides? "Thanks."

"Oh, and Zo?"

Zoey froze, half in, half out of the car, and looked at her sister.

"Mama would be proud to know you're singing on a stage, in front of a crowd, with your band."

With her band. That mattered most. Fame

wouldn't be worth it without her friends, and if Mama were here, Zoey was sure she'd agree.

Zoey left her bass and amp in the car and made her way to the bright green field. Booths constructed of white poles and blue canvas edged the giant square where people had spread out blankets and one group had set up a camping tent. Dogs romped around, and kids darted in the sunshine. Zoey squinted and scanned the crowds for Sawyer's spiked hair and Chey's flashy clothes.

"Fi-nally."

At the desperate voice, Zoey jumped. Chey had sneaked up behind her.

"Sorry." Zoey tucked black and green hair behind her ear. "But I'm not late."

"Yeah, I know." Chey glanced over her shoulder at Sawyer lurking in her shadow. "Girl time. Go do something grossly male."

"Like what?" Sawyer sounded offended as if he never did anything gross.

"Whatever." Chey waved him away and then linked arms with Zoey and dragged her toward a booth speaking when they were out of Sawyer's earshot. "He's driving me crazy. We've been wandering around, looking at stuff, and every time I say I like something, he's offering to buy it for me. Did he come into an inheritance? Or do I just look that poor?"

"I think it's because he likes you."

Chey's eyes narrowed. "I thought you wanted us to be friends."

"And I thought you liked him." Zoey hip-bumped Chey.

"I do. Too much. And he knows it." Chey's voice

faded in a way that sounded disappointed or maybe wistful. She fingered fabric bags hanging from a white tent post. "But I don't want him thinking I'm ready to date him. Because I'm not. Not until I'm sure there's something more than physical attraction."

That sounded familiar. "You been talking to my sister?"

"Huh?"

"Never mind."

"Anyway." Chey led the way to another booth filled with tie-dyed everything. "He was annoying me."

"I think you're smart." Zoey examined a bag. Twenty dollars? She could make one at home for less. Wasn't that kind of the point of tie-dye? And why couldn't she ever find tie-dye in black? "I didn't tell you this before because I didn't want you to blame me for Justin not agreeing, but he wanted to get back together. And before I went over to his house Tuesday, I thought I did too." The psychotic moths moved into her chest flapping against her lungs and making it hard to breathe. She walked out from under the booth's shade and into the sun. "But I couldn't."

"Why not?"

"Because when I looked into his eyes, I knew he'd do anything for me, and I don't know if I feel that. I still care about him, but I can't return that kind of love. I don't know that I ever could, even when we were together." Who claimed not to love the guy she'd been dating? She chuckled to hide her embarrassment. "But if I felt differently, maybe he'd be playing with us today."

"If he's not willing to be friends with you, then you did the right thing."

Zoey took a deep breath. The psychotic moths calmed a little. Did she agree? Yeah. Love wasn't just about finding someone who loved her, but about being willing to return that love. Until she straightened out her complicated feelings, she wouldn't be dating anybody. That decision was freeing.

"OK, you've done this before, right?" Chey looked at her, the stud in her lower lip jiggling. "The concert thing?"

"Yeah. A few times."

"Is it normal to want to hurl? Because I feel like my stepmom dealing with morning sickness—which is definitely not my problem."

"Yeah. I feel about like that every time."

"Great. So if today goes well, I'll be able to look forward to this." Chey pressed a hand against her stomach. "Do you think we'll totally humiliate ourselves?"

"Not totally..."

Chey sighed and glanced at the stage where a guy with eyeliner screamed into a mic. "You and Sawyer are going to hate me forever after today, aren't you?"

"Not forever." Zoey couldn't help teasing Chey. This is what she'd missed most since breaking up with Justin—having a best friend. "But maybe until next week."

"Thanks." Chey turned scanning the crowds. "Think we've punished Sawyer long enough? He's shopping in the free clothes."

Zoey followed Chey's gaze to a corner of the field. Clothes were stacked on folding tables, on the ground underneath and overflowing boxes. A sign fashioned out of a cardboard box read, "Free Clothes." "He's probably searching for old band T-shirts. He found a couple last year."

"Really? Maybe we should help him." Chey started toward the booth. "There's gotta be a thousand items. Maybe I can find something."

Was Chey motivated by the possibility of a good find? Or had fifteen minutes away from Sawyer been long enough? Zoey kept those questions to herself. Chey had more self-control than Zoey. She still half-wanted to call Justin up and hang out with him too.

Zoey hurried to catch up with Chey. "Hey, thanks for making us do this concert."

"No problem." Chey sounded confident despite her earlier confession. "I have a talent for forcing people into doing things they'll regret."

"Don't worry, I won't regret this." The psychotic moths settled back into her stomach. A familiar and oddly comforting feeling.

Even if they were booed off the stage being reunited as a band was enough.

If only Justin could see that too.

51

The Note from Which a Chord is Built

The acoustic chords from the festival emcee, entertaining the crowd between acts, drifted through the thin curtain. On the stage, Zoey, Chey, and Sawyer rushed to set up their gear.

Sawyer crouched by his drums twisting the brackets.

"Want help?"

He glanced up at Chey. Her face was pale. "Sure. Finish this one."

She took his place, and he started attaching a floor tom.

"You're going to be great," he said.

"I can't even remember the titles of the songs."

"That's why we wrote a set list."

"Yeah, but the names don't mean anything if I can't remember the songs."

He almost laughed. She sounded like Zoey before a performance—completely freaked. He suddenly understood why Justin had never told Zoey to shut up and deal.

"You'll remember."

"If you say so." She didn't sound as if she believed him.

"Just pretend it's another practice."

"But it's not. There are people—strangers—listening."

"Yeah, but it's free. Their expectations are low."

She shifted her gaze from the drum set to him. "So you're saying they expect us to sound bad?"

"Something like that."

"And that makes you feel better about playing?"

"I don't need to feel better. I remember the song titles."

She slapped his shin.

"Are you guys ready?" Zoey, carrying her bass, stepped over and around snaking cords to stand in front of the drums.

"Almost." Sawyer twisted the final brackets.

"Who's introducing us?" Zoey asked.

"You," Sawyer said.

"I was afraid of that." A tiny moan attached itself to Zoey's words. "One of you want to do it instead?"

Chey shook her head, her face almost the same shade as her blonde hair.

"You're the vocalist. Be vocal," Sawyer said.

"Introductions were Justin's job." Zoey licked her lips. Her bass trembled in her hands. "He was good at that."

The words "shut up and deal" hovered on the tip of Sawyer's tongue. He might not want to say them to Chey, but he wouldn't have any trouble saying them to Zoey.

"Well, you're gonna have to." If Sawyer spoke into the mic, the audience would think he was threatening them. He tightened the last bracket. "'Cause we're ready."

Chey and Zoey stared at him, as though they expected him to do or say something. Like what? Did they want him to give some sort of pre-concert prep talk? Or were they hoping he'd offer to go solo so they didn't have to be on stage?

"Go." He gave commands, not encouragement. "Get to your spots so we can play."

They scurried off, not looking inspired.

Sawyer sat behind the drums and raked a hand through his spiked hair. Epic Fail would be a better band name.

The emcee and another guy pulled back the black fabric curtain and wrapped it around the posts on either side.

"Uh, hi." Zoey cleared her throat, and the microphone squeaked. "So we're next. The three of us. I'm Zoey, that's Chey, and Sawyer's on the drums."

He resisted the urge to duck or dive off the stage. Why had he ever let Chey talk him into this?

"We're kind of new at this. Actually, Sawyer and I have been playing together for a while. A couple of years. We had another band, with my boyfriend, but he and I broke up because—"

What was she doing? He was ready to tackle her off the stage. Even he could do a better job.

"You probably don't care about that. Anyway, I left the band."

He rolled his eyes away from the disaster. Zoey launched into talking about Aurora Fire for some reason, but he blocked her out when he saw someone walking toward the stage. The one person he never expected to see today.

Justin.

Sawyer slipped away from the drums and jumped onto the grass. "Hey."

"Hey." Justin slipped the strap of his guitar case

over his head.

"What're you doing here?" Sawyer didn't mean to sound defensive, but Justin hadn't exactly wanted to be around him lately.

"Heard you needed a guitarist." Justin smiled, but it didn't quite reach his eyes. He set the black case on the edge of the stage.

"You're volunteering?" Sawyer's heart pounded in his throat threatening to choke him. He waited for the catch.

"Yeah, I guess so." Justin toyed with one of the straps. He glanced up, his eyes guarded. "But I haven't forgiven you."

"OK." How was he supposed to react to that? Quit and let Justin play in his place? They'd sound better without him than they did without Justin.

He looked across the stage. Chey stared at them, the nervousness from earlier replaced by confusion.

He wouldn't quit and abandon her.

"But I'm trying to," Justin added.

"Oh. Thanks." That was good news, right? Maybe he should try apologizing again. No, maybe if they all stopped talking about it, they could move on. Except Zoey seemed to be telling half of Fairbanks about their big breakup.

Justin undid the latches and zippers and removed his blue and white electric guitar. Then he glanced up at the stage, his forehead bunching together. "What's she doing up there?"

Sawyer tuned in to what Zoey was saying. "But it turns out that being a band isn't just about music. It's about relationships—friendships."

"Yeah," he heard himself say.

"You agree with her?" Justin looked more shocked

by that than when Sawyer had apologized at Rhythm and Notes. "What happened to music being the only thing that mattered?"

Sawyer shrugged. "I was wrong."

"You really like her, don't you?"

"What? No." He stepped back raising his hands, palms out. No need to go there again. "I told you it was a mistake."

"Not Zoey." Justin's voice was sharp and angry at the reminder. "The new girl. Chey."

"Oh, her." He looked at Chey again. He felt something lighten inside him. Like helium filled his lungs. Or his heart.

She stared at her keyboard fingering the notes. She was here because of him, and he really hoped he didn't mess things up and run her off again. "Yeah, maybe."

A genuine grin cracked Justin's face, and he met Sawyer's gaze with that understanding look—the look that said he knew Sawyer better than Sawyer knew himself.

Maybe forgiveness and friendship were possible.

"C'mon." Justin climbed onto the stage. "Let's put the crowd out of their misery."

Sawyer grabbed Justin's amp and moved to plug it in. The missing piece was finally in place. They were a band again.

"And we're all friends." Zoey's pathetic speech continued. "Well, except for my boyfriend, but who can blame him, since I dumped him three times in as many wee—"

"Sorry about that." Justin marched up to the mic with the confidence of a rock star expecting cheers.

The crowd was silent. They'd probably fallen asleep listening to Zoey.

But she stared at Justin, mouth hanging open.

"My band mates here were covering for me, since I was late. Thanks for listening to all...that. Anyway, we're..." Justin glanced at Zoey.

"Uh, You, Me and a CD?" she said.

"Really?" Justin shot Sawyer a look that said, after all the names you've shot down, you agreed to this one?

Sawyer shrugged. Yeah, it was lame, but if it brought the four of them together, he'd grow to like it.

"Well, I guess that's us." Justin faced the crowd again. "So let's play."

Justin, Zoey, and Chey eyed Sawyer waiting for his cue.

He raised his sticks into the air. They were all here, on a stage playing in front of strangers. Nothing could be better than this moment.

"One! Two! Three! Four!"

Thank you…

for purchasing this Watershed Books title. For other
inspirational stories, please visit our on-line bookstore
at www.pelicanbookgroup.com.

For questions or more information, contact us at
customer@pelicanbookgroup.com.

Watershed Books
Make a Splash!™
an imprint of Pelican Book Group
www.PelicanBookGroup.com

Connect with Us
www.facebook.com/Pelicanbookgroup
www.twitter.com/pelicanbookgrp

To receive news and specials, subscribe to our bulletin
http://pelink.us/bulletin

May God's glory shine through
this inspirational work of fiction.

AMDG

You Can Help!

At Pelican Book Group it is our mission to entertain readers with fiction that uplifts the Gospel. It is our privilege to spend time with you awhile as you read our stories.

We believe you can help us to bring Christ into the lives of people across the globe. And you don't have to open your wallet or even leave your house!

Here are 3 simple things you can do to help us bring illuminating fiction™ to people everywhere.

1) If you enjoyed this book, write a positive review. Post it at online retailers and websites where readers gather. And share your review with us at reviews@pelicanbookgroup.com (this does give us permission to reprint your review in whole or in part.)

2) If you enjoyed this book, recommend it to a friend in person, at a book club or on social media.

3) If you have suggestions on how we can improve or expand our selection, let us know. We value your opinion. Use the contact form on our web site or e-mail us at customer@pelicanbookgroup.com

God Can Help!

Are you in need? The Almighty can do great things for you. Holy is His Name! He has mercy in every generation. He can lift up the lowly and accomplish all things. Reach out today.

> *Do not fear: I am with you; do not be anxious: I am your God. I will strengthen you, I will help you, I will uphold you with my victorious right hand.*
>
> ~Isaiah 41:10 (NAB)

We pray daily, and we especially pray for everyone connected to Pelican Book Group—that includes you! If you have a specific need, we welcome the opportunity to pray for you. Share your needs or praise reports at http://pelink.us/pray4us

Free Book Offer

We're looking for booklovers like you to partner with us! Join our team of influencers today and periodically receive free eBooks!

For more information
Visit http://pelicanbookgroup.com/booklovers